WHEN ANYONE CAME UP AND SAID, "WHO'S YOUR FRIEND?" I would answer, "Um, this is my sister Caitlin."

Mostly she shrugged, and so did I. I was thankful she wasn't curling her lip at everybody and throwing insulting remarks in people's faces. Until I introduced her to Adam.

Tobey had taken the comatose Caitlin over to meet Holly, when Adam said at my elbow, "So who's that?"

I looked up...and up...and up into his freckled face and gap-toothed smile.

"Oh, that's my sister Caitlin."

"Cool," he said. Then he left me standing there while he strode across the room in two long steps and said, "Hi. I'm Adam."

Caitlin took one look at him and stuck out her hand and shook his. You could see her face waking up.

Adam stuffed his hands into his pockets and curved his back over the way tall guys do when they're talking to short girls they really want to hear. I had a deep, green pang of envy.

Dear Parent,

Thank you for considering Nancy Rue's book for your teen. We are pleased to publish her Raise the Flag series and believe these books are different than most you will find for teens.

Tragically, some of the things our teens face today are not easy to discuss. Nancy has created stories and characters that depict real kids, facing real-life issues with real faith. Our desire is to help you equip your children to act in a God-pleasing way no matter what they face.

Nancy has beautifully woven scriptural truth and direction into the choices and actions of her characters. She has worked hard to depict the issues in a sensitive way. However, I would recommend that you scan the book to determine if the subject matter is appropriate for your teen.

Sincerely,

Dan Rich
Publisher

Raise the Flag Series BOOK 6

WHEN IS PERFECT, PERFECT ENOUGH?

Nancy Rue

WATERBROOK
P R E S S

WHEN IS PERFECT, PERFECT ENOUGH?
PUBLISHED BY WATERBROOK PRESS
5446 North Academy Boulevard, Suite 200
Colorado Springs, Colorado 80918
A division of Random House, Inc.

Scripture taken from the *Holy Bible, New International Version*®. NIV®
Copyright © 1973, 1978, 1984 by International Bible Society. Used by permission of Zondervan Publishing House. All rights reserved.

The characters and events in this book are fictional, and any resemblance to
actual persons or events is coincidental.

ISBN 1-57856-088-8

Published in association with the literary agency of Alive Communications, Inc.,
1465 Kelly Johnson Blvd., Suite 320, Colorado Springs, Colorado 80920

Rue, Nancy N.
    When is perfect, perfect enough? / Nancy Rue.
        p.   cm.—(Raise the flag series : bk. 6)
    Summary: Shannon suffers in the shadow of her wild and uncontrol-
lable younger sister Caitlin, who seems ready to tear their Christian family
apart, and finds herself developing an eating disorder.
    ISBN 1-57856-088-8 (pbk.)
    1. Bulimia—Fiction. [1. Behavior—Fiction. 2. Sisters—Fiction.
3. Christian life—Fiction.] I. Title. II. Series: Rue, Nancy N. Raise the
flag series : bk. 6.
PZ7.R88515Wh 1999
[Fic]--dc21   99-10709
                                                                  CIP

Printed in the United States of America
1999—First Edition

10 9 8 7 6 5 4 3 2 1

To Marijean Rue,
who is blond enough, thin enough—
just wonderful enough!

UNTIL I WAS SIXTEEN, I, SHANNON D'ANGELO, WAS PER-
FECT.

Now, I know you're saying, "Nobody's perfect. She's lying!"
And you're right. The whole truth, the real truth, about me only
started to come out the day Brianna and Diesel graduated from
high school.

We were all in a pavilion at Rancho San Rafael celebrating after
the ceremony. The adults had left except for Ms. Race, and everybody was pigging out on this enormous cake Marissa had made.
Well, everybody *else* was pigging out. I was pushing my piece
around on a paper plate and waiting for an opportunity when nobody was looking to pitch it into the trash can.

"Dude, this is *great*," Fletcher said. He was Tobey's little brother.
Also Cheyenne's boyfriend. Also the skinniest kid on the planet,
even though he devoured whole cakes in a single sitting.

"You ought to know," Tobey told him. "That's your fourth piece."

"Hey, it's the last party of the school year," he said.

Norie grunted from the corner of the picnic table where she sat
with Wyatt, her boyfriend. "Oh, that explains it," she said. "Clearly
you won't get another bite of cake until school starts again."

"Right," Tobey said. She whacked Fletcher cheerfully across
the top of the head. "He'll go home after this and head for the
Hostess Twinkies."

Fletcher's mouth was full, which gave Cheyenne the perfect
in. "I'm not going to eat a single bite of junk food all summer."
She gave her dark brown bangs a shake.

Diesel grunted, which sounded like a chain saw starting up.

Diesel was Cheyenne's foster brother, and he kind of talked in mechanical sounds, which matched his bulldozer body.

"What's that supposed to mean?" Cheyenne said.

"It means I'll believe it when I see it," Diesel said, vocal pistons tapping. "You won't make it through the afternoon without dipping your hand into those tortilla chips."

Cheyenne looked blankly at the bag of Doritos on the table. "Chips are junk food?"

Ms. Race's voice rose above the good-natured hooting that ensued. Ms. Race was sort of our mentor. Her real job was being our principal's secretary.

"Cheyenne, honey, I'm impressed," she said. She wrinkled her faintly freckled nose in that playful way she had.

Brianna looked up from the arm of Ira's wheelchair where she was perched and arched one of her beautiful eyebrows. "Impressed by what?" Her black eyes were sparkling, her signal that she was kidding. If you didn't know her, she sure could make you think she was about to rip you a new pair of nostrils. Must have been from growing up African-American in East Oakland.

"I'm impressed that Cheyenne has a goal for the summer," Ms. Race said.

Beside me, Marissa gave her soft laugh. "I wish I were that ambitious. I don't have any goals for the summer."

"I have a hard time believing you're going to veg in front of the TV for three months," Norie said.

Marissa shrugged. "No, I have to take care of my little brothers and sisters, but I'm hoping to write some more poetry—"

"And make enchiladas for us," Fletcher put in.

"We know *your* goal, Fletch," Ira said from the wheelchair. In spite of the injuries that limited his life to that chair, he still had this incredible attitude. It flashed out at us from his smile. "He's going to consume as much food as possible."

"That's not a goal, that's a *fait accompli*," Norie said.

Cheyenne pushed her just-big-enough-to-be-beautiful lips into a frown. "What's that?"

Probably none of the rest of us knew either, but we always counted on Cheyenne to ask.

While all eyes were on Norie as she held forth about French

phrases, I edged my way over to the garbage can and worked on *my* one and only summer goal. I slid my still full plate inside. I had become pretty slick at those moves.

But not slick enough. Marissa was right at my elbow.

"Shannon," she said, "are you okay?"

If you have noticed, up until that point I hadn't uttered a word, which is why she would ask. She was also asking because she and I knew I had been throwing away food—all food—for about two months, and I had promised her I would stop. I had also promised her I would tell my parents I had a problem, which I hadn't done yet. In fact, I hadn't told even Marissa much of anything since then. I had been avoiding her like she was the food police. Her and everybody else.

"I'm fine," I said. "I was just throwing away my trash."

She looked doubtfully at the garbage can. "We haven't talked in so long."

"Finals and stuff," I said.

She forced a smile. She knew that wasn't the reason as well as I did. "Can you spend the night at my house? We could celebrate the beginning of vacation."

That caught me off guard, and my head started to spin.

It would be wonderful to be with Marissa. I could probably steer the conversation away from me and my family and all that stuff, and we could actually have fun.

No way. All those brown brothers of hers grabbing stuff out of the refrigerator, and Marissa pulling enchiladas and chile rellenos out of the oven. The Martinezes' whole life revolves around cuisine. You won't be able to resist, and you know it.

"I don't know," I said. "I have to ask."

"I know how that is. Your parents are about as strict as mine."

"Okay, everybody tell their summer goals," Tobey was saying as we moved back to the picnic table. Everything on her was shining—honey-brown eyes, strawberry-blond bob, clear skin—which meant this was a topic she could clamp her teeth into.

I definitely didn't want to plunge into the discussion, with my molars or any other part of me. Norie was talking, spitting out her words in that way she had that demanded you listen. But what I heard was the Voice in my own head.

Don't even bother to try to think of something to say. You wouldn't know a goal if it came to your house FedEx.

"I want to come back from Costa Rica changed in some way," Norie was saying. "I don't know *how*, but I'm, like, leaving that up to God."

"When do you guys leave?" Tobey said.

Ms. Race answered that one. She and Norie had been planning this mission trip since about December. "July 18," she said. "We'll be there three weeks."

"We're going to miss you," Tobey said.

"You'll survive," Norie said.

"Yeah, but will Wyatt?" Cheyenne said. She clung to Fletcher as if he, too, were about to leave the country.

"I'll probably go into some kind of blue funk," Wyatt said, eyes twinkling behind his glasses. I personally had never seen Wyatt in a funk. I didn't think he was capable of one. I didn't think any of them even knew what a real funk was. Not like I did.

Oh, stop feeling sorry for yourself, the Voice in my head said. *If you had your act together—*

"I have one," Tobey said. "I want to find somebody who's ready to meet Christ, and I want to bring that person to Him."

We all stared at her. Of all of us, Tobey was the furthest along on what Ms. Race called "the spiritual journey." The way Tobey said it was what surprised us. It wasn't that flippant, offhand manner we had with each other. It sounded so…serious, so adult.

The Voice was practically shouting in my head. *You're not that far along on your spiritual journey. You don't even have a spiritual journey!*

"Wow," Norie said.

"Yeah," Cheyenne said.

Tobey hitched up her shoulders and grinned, almost sheepishly. "I didn't mean to drop the heavies on you guys. This is supposed to be a party, right?"

"And it's my party and Diesel's," Brianna said, neck arching. "I say if you want to bring the heavies in, you do it, girl. What are we, some lightweight group?"

Ms. Race laughed. "No, I wouldn't call you lightweights. We have Norie going on a mission trip. Brianna, you're headed off to art school in, what, six weeks? You'll be creating who knows what that will rock the world. Tobey wants to bring someone to the Lord. Diesel, you're starting your first real job Monday. Ira has a court trial to deal with. Marissa's going to write poetry. I mean, my gosh, I'm used to teenage girls saying their summer goal is to be blonder, tanner, and thinner!"

"Then there's me," Cheyenne said. But she was grinning, dark eyes expectant, awaiting Ms. Race's edict about her, which was sure to be soul inspiring.

"Cheyenne, you have grown so much this year," Ms. Race said without even blinking. "Who knows what's going to happen to you this summer!"

That satisfied Cheyenne—enough so she whipped her dark head right toward me and riveted a look from under her fringed bangs. "How about Shannon?" she said.

The Voice screamed right in my ear. *How about Shannon? Neither Ms. Race nor anybody else can say anything about you that would make you even come close to the rest of them.*

"I know what her goal *ought* to be," Fletcher said. "She ought to gain about twenty pounds. Maybe thirty."

"Fletch-*er!*" Tobey said.

"She *could* use a little meat on her bones—" Ira started to say.

"But we are *not* going to critique the girl's looks, now, are we?" Brianna said.

Her teeth were clenched so hard, I doubt anybody would have argued with her, even if Ms. Race hadn't chimed in with, "You are beautiful, Shannon, you know that. I would just love to see you happier, that's all."

"I'm happy," I said automatically. They all stared at me as if I had just said, "I'm an alien." I stammered for something to say. "I'm working on the staff for our church's summer program. It's a six-week thing. Of course, a whole team of people are coming in from Montana or someplace to actually run it because we've never had one at our church before. I'll just be a gofer or something. Besides, Tobey and Marissa and Cheyenne are working on it too, so it's not really my goal to claim—"

"So now that you have talked yourself out of taking any credit...," Wyatt said.

Norie leaned in toward me. "Your sister is coming home for the summer, right? Getting her straightened out could take you at least till school starts."

"Why is that Shannon's job?" Brianna said. "Seems to me that Caitlin girl ought to take some responsibility for herself for a change."

I shook my head. "She can't. She needs a lot of help."

Brianna started to say something, but she closed her mouth firmly and gave one of her sounds, the one that came out, "Mmm-*mmm.*"

"I'm having another piece of cake," Fletcher said.

Nobody protested. Everyone was glad to change the topic— and none of them was gladder than I was.

"I'm going for a walk," I whispered to Marissa.

I took off at a punishing pace, running away from the on-slaught, burning off guilty calories, separating myself yet again from the people who were so much better—

Yeah, and stronger and smarter, the Voice added.

And happier, I thought.

Well, dream on. You don't have the right to that kind of happi-ness—not yet.

You see? I told you the truth was starting to come out. And, believe me, it got worse before it got better.

CHAPTER ONE

BEFORE I GO ANY FURTHER, I NEED TO TELL YOU ABOUT my sister. My younger sister, Caitlin, not my older sister, Colleen.

Colleen is three years older than I am, and about three light-years more mature. She always did everything way ahead of the age I did it—shaving her legs, wearing a bra, starting her period. Good grief, she even opened her own checking account at sixteen. She did that when she started to work in a music store so she could save up extra money for college. Turns out she received a partial scholarship to William and Mary, in Virginia. Then she started to save extra money for graduate school. Colleen never did anything less than independently.

Now Caitlin, she never did anything less than infuriatingly. I mean it. From the time she could pull herself up to the coffee table, when I was three and she was a year old, she would look right at my mother and reach for the Lenox china candy dish. Mom or Dad would tell her no, but she would keep looking at them, keep reaching, and keep nodding her little dark curly head yes. Colleen, at six, would roll her eyes in disgust.

I would pick up the forbidden object, carry it to a higher surface, and say, "I don't think she understood you, Mommy."

That's kind of why I felt responsible when puberty hit cute little Caitlin at twelve, and she turned into the Adolescent from Hades. First it was clothes. Mom made all our stuff. She liked to buy fabric and patterns on the sly, whip up outfits for us girls while we were at school, and then surprise us with them.

Caitlin started to make little comments about them under her breath. Stuff like "You, too, can be laughed right out of your middle school." Then, in the morning, she would put on that homemade garment, but on the school bus, she would turn up the hem about ten times and secure it with Scotch tape. From there she went on to borrowing clothes from her friends and changing into them at school. Mom showed up unexpectedly one day to take Caitlin the homework she had forgotten and found her in a crop top and ripped jeans hanging down below her belly button.

That's when the fighting started—and the grounding and the taking away of everything precious to Caitlin, including her Walkman, her Metallica posters, and her telephone privileges. But my parents were no match for Caitlin.

She convinced them she was practicing soccer at school, but she would go to Meadowood Mall so she could call her friends on the phone and meet up with boys that made Metallica look like they were in your Sunday school class.

During that period, my mom and dad thought they had her all straightened out. But she was way smarter than they were. When they gave her Walkman back to her, she taped her friends' CDs of The Spin Doctors and Nine-Inch Nails but marked the tapes Michael W. Smith and the Newsboys. She cut classes and took up smoking in the rest rooms.

Naturally, all that creativity took time, leaving her virtually none for doing homework. When report cards came out, when Dad called the soccer coach to ask what the game schedule was, and when Mom thought she would like to listen to a little Michael W. Smith while she dusted the living room, the sun went down on Caitlin.

And did she show even an ounce of remorse?

Guess again. It was like she was back at the coffee table at age one, reaching for the candy dish and nodding her head yes—minus the drool and the curly head. She had her friend shave her hair up one side.

When my parents confined her to her room, Caitlin burned incense and candles until Mom thought her daughter was practicing satanic rites and took them all away from her. Then Caitlin sneaked out the window.

They ordered weekly progress reports from the school, and

Caitlin forged them. They drove her to school every day, in an approved outfit, and quickly learned to drive to the back of the building to make sure she didn't split through the rear door. Sometimes she beat them.

Colleen stopped speaking to her and started making plans to go far away to college. I talked to Caitlin plenty. I begged her not to mess up her life. I tried to bribe her into behaving by offering her anything of mine she wanted, although she said she wouldn't have any of my juvenile garbage if I gift-wrapped it for her. And I stayed awake nights listening for her so I could stop her if she tried to sneak out.

In spite of my efforts, Caitlin got worse.

By the time she was in the eighth grade, she had graduated to marijuana. A bunch of high-school kids "adopted" her and took her to coffee shops where she hung out with dudes old enough to be too old for Colleen. Caitlin developed a wardrobe made up of obscene T-shirts, jeans that were more rip than denim, and tons of jewelry that looked as if it belonged on the neighbors' Doberman. Somewhere she acquired this red-and-black-plaid flannel that she wore even when it was ninety degrees. Just like she refused to do anything else that was expected of her, she refused to sweat.

So the first semester of her eighth-grade year, my sophomore year, and Colleen's first year away at college was a living nightmare nobody could seem to wake up from. She was busted for pot, and only because my parents had our pastor and half of our congregation vouch for them were they allowed to keep her out of juvie. When she ran away and was caught, the judge still let her stay home but ordered that she undergo psychiatric treatment. He—and everybody else—had no clue why a girl from such a wonderful, Christian, moral family would behave this way. Something had to be wrong with her.

If there was, Caitlin wasn't telling the psychiatrist. She would sit in his office with her lips pressed together, three times a week, at a hundred and fifty dollars an hour. Then she would come home and swear at my parents. My mother would cry and start to clean, and my father would explode and then go out in the garage and pretend to change the oil so he could throw tools around. When the linoleum's pattern was practically scrubbed off and the cars looked as if they belonged in a showroom, my parents decided to send Caitlin away to a Christian boarding school. She wouldn't be able to get away with anything there, they thought, and she would be surrounded by stable, maturing Christian young women twenty-four hours a day.

They sent her in January. By April, I was wondering how those stable, maturing Christian young women were holding up.

Practically every week a phone call came from the school, reporting that Caitlin had been caught trying to steal glue from the art room or bumming a cigarette from the man who washed the dorm windows. The school was going to keep working with her, the administrators said. Our church congregation was going to keep praying for her. My parents were going to continue to drive themselves nuts agonizing over her. Colleen was going to stay with her program of cold, steely silence. And I was going to keep being as near perfect as I could so my parents wouldn't have to worry about me.

Like I said before, perfect I was, too. I made straight A's my sophomore year. I wore every outfit my mother cranked out for me. I practiced the piano two hours a day even when I had to stop taking lessons because they were too expensive with Caitlin's boarding-school tuition. I fixed meals when Mom was too upset to decide between pork chops and Hamburger Helper. I didn't argue with my dad even when he made decisions about my life I thought were unfair—like not letting me help Brianna when the skinheads were after her and Ira. My dad was racially prejudiced—another whole story.

When I had to cry about the chaos our household had turned into, I went to my room on the third floor. It was the only room up there—the coveted attic-turned-bedroom that had been Colleen's and was passed on to me when she went off to college.

It looked like something out of *House Beautiful*. Mom had made the off-white swags and the cream-and-apricot duvet cover and dust ruffle, and she had carefully coordinated the posters and knickknacks, right down to the china saucer on the dresser for my birthstone ring and wristwatch when I took them off at night. The two things I wanted on the walls, the poem Marissa had written for me and the poster Norie had made, Mom hadn't framed yet. Sticking them up with thumbtacks was out of the question.

The Voice in my head told me that poem was hogwash anyway. In fact, right after Marissa gave it to me, I started to think maybe I was in trouble with the eating thing. That's about when the Voice really started to bug me.

Anyway, I wouldn't exactly have called my room a haven. It was just that when I went up there and sobbed into my pillow, Mom and Dad couldn't hear me. They had enough to worry about.

The week before Caitlin was supposed to come home, though, I promised Marissa I would tell them I thought I might have an eating disorder. I would tell them before Caitlin came home so we could fix it. Then it would be out of the way so they could concentrate on her.

But I couldn't even do that much because of what happened that Sunday, the Sunday before Brianna and Diesel's graduation. I'll take you back to that.

We were getting ready to go to church, as usual like the perfect little family of three—me in a flowered dress with puffed sleeves, a sash in back, and lace that Mom had tatted by hand on the collar.

As I hurried past the kitchen to escape eating one of the blueberry muffins whose smell beckoned from the oven, Mom poked her head out and said, "Come here, Shannon. Let me fix that sash."

"Isn't it okay?" I said. I glanced over my shoulder at it, but she was already untying it and deftly making a big loop out of one side of it.

"It's supposed to be in a bow, not trailing after you like a horse's tail," she said. She pressed back a permed tendril of her graying hair from her forehead and narrowed her pale blue eyes—like mine—at the sash. "You have it all wrinkled where you knotted it."

"Colleen says a bow in the back makes your behind look bigger," I said.

"You could use a little bigger behind." She gave a frustrated sigh and yanked out the attempt at a bow to start over. Since it looked as if I would be facing away from her for a while—and since she had brought it up—this seemed like the perfect time to do what I had promised Marissa I would do.

"Can we talk about something, Mom?" I said.

"Of course, don't be silly," she said. "How many times have I told you that you can talk to me about anything?"

I took in an anxious breath. "Um, you know how you just said I could use a bigger behind?"

"Yes. You didn't get Colleen's rump, that's for sure. You take after the McBrien side. Colleen and Caitlin are both D'Angelos."

"No, Mom. It isn't because of my genes, okay?"

She tightened the bow like it was corset strings. I automatically reached my fingers in there to loosen it.

Yeah, do that, the Voice said. *Tight clothes make you look fat.*

"What are you doing, Shannon?" Mom said. "I just got it right, and you mess with it. Keep your hands down!"

She took the whole thing out and started over. I started over too. "My behind isn't small because I'm part McBrien. My buns are skinny because I'm not eating," I blurted out.

"Don't be ridiculous," Mom said. "Of course you're eating. You loved that pasta salad I made last night."

"I went into the bathroom and threw it all up," I said.

Finally, she stopped working on that stupid bow. But now that I had her attention, I wasn't sure I could go on with the rest of it.

"Why didn't you tell me you were sick?" Mom said. I could feel her standing up, and I stared straight at the grandfather clock in the entrance hall. "I could have given you something—"

"It's not that kind of sick," I said to the swinging pendulum. "I think it's in my head. I don't eat."

I heard a creaking on the steps, and I could feel my dad coming down. Man, I had hoped just to talk to Mom and let her pass it on to Dad. He had a way of exploding that could put the average fireworks display to shame.

"What's this?" he said.

He stood right in front of me. He was only about my height so he could look straight into my eyes with his snappy brown ones. His eyebrows were coming down lower, a sure sign he was about to drop a cherry bomb.

"She says she thinks she's sick," Mom said. "It's the first I've heard about it." She went back to cutting off my breathing with the sash.

"What do you mean, you're sick?" he thundered at me. "Do you need to see a doctor?"

"No," I said. "I think I need, like, a counselor just, like, one time so I know how to stop this—"

"A counselor!" Dad's dark, bushy eyebrows lowered like a pair of storm clouds. "I've had enough counselors to last me till doomsday!"

"She doesn't need any counselor," Mom said. She punctuated that with a final snap on the bow and joined Dad in front of me. "Now this is ridiculous, Shannon. If you're upset about something, we can talk about it right here in our own home. I've been humiliated enough by Caitlin's dragging our dirty laundry all over Reno."

"Nobody else is going to a shrink," Dad said, voice still at storm-watch level. "Now, if somebody would just tell me what's going on...What's wrong with you, Shannon?"

I stood there blinking at them. I'm sure I looked like somebody slowly going under general anesthesia. *If I knew what was wrong with me,* I wanted to say, *we wouldn't be having this conversation.*

The phone rang and jangled all three of us. Dad, who almost never answers the phone, snatched it up as if it were some kind of lifeline. Immediately his face went ashen, and he smeared his hand across his eyes.

"John," Mom said. She pursed her lips together. "John, what's wrong?"

It was classic déjà vu. How many times since Caitlin decided she was the Rebel Without a Cause had I stood there while my parents received some bad-news phone call? As soon as Dad hung up, they would yell and cry.

But when Dad set down the phone this time, he held out his arms to my mother. She stood there stiff as a pole while he held her.

"Caitlin's in the hospital," he said. "In Grass Valley. She was in a car accident."

Mom struggled free of his grasp. "How bad is she, John? Don't you lie to me."

"Bumps, bruises, some stitches. A broken rib," he said. "But she was unconscious for a couple of hours so they want to keep her for—"

"Head injuries?" Mom said. She was pursing her lips fast and furious, and her eyes were wild. My own heart was thrashing inside my chest.

"No," Dad said. "They just want to keep her for observation."

"We're going," Mom said. She was already taking the steps two at a time.

"Of course we're going. What did you think?" Dad said as he followed her.

I stood helplessly at the bottom of the stairs until, on the first landing, he stopped and leaned over the banister. "Find your mother's purse. Meet us in the car."

The drive to Grass Valley–Nevada City where Caitlin went to boarding school usually takes two hours, but that day Dad made it in just under an hour and a half. The more he and my mother "talked," the harder he pushed his foot down on the accelerator. I sat in the backseat white-knuckling the door handle.

"This may just be the wake-up call Caitlin needs," Dad said. "I mean, God works in mysterious ways."

"Well, this is about as mysterious as it gets," Mom said. She sneaked a glance at him as he frowned through the windshield. I could see his eyes smoldering in the rearview mirror.

"She isn't hurt that bad, but she could have been. If she has any sense, she will see this as a second chance." Dad gave a loud sniff through his sizable Roman nose. "Course, if she had any sense, she wouldn't be where she is in the first place."

"Let's give her a little credit," Mom said. "It wasn't her fault this time."

"What? That she got into the car with some kid who was drunk?"

"What are you talking about?"

"That headmistress—what's her name—said Caitlin was riding with a kid who had been drinking. He flipped the car off one of those hairpin turns—"

"Why didn't you tell me?"

"I'm telling you now."

"Did she say what Caitlin was doing off campus in the first place?"

"What do you think she was doing, Bronwyn? What is she always doing? Fouling up her life!"

By that time, I had released my death grip on the door handle and was applying it to my own wrists, wringing them out as if they were turkey necks.

"Well, this school obviously isn't working," Mom said. "I just want to bring her home and *make* her behave."

"You better buy some handcuffs and leg irons then," Dad said.

I cleared my throat uncertainly. "Um, I don't think she needs that."

They both looked at me as if they just realized I was with them.

"No?" Dad said. "What does she need, Shan?"

"Don't you dare say she needs counseling," Mom said. The pinch lines between her eyes, right at the top of her nose, deepened like scars. "It's ridiculous for a girl from a family like this to need some stranger telling her—telling us—how to run our lives. She doesn't need any more counseling; you don't need counseling. I don't go for all that."

She turned stiffly forward and rifled through her purse, pulling out half-used Kleenex and wadded up store coupons and filling the litterbag with them. She was stony silent. Dad glanced at me in his mirror, and the wrinkles around his eyes softened.

"You're all right, Shan,'" he said. "Whatever you have going on, you'll work it out." He shifted his eyes back to the road. "You're not like Caitlin. We can always count on you."

Mom looked up from the litterbag at me. She gave a shaky, it's-all-right-for-the-moment smile and reached back to pat my knee. If I had been standing up, she would have patted my nonexistent buttocks. That was Mom-language for "You're a good girl, Shannon. You're such a good girl."

Oh, you're good, all right. Just not good enough.

When we arrived at the hospital, I dutifully followed my parents. I didn't believe this was a wake-up call for Caitlin, and it turned out I was right. The first thing Caitlin did when she opened her somewhat foggy brown eyes from the middle of that sterile white pillow was laugh.

"Cheated death again, huh, guys?" she said.

She turned on the dimples for Dad's benefit, the bite-the-bottom-lip smile for Mom, and directed a see-I-can-pull-anything-off look at me.

Mom brushed Caitlin's short, milk-chocolate-colored curls back from her forehead. "This isn't funny, Caitlin. Your father and I are very upset."

"What was my first clue?" Caitlin snatched the smile right off her face and glowered at them both. So far Dad hadn't spoken, but his facial muscles were working up to it. I stammered around in my brain for something neutralizing to say.

"This isn't the time to be a smart-mouth either," Mom said. "You could have been killed."

"But I had my little seat belt on like a good Doobie." Even under the influence of pretty heavy pain medication, Caitlin could be sharply mocking.

"Well, that's good at least," I said quickly.

"Wow," Caitlin said. "Goody Two-Shoes gives me a compliment. What, am I supposed to write that in my memory book?"

"I was just trying to help," I said lamely.

"What do I need help for? I didn't do anything wrong. This wasn't my fault!"

"It's never your fault, is it, Caitlin?" Dad said. "Somebody else is always to blame."

"Well, what the...You send me off to this school where I have to ask permission every time I have to go to the bathroom, and then you wonder why I sneak out to have a little fun?"

At that point, I stepped away from the bed and went into the bathroom myself. If I had eaten anything that day, I would have made myself throw up. As it was, I sat down on the closed toilet seat and grabbed at the sink with both hands.

The Voice was right there. *You want to chew Caitlin's head off, and you know it.*

I can't do that.

Of course you can't, and you had better not. You would lose control. You've seen your father do it a billion times.

It's hard to stay in control!

Well, you better try.

So, for about the thousandth time in my life, I stood up and went back to my family and tried. I tried really hard to make everything perfect.

CHAPTER TWO

DAD AND I WENT BACK HOME TO RENO THAT NIGHT, BUT Mom stayed in Grass Valley with Caitlin. The doctor was releasing her from the hospital in a few days, but then everything had to be settled at the school and all that.

Dad didn't say too much on the way home beyond "Are you hungry?" and "Do you need to stop and use the rest room?"

I said, "No thanks" to both. I wanted to make as few waves for my father as possible. When my parents had called Colleen to ask her to come home and help, she had flatly said she was taking summer classes and, gee, just couldn't make it. As usual it was all up to me.

I decided to start by getting the eating thing under control.

The Monday before Diesel and Brianna graduated, I went home after my last final and defrosted a package of ground sirloin and made a meatloaf, baked potatoes, and asparagus with hollandaise sauce. I was chopping apples for a Waldorf salad and trying to imagine myself across the dining room table from Dad, eating the first real meal I had had in about two months, when the phone rang. Dad was calling to tell me he had to work late and to eat without him.

The minute I hung up, the Voice nagged at me. *Good. Now you have no excuse to eat.*

I cut off a hunk of meatloaf, put it on a plate, and loaded a potato with butter and chives. Then I dribbled some hollandaise over a helping of asparagus.

Go ahead, glutton. You don't have any self-control, and this proves it. You are actually thinking about putting that slimy green stuff into your mouth.

My stomach turned over.

How do you expect to get below ninety pounds filling your gut with butter, huh? It's disgusting.

I gagged.

Yeah, that's more like it.

I dashed for the powder room in the entrance hall and hurled myself at the open toilet. Face in the bowl, I threw up. Then I tore up to the second-floor bathroom where the scales were.

Ninety-one pounds, they told me.

Ninety-one fat, disgusting pounds.

What's going on? Why can't I get down to ninety?

It sure isn't going to happen if you eat meatloaf and baked potatoes! What were you thinking? You have two torn-up parents, one messed-up sister, and another who's about to abandon the whole family, and you can think about food? What's the matter with you?

I sank down in the corner of the bathroom, under the towel rack hung with thick, peach-colored towels that smelled like Downy, and squeezed my eyes shut. I could feel my shoulders shaking.

I wasn't crying though, not with tears. I hadn't cried with tears for a while. They seemed to have all dried up.

Where do you get off feeling sorry for yourself? the Voice said. *You have nobody to blame but yourself for any of this.*

When my shoulders stopped shaking, I went down to the kitchen, put my portion of dinner into the garbage disposal, and kept Dad's warm in the oven. Then I took out the fat-free, unsalted crackers and put them in the outside garbage can for tomorrow's trash pickup. I would consume water and nothing else from now on.

Mom called two days later, on Wednesday, to say they were releasing Caitlin from the hospital and the two of them would be home next Tuesday after Caitlin made up her finals.

"Make her study," Dad said to Mom on the phone.

I left the room before another argument ensued. And before the Voice could start screaming in my head.

That was the state I was in on Friday when Diesel and Brianna graduated and we had our party—the one I've told you about. I didn't fill Marissa in on all that, and yet somehow she knew I was leaving things out. I think that's why she called me when I got home from the park.

"I just saw you an hour ago," I said glibly.

"But you didn't answer my question," she said. "Can you spend the night tonight?"

"My dad isn't coming home for dinner again," I said slowly.

"Then there you go; you can eat here," Marissa said. "You are eating, aren't you?"

"Oh yeah," I lied.

I could hear pans clanging around on her end of the phone. I could also hear my own stomach growling.

"So what are you cooking?" I said. Maybe if I just heard about it that would stop the gnawing in my insides.

"Chile relleno," Marissa said. "I'm putting three kinds of cheese in it. You like cheese?"

"Love it," I said.

Yeah, to the tune of thirty percent fat content. You might as well stick it right on your thighs. Splat—like lard.

"Shannon?"

"Huh?"

"So, can you come?"

By then I could hear her grating the cheese. I could practically smell the salsa, feel the jalapeños nipping my tongue…

You are losing control. What are you, a pig?

"I can't, really," I said. "So much is going on with my sister. I have to be here when Dad comes home. It's, you know, family stuff."

"Again?" she said, voice sympathetic.

"Still," I said. "It never ends. But I think it might get better now."

"I hope so," she said. "What about you? Are you—"

"I really have to go," I said. "I'll call you tomorrow."

Then I forgot that, too. I forgot everything as I went back into the kitchen and checked the bubbling cheddar on the tuna casserole I had in the oven. I fixed myself a glass of ice water and drank half of it. Then I dumped out the ice. Then I dumped out the rest of it. Then I set a stunning table for my dad.

Cheyenne called me Saturday, about to bust the proverbial gasket, and told me she was coming to our church over the summer since she was going to be working there.

"You want me to save you a seat?" I said.

"Yeah. Where should I look for you?" she said.

Well, right in the middle, of course. We D'Angelos were pillars of the church. We were always right in the middle of things. That's where Cheyenne found Dad and me the next morning. After she hugged me eight times, she told me everything that had happened to her since I had seen her on Friday, which included such monumental events as an old episode of *Mad About You* and a trip to the bead store for new stuff to make jewelry.

"I need to make you some earrings," she said, bobbing the pair of purple glass beads she was sporting. "You wear mostly pastels, right?"

I hadn't thought about it, but I shrugged. I guessed I did at that.

The service finally started, and I remembered we were doing a series on the Beatitudes. We were up to "Blessed are the peacemakers" that Sunday. Reverend Winston was anything but peaceful as he roared at us from the pulpit. You could even see his spit flying.

"What is this about peacemakers?" he said. "Jesus said He came to make war, not peace. But then He turned around and said blessed are the peacemakers. What's that about?"

That's what I'm supposed to be doing, I thought. *Making peace in my family.*

Hey, you're doing a great job of it so far, aren't you? They ought to bring the Nobel Prize to your door any day now.

The argument must have gone on in my head for some time. The next thing I heard was "Blessed are the peacemakers." Reverend Winston was reading again as he closed his sermon. "For they shall be called the children of God."

Oh, that's you all right. One of God's favorites.

"Let us bow our heads in prayer."

I obediently bowed my head, but no prayers were there. Only a blank.

That wasn't new. I hadn't been able to pray for three or four weeks. Not that I hadn't tried. I had even gotten down on my knees and pounded on the bed. But nothing would come.

Except, of course, the Voice. *What did you expect? You can't talk to Him, messed up as you are.*

Just then, as we sat in church, I could feel my heart pounding really fast, so hard my throat throbbed.

"Let us sing hymn number 120," the pastor was calling out.

I lurched to my feet, and that's the last thing I remember until I heard Dad whispering, "Come on, Shan. Come around."

"Why?" I muttered. "Are you hungry? Do you want me to fix you something to eat?"

"What did she say?" somebody else whispered.

Why were they whispering? Where were we?

I opened my eyes and saw a vaulted ceiling far above me. A light fixture was spinning crazily from it. No, my *head* was spinning.

I tried to sit up, but Dad caught me by the shoulder and forced me back down.

"What happened?" I said.

"You passed out cold," Cheyenne whispered hoarsely. "I leaned over to ask you what page, and you sank out of sight!"

"Does it hurt?" Dad said. He was running his fingers across the back of my head, which I shook.

"I'm fine," I said. "I must have just fainted. I'm okay."

"You are no such thing," Dad said. "Nobody 'just faints.' I'm taking you to the hospital."

"No, I'm okay!" I said.

Dad ignored that and every other protest I lodged between the church and St. Mary's Hospital. When he walked into the ER waiting room carrying me, three nurses practically attacked us and swept me away from him. I was relieved that they tucked me into an examining area alone while he filled out a bunch of forms. Maybe some doctor could tell me nothing was wrong and get me out of there before Dad could finish the forms.

"So, I hear you're having a little trouble saying vertical," a voice said, preceding a tall, lanky, curls-cut-short doctor into the curtained cubicle.

"I just passed out is all," I said. I forced myself to stop wringing my wrists and sat up as straight as I could with the room swaying. "See? I'm upright now."

"Yeah, well, why don't you lie down," he said, "before you conk out again."

"I feel fine now, really," I said.

"Uh-huh. Let me just have a listen."

He pressed a cold stethoscope against my chest while I concentrated on his nametag—Kevin J. Bogen, M.D.—and pretended he wasn't staring at my flat chest. He squeezed my arm with the blood-pressure cuff and then did it again as if he hadn't gotten it right the first time. Then he looked at my fingernails and frowned. I licked my lips and tried to look healthy.

He pulled up a stool next to the examining table, closed my chart on his thigh, and leaned on it. "How much do you weigh?"

"Ninety-one," I said.

"When was the date of your last menstrual period?"

"I know I'm not pregnant, if that's what you're thinking," I said.

"That's not what I'm thinking. When was it?"

I fiddled with my birthstone ring. "Sometime in April."

"First part of April or last part of April?"

"Okay, maybe it was the end of March," I said.

"Any constipation?"

Could this get any more embarrassing? I shook my head, although I couldn't remember anything about that.

"Headaches?"

"No."

"How are you sleeping?"

"Fine."

"You don't wake up early in the morning? Have trouble falling asleep?"

"A lot is going on in our family right now," I said.

"So you're not sleeping well?"

Dr. Bogen looked at me over the top of my chart. His gray eyes were kind of droopy at the corners, and his mouth was soft. I tried to smile at him.

"I guess not," I said. "That must be why I fainted, huh?"

He covered my hand with one of his, which was warm.

"Are you always this cold?" he said.

"Most of the time," I said.

"I think you know why you fainted, Shannon," he said. "Why don't you tell me?"

Dr. Bogen didn't seem to expect an answer really. He put his hand up to my hair and gave a gentle tug. He came out with a palmful of pale blond.

"We learned in biology that you lose a hundred hairs a day," I said.

"You like biology?" he said.

"It's okay," I said.

"What grade did you get in it?"

I looked at him in surprise. He was still wearing that sincere face.

"An A," I said.

"Then you probably also know that blue fingernails probably mean you're anemic, and a sunken-looking body, dry skin, very low blood pressure, and a slow heart rate are evidence that you're anorexic. Am I right?"

I tried not to gnaw on my lower lip, wring my wrists, or look down into my lap like a bad little kid. I looked at him, and I tried to smile again.

"Oh, I know that," I said. "But I'm working on it."

"Working on it how?" he said. "Do you have a therapist?"

"Not exactly."

He nodded. "Who's here with you?"

"My dad," I said. "I've already told him about my problem. He knows."

He drummed his fingers softly on the top of my chart. "So if I put this all to him, he won't be surprised."

I shook my head. *But please don't. Oh man, please don't.*

"I tell you what I'm going to do," Dr. Bogen said finally. "I'm going to recommend to your father he take you to your family doctor and get you a complete physical—EKG, blood count, electrolytes, chemistry panel, hormones, the whole bit. Now, I tell you, they may not show anything abnormal. Your weight isn't so dangerously low yet that any real damage has been done. But if you keep on like this, you will hurt yourself. You'll do worse than faint, Shannon; you'll eventually die."

"I'm not going to die!" I said.

He gave me a long look, one so long I had to turn away.

"No, I don't think you will," he said. "I think you're smart, and you have a lot going for you. But take care of this, you hear me?"

"I do," I said.

"All right. I'm going to get your dad in here."

He did, and while I listened he told Dad to take me to our family doctor for a checkup, have this list of tests run, take me home, and make sure I ate a dinner of no less than four hundred calories—plenty of carbohydrates, protein, and fat.

You will not do that, do you hear me? No way! You'll blow up like the Goodyear blimp! the Voice screamed at me.

I almost barfed right there.

"I'm sorry, Dad," I said as we headed for the car.

He shook his head. "No need to be sorry."

"But you have all this stuff going on with Caitlin. I'll do better, I promise. I'll eat. You don't need to take me to the doctor."

He waited until he had pulled the car out of the parking lot to respond. "I'll have to discuss this with your mother."

I wanted to groan. Discuss? Right. At the top of their voices.

"She'll say the same thing, I know she will," I said.

But Mom didn't have a chance to say anything. She was there, with Caitlin, when we arrived, and Caitlin was pitching a fit.

"I didn't come home so you could lock me up like a prisoner!" she was screaming at the top of her voice. She had learned from the best.

"If you act like a felon, we treat you like a prisoner," my dad said, jumping right in midfight. "Funny how that works out, huh?"

"Oh, excuse me for not being your idea of perfect!" Caitlin screamed back. For an instant, her eyes blazed across me.

Mom and Dad were so busy going after Caitlin—practically with whip and chair—that no mention was made of the four-hundred-calorie meal I was supposed to eat or the doctor I was supposed to see or the list Dad had conveniently left on the table by the front door. I tore it into little pieces and deposited them in the trash can.

CHAPTER THREE

THE NEXT DAY, MONDAY, WAS THE FIRST DAY OF TRAINING for those of us who were supposed to help the Montana team with Vacation Bible School. Cheyenne, Tobey, and Marissa were picking me up. I woke up thinking about that, but my thoughts were shoved into another line when the smell of bacon infiltrated the upstairs.

Maybe if I take a long time to get dressed, I won't have time to eat, I thought.

No such luck. Dad tapped on my doorframe when I was buckling my sandals for the third time and said, "Your mother has breakfast on the table. Let's go, Shan." Then he waited for me like an usher at a wedding and saw me down the two flights of stairs. Talk about wringing my wrists, they were like dishrags.

My mother put a larger-than-life plateful of scrambled eggs in front of me and instead of "Good morning, Shannon" said, "You eat every bit of that."

"That's a lot," I said carefully.

"I put cheese in them," she said. "You always liked them with cheese. You're going to have bacon, too, and toast."

I could feel the bile rising from my esophagus. I would never make it to the powder room if I ate even half of that.

I smiled faintly at my mother, but as soon as she went back to her Jenn-Air, I divided the eggs into three parts and proceeded to smash and scatter them so it would look like I was eating. Dad was busy with the local news section so he didn't notice.

"I'm not fooling with you, Shannon," my mother was saying over the sputtering bacon. "It's ridiculous that we had to have somebody in an emergency room tell us you aren't eating enough."

I glared at my fork. *I tried to tell you that myself.*

"I don't think we need to run to Dr. Chadwick. I'd be so embarrassed. You are just going to have to eat better. That's all there is to it."

The toaster popped up as if on cue, and she went after a slice of whole wheat bread with a knife and a blob of butter. I took a drink of orange juice, swished it around in my mouth, and spit it back into the glass. The eggs were growing cold on the plate in front of me.

"Speaking of food," Mom went on, "I need to know what you want for your birthday dinner. It's next Tuesday, you know."

I watched the egg come up between the fork tines as I held them down hard. My throat closed.

"You always wanted spaghetti when you were little. With Colleen it was steak."

Dad grunted. "Leave it to her to want something expensive."

"Don't you start in on Colleen," Mom said. "She is paying her own way, if you'll recall."

"I don't need to recall. You remind me every ten minutes." Dad scowled at the newspaper and sipped noisily at his coffee. I watched Mom put bacon on my plate with tongs and set it all off with two triangles of buttered and jellied toast.

"Every bite," she said.

She brushed back the always-falling-down-on-her-forehead tendrils of permed hair and went back to the stove yet again. What else could she be cooking? Enough nauseating food was already on the table to feed us and a small Vietnamese family.

"You don't have to fix me a big birthday dinner," I said. "You have enough going on with Caitlin."

"Caitlin is going to be fine. She's home, and that's where she needs to be."

I ripped off a hunk from the toast and played with it. She was acting as if Caitlin *hadn't* hurled three throw pillows across the living room while she screamed last night.

"Do I hear a car?" Dad said.

"That's probably Tobey and them," I said. I pushed back my

chair and wiped my mouth needlessly with a gingham napkin. "I'll see you this afternoon, Mom."

"You're not going anywhere until that plate is empty," she said. She turned toward me, forehead pinched between her eyes like the solid lines on a highway.

"I'll make everybody late!" I said.

"Then they can go on, and I'll take you," Mom said. "I have to take Caitlin anyway. I'm having trouble getting her out of bed."

"Where's she going?" I said.

"To the church."

Mom said it as if I had just asked a stupid question. I asked another one.

"For what?"

"Same reason you're going," Mom said. "They said she could help, provided she didn't make any trouble, which she won't. She can't sit here on her fanny all summer. The more she has to do, the less trouble she can get into."

A honk sounded from Tobey's horn.

"Let me just tell them to come on in," I said. I picked up my plate and took it with me to the front door, burying the bacon in the potted plant next to the grandfather clock. Then I went out to meet them.

"That looks good," Cheyenne said, eyeing my plate.

"Want some?" I said. I shoved a piece of toast at her and walked slowly so she would have it consumed before we reached the door.

Mom, of course, put a whole pile of the stuff on the table for everybody and filled juice glasses even as she inspected my plate. The lines between her eyes smoothed out a little when she saw that the bacon and toast were gone. I scooped up a forkful of egg and lifted it to my lips. When she turned away, I set it back down.

"Cheyenne told us you had to go to the hospital yesterday," Tobey said.

"I'm fine," I said and then glanced warily at my father. He was intent on some article.

"So you don't have, like, some kind of disease or something?" Cheyenne said.

Marissa nudged her.

"No," I said. "It wasn't anything."

Out of the corner of my eye, I saw Mom turning back toward us so I grabbed on to the first new topic I could think of. "When does Ira's trial start?"

"Next Wednesday," Tobey said.

"Why couldn't that be settled out of court?" Mom said.

"They tried that," Tobey said. "But the way my father explained it to me, everybody involved on a higher level—the district attorney and all those people—want it to go to trial because then nobody can say they were siding with the skinheads or siding with the blacks."

"Have to keep the politicians off the hook," Dad mumbled. "God forbid anybody should take responsibility."

"What does your dad think is going to happen?" I said.

"He's not sure. I mean, he's not a lawyer or anything, but he's been talking to some attorneys at our church. Anyway, he says the district attorney has to prove beyond a reasonable doubt that Ira went up into the mountains that day intending to injure the skinheads."

"What's he charged with?" Dad said. Tobey had his full attention now, and that made my stomach churn. I set down my fork.

"Attempted murder. His lawyer tried to get it changed because of some comparative something or other—"

"Comparative fault," Dad said.

"What's that?" Cheyenne said. She offered me the bacon plate, and I shook my head.

"They compare the faults of both people involved, and if it comes out fifty percent on each side, then nobody is charged," Dad said.

"And that didn't happen?" Marissa said.

Tobey shook her head.

"So if they prove that, will he go to prison?" Cheyenne said. "I mean, we don't want that, no way. I've been in prisons, when my stepfather was there. It's so gross—"

"He could get twenty to life," Dad said. He snapped the newspaper back into place and started to read again. I could feel myself stiffening.

"But that isn't going to happen," Tobey said. "He has a good lawyer, and Ira didn't go up there to hurt anybody, and that's going to come out."

"I bet he's scared," Cheyenne said.

Marissa nodded. "I would be."

"That's why we're all meeting with him tonight, to see what he wants us to pray for," Tobey said. "You want me to pick you up, Shannon?"

"No," Dad said.

I stared at the back of his newspaper. Tobey shifted in her seat. "Okay," she said. "If you have another ride—"

"She isn't going."

"My dad's letting me go so you know it isn't going to be late," Marissa said.

They all glanced at my father and then busied themselves with butter and toast. I shoved aside my plate and leaned against the table.

"I'm just trying to support Ira," I said.

He sighed and put down the newspaper as if I were interrupting a board meeting or something. "Why? Because he was messing around up in the mountains and hit some white kid head-on and killed him?"

"There was more to it than that," I said.

"We're not going to have this discussion," Dad said. "I didn't let you get involved in this before, and I'm not going to change my mind now."

He started to pick up the newspaper again, then gave it an impatient tap and stood up. "I have to get to work," he said and pecked my mother on the cheek.

She kept her eyes on me, with a why-did-you-even-bring-that-up look on her face. Then she nodded firmly at my plate. "I still see eggs in front of you, Shannon. You're not leaving here until you eat every bite."

I thought I was going to die. Just die, right there at the table in front of my three best friends.

Tobey, God bless her, tried to save me. "Do it, girl," she said, glancing at her watch. "We're going to be late. Want some help?"

"No help," Mom said. "Come on, let me see you take a mouthful."

"Okay, Mom," I said, my lips tight. "You don't have to stand there and watch me. I'll eat it."

She just raised an eyebrow at me. She *was* going to stand there and watch me. All I could do was shove that disgusting, rubber, yellow mass into my mouth. I did—and chewed and fought against the gagging of my throat muscles. She kept watching. My friends stared at their shoelaces. I put in one more bite and chewed solemnly. Mom gave a satisfied nod and headed for the doorway. "I'm going to try to get your sister out of bed. I want that plate clean when I come back."

I couldn't look at anybody when she left the room.

"Dude, she treats you like a five-year-old," Cheyenne said.

Tobey glared at her, and Marissa gave her a gentle nudge.

I shoved one more forkful of egg into my mouth and choked. I grabbed a napkin and spit the whole mess into it. Then I marched to the trash can and dumped it in, napkin and all. When I turned back to the table, the eggs were gone. The three of them looked at me like a trio of caught cats.

"Let's go," Tobey said, mouth stuffed. "We're already going to be late if we don't *run* to the car."

I never loved them more than I did at that moment. Unless it was the next moment when we could hear Caitlin cussing at my mother from upstairs, and they all acted as if they hadn't noticed a thing. In fact, they all started to talk at the same time as soon as we climbed into the car.

I sat there and smiled and put in an occasional snicker, but I had no idea what they were talking about. My mind was racing like a pack of greyhounds.

Why can't Mom and Dad leave me alone?

Because you don't have the brains of a two-year-old. If you were halfway mature, they wouldn't get on your case. Just grow up. Meanwhile, get rid of those eggs. You don't deserve them, the way you've messed up.

As soon as we pulled into the church parking lot, I made tracks for the rest room. "I'll meet you guys in there," I called to Tobey.

She nodded and led the way into the main meeting room downstairs. When they were out of sight, I broke into a run, flinging open the door to the girls' bathroom and diving for the stalls. The door to the first one was closed, so I bent over and looked underneath for feet. Nothing.

I tugged at the stall door.

It didn't come open at first, just like usual. Everything in that church was old. Every door stuck.

I gave a determined yank, and the thing came open with a wood-ripping sound. I would have been dismayed that I had torn half the latch off, if a guy hadn't been standing on the toilet seat.

Seriously. There stood a dude dressed in shorts, a striped T-shirt, and Tivas, feet planted on either side of the seat, hands pressed against the sides of the stall. Oh, and face scarlet all the way to the roots of his reddish hair.

I let out a yelp, and so did he. I took a step backward, and he looked down at me from the seat, grinning. Only later did I notice the cute gap between his two front teeth.

"I can explain," he said.

"Okay," I said.

"The guys' rest room is all messed up. Both toilets are stopped up. It's gross in there."

"Okay."

"But I had to, you know, go, so I came in here. Then I heard somebody come in, and I knew whoever it was would be as embarrassed as I was, so I was going to hide and then leave once you went into the other stall. Only...you...didn't."

He shut his mouth and shrugged and looked as if he really wanted to bolt out of there. So did I.

"Oh," I said.

"So I guess I'll leave now," he said.

With that, he took a step forward and landed his left Tiva right smack into the toilet. Water splashed over the sides, and I stood there hoping against hope that he had never gotten around to using the thing.

"Aw, man!" he said. "Can you stand it!"

I shook my head, for no apparent reason, and he leaped down, onto the floor this time, and stood there for a second, still looking down at me. He had to be six foot three and not an ounce over 150 pounds. Somehow he got past me, dragging toilet water en route to the door. I could hear his sandal squishing all the way down the hall.

"What was *that?*" I said out loud.

It was a boy, stupid, about which you know nothing and never will, so give it up. Now that you've messed that up, you have no time to throw up and clean up. You're going to have to keep those foul eggs you ate. You don't even have the backbone to stand up to your parents. They have no respect for you.

I put my hands over my ears and made for the bathroom door.

By the time I reached the meeting room, the whole group was sitting in a circle, passing a box of donuts around and introducing themselves. A man with very hairy legs and a face that would have been just as hairy if he hadn't recently shaved was sitting on a table at the front, and he smiled at me when I arrived.

"Come on in," he said.

I nodded and made a beeline for a chair next to Tobey.

"I'm Doug," he said. "You'll have to catch up on the names you've missed—and look out, there's going to be a test."

I nodded again and pulled a pad and paper out of my purse to take notes. Test? Okay, I could do test. Perfectly. Straight-A.

"I'm Adam," a familiar voice said.

I looked up to see Toilet Boy standing up, grinning his gap-toothed smile at the group. If I had just stuck my foot in a toilet, I couldn't look as poised as he did. Especially when the girl next to him nudged him on the knee and said, "Adam, why is your shoe making a puddle on the floor?"

Everybody leaned over to look and snickered.

"I had a little accident in the bathroom," he said.

"Oh, gross!" the girl said. She squeezed her eyes shut and shook her mahogany-red ponytail.

"No, not that, Holly," Adam said. "I didn't wet on myself."

"Thanks for sharing," Tobey said.

Adam turned and grinned at her, and at the same time caught me in his sights. He grinned even bigger. I looked studiously down at my pad.

"Let's not go there," Doug said. "Moving on…who's next?"

People continued to introduce themselves—the six people on the traveling team, the twelve from our church, and some others.

I wrote them all down and started to commit them to memory. Of course, I practically forgot my own when Doug called on me.

"Shannon," I said. My voice wavered, the way it did when I was nervous. I really hated that about myself. "D'Angelo," I added.

"Cool name," Holly said. "I'd love to have a name like that."

"What's wrong with your name?" Cheyenne said.

"Holly Schwartz?" the girl said. "I can't wait to get married."

"Marry me," Adam said, holding up his hand and grinning.

"You don't want to do that," Doug said. "Then you would be Holly Polley."

"I love that!" Tobey said.

"Uh, no thanks," Holly said. She patted Adam's thigh. "Sorry, pal."

Adam didn't look all that sorry. He just grinned. He seemed to do that a lot. He even directed another one at me. I started to smile back, but I felt as if my lips were going way above my gums, and I felt stupid. I looked back down at my notes.

And you wonder why guys aren't part of your life. Gee, what was your first clue?

"Okay," Doug said, pressing the fingertips of both hands together like a spider doing push-ups on a mirror. "Let me just tell you what our team is about here, and then we're going to do some exercises to see if we can't meld with what you guys are about. How does that sound?"

I didn't participate verbally in the meeting, which turned into a lively discussion. Tobey and Cheyenne were right in there. Marissa was, too, kind of, I mean, in her Marissa-way. She is about the best listener on the planet. You never feel like she's thinking about what she's going to say next when you're talking. I felt a pang of guilt. I had stopped talking to her.

About what? You don't need to load your problems onto your friends. You've done that enough. Get a grip.

The next thing I had to do was get through lunch under my mother's eagle eye. I didn't have to worry though. When I reached home, she had other things on her mind.

"Shannon, is that you, honey?" she said, when I closed the kitchen door behind me.

"It's me," I said. No soup-and-sandwich platter waited on the table. That was good news. I could just say there had been food at the church, which was true.

"Come on up here. I want to show you something," she said.

I went all the way upstairs to my attic room, hoping she didn't have the chicken clubs ready beside my bed.

Nope. Nothing was next to my bed—at least, where my bed used to be.

"What happened?" I said.

My room looked about half its former size, and it only took ten seconds to figure out a second bed was squeezed in there with a second dresser.

"Surprise," Mom said. "Caitlin's moved in with you!"

MOM WAFTED HER HAND OVER WHAT NOW LOOKED LIKE the showroom at Gruner's Furniture Store.

"Why?" I said.

"She's in the shower," she said in a half whisper. She nodded me toward the bed.

"Who?" I said.

"Caitlin. It's been a long morning, but we're making progress."

She sat on the edge of what I assumed was Caitlin's bed, across from me, and looked right into my face. Like she could help it. The beds were so close together I could see where she needed to pluck a few eyebrow hairs.

"After you left, Caitlin threw one of her hissy fits, and I just sat her down, and I said, 'Look, young lady, you tell me what's eating you and you tell me now. I'm sick of this.' She knew I meant business. So we wrestled around with that for a while and finally..." Mom rolled her eyes, and I could see tears forming a filmy line across her irises. "She just blurted it out. 'I don't feel like I'm part of this family anymore.'"

Mom looked at me, but I just looked back. What was I supposed to say?

"I can see her point," Mom said. "I mean, she's been separated from us, and we've just gone on with life. How is she supposed to feel coming back to us now?"

"I don't know," I said.

"So she went back to sleep on the sofa for a while," Mom went on. "She was exhausted from all that hysteria, and I thought, What if I moved her in here with you? That way you could focus on including her in things and making her feel like she's your sister again. I moved everything in here, and then she woke up and went to shower before I could show her. So I went ahead and put on the finishing touches."

"Finishing touches" wasn't the word for it. My mother is like a Tasmanian devil when it comes to getting things done. It didn't even have to be a very long shower for her to take down all my posters of piano keyboards with roses on them, an angel playing the flute and all that stuff, and put them back up on what I could only assume was now "my side" of the room. And then for her to fill Caitlin's side with the least disturbing of her stuff: a poster for the movie *The Crow,* another poster that read "This is your brain, this is your brain on drugs, this is your brain on drugs with a side order of bacon," featuring two fried eggs with bacon forming a smiley face (enough to make me gag every time I looked at it), and a fantasy art poster with a chick in a cloak on a horse, riding past a dark mountain, which if you looked at it closely, you saw was made out of skulls, snakes, and scorpions. My mother obviously hadn't looked at it closely. I shuddered.

There's no way I'm going to be able to live in here! I wanted to scream at her.

Just then, Caitlin appeared in the doorway wrapped in a peach-colored towel. It didn't take her five seconds to start screaming. "What the—"

"You have a roommate now," Mom said crisply. She smoothed out a nonexistent wrinkle on the bedspread and gave Caitlin a plastic smile. "You don't even have to unpack. I've done it for you."

"Well, you can just pack it right back up!" Caitlin shouted. "I am not living with her!"

"Caitlin, you have no reason to be jealous of Shannon," Mom said.

I blinked.

"Who said anything about jealous?" Caitlin said, upper lip curled. "Why would I be jealous of her? She's a nerd."

"There will be no name-calling," Mom said. "We don't do that in this house."

"So, are you going to tell us what we *do* 'do in this house'?" Caitlin said.

I had to admit I was thinking something like that myself. It would be nice if Mom would give us the script for the play she had written when we weren't looking.

"You're going to rediscover each other," Mom said. She headed for the door, rewarded us with another plastic smile, and stepped out into the hall, pulling the door almost all the way shut behind her. We didn't close doors all the way shut "in this house" either.

Caitlin stomped over to the door, gave it a good, swift kick with the ball of her foot, and set the whole upstairs shaking. In the process, she also dropped her towel, revealing the entire back of her curvy, olive-skinned, pixie-short body. She was a perfectly proportioned D'Angelo. I was a wiry McBrien.

Caitlin swore as she snatched up the towel and wrapped it back around her, just below the outbreak of acne scattered across her back and the tattoo of a scorpion on her shoulder blade.

"What are you looking at?" she said. "Are you some kind of pervert?"

"No," I said. Now, if I had been Colleen, I wouldn't have dignified that question with an answer. But I was not Colleen.

"I hate this place!" Caitlin shouted. She took a leap out over her bed and landed squarely on her back.

"Just so you know," I said, "this wasn't my idea."

"I didn't hear you disagreeing with her," Caitlin said. She directed her angry brown eyes at me for a second and then looked away as she rolled them.

"What good would that do?" I said. "You know she's going to do exactly what she wants. If you argue with her, all you get is the silent treatment."

"Good," Caitlin said. "Anything to shut her up."

She sat up cross-legged on the bed and inspected her toenails, which, I noticed, were painted black.

"Do you always paint your toenails black?" I said.

"What do you care?"

"Just wondered."

She sniffed. "No. Depends what mood I'm in."

"What kind of mood is black?" I said.

Caitlin's eyes closed into slits, and her full upper lip curled. She was no longer pixie-cute. Charles Manson was more adorable.

"The kind of mood I'm in right now," she said. "Like I want to slash things."

She stood up, and for a second I thought she was going to grab a nail file and go after the posters. But she discarded the towel and rifled through a dresser drawer.

"You can't tell me this doesn't tick you off," Caitlin said.

I shrugged. "Sure it does. I mean, this is my room."

"The woman is losing it, that's all I have to say," Caitlin said into the drawer. "If I learned anything from that shrink they sent me to, it's what crazy is and what crazy isn't. Mother is what crazy is."

I looked at her sharply, just in time to see a gold ring shining from her navel, before she pulled on a pair of cutoff jeans. *Way* cut off.

"Did you learn anything from that psychiatrist? I mean, did he help you?" I asked.

"With what? I wasn't the one who thought I needed help. It was Mom and Dad and that stupid judge."

I took a breath. "You have to admit you were pretty much messing up your life—"

"Was I? Or was I messing up what *they* thought was supposed to be my life?" She pulled a too-small white T-shirt over her bra-less chest and flopped back down on the bed, hairbrush in hand. I tried not to watch as she went after her lopsided crop of dark hair. It seemed to me it would hurt to brush the side that was shaved. I also tried not to smell. The clothes she had just put on, miniscule as they were, had a funky odor, a combination of cigarette smoke and greasy cooking, neither of which came from our house, believe me.

"I know you think you're supposed to fit into their little mold—you and Colleen both," she said. "But I'm not going to do that."

"What mold?" I said.

"Oh, come on, Shannon. Man, you really are dense. But then, it didn't happen the same with you, so how would you know?"

"What didn't happen?" I said. She was talking in downward, spiraling circles that were making me nauseous. I pulled out a pillow and hugged it against me.

Caitlin tossed the brush aside and sprawled on the bed in that

I-could-care-less position she liked to take—legs spread-eagle, arms free to gesticulate. "Okay, it's like this. Mom doesn't want any of us to grow up. Haven't you figured that out yet? Colleen escaped it by getting out of here. You, you just go, 'Oh, I'm not supposed to grow up? Okay.'"

I dug my fingernails into the pillow, but I let her go on.

"I'm almost fifteen. I'm supposed to have more freedom and responsibility, and here they are shoving all these rules and regulations down my throat—unreasonable rules."

"What's unreasonable about them?" I said.

She narrowed her eyes at me. "Don't start with me, okay? You sound like that shrink. 'Just what strikes you as unfair, Kalyn?' I went to the dude five times before he ever got my name right." She waved her arms around like she was erasing something in the air. "Anyway, the point is, if you're going to grow up, you have to, like, totally give up your security and go for it. I see that—anybody with brains sees that—but *they* don't see that. Plus they don't trust me. So if I'm going to break away, I have to just do it. I'm not going to stay here like a caged animal the way you do."

"I'm not a caged animal!"

"You just don't see it because you're Daddy's little girl. And Colleen is Mommy's precious angel. Which leaves me to fend for myself, which I'm trying to do. Only nobody wants to let me." Her voice rose to a shout, and she hurled the brush across the room where it connected with my desk chair and dropped neatly into the wastepaper basket. While she was retrieving it, I squeezed the pillow more firmly so I could wring my wrists. This was getting freaky. I actually *did* feel like a small creature behind bars, although Caitlin was the one who was acting like it. She flung her hairbrush onto her dresser and paced around "our" room like some entrapped, wild feline. She was snarling too. Any minute now I figured she would start slashing—with her black toenails.

"It's the truth, you know," she said. "You can't deny it."

"What?" I said.

"That I even *look* more developed than you." She stopped in front of me, and for an awful second I thought she was going to whip off her shirt to compare her chest with mine.

"Did your psychiatrist tell you all that stuff?" I said.

Caitlin rolled her eyes. "No. All he told me was that I felt like Mom and Dad's restrictions were evidence of a lack of trust, even when I myself knew that my rebellious, hostile behavior was wrong and dangerous." She hooted. "Right."

"Well, wasn't it? It was."

"Make up your mind: Are you asking me or telling me?"

"Mom and Dad were doing what they thought was right. They were just trying to help you—"

"Oh, please!" Caitlin went fanny first onto the bed, wet curls bouncing out of one side of her head. "Let me tell you about their 'help.' I went to them once, okay, when I was feeling really crummy about myself, and I told them I hated the way I was acting. I just wanted a way to work things out with them. You know what they did?"

I shook my head. It was the first I had ever heard about this conversation.

"They told me to keep going to the shrink, who sat there and looked at me for six weeks in a row and then told them I needed to go to boarding school. So they didn't even ask me what I wanted. They just shipped me off like a FedEx package—the faster the better."

She yanked open the drawer of the bedside table, pulled out a pack of gum, and peeled pieces open. I watched as she stuffed three of them into her mouth.

"Man, I wish I had a cigarette," she said.

"You wouldn't smoke it in here," I said.

"Are you telling me or asking me?" She chewed noisily. "No, Mom and Dad never tried to 'help.' What Mom and Dad do—especially Mom—what she does supposedly for us, she does for herself. So she won't look bad in front of the rest of the church ladies. If you went to Mom and Dad and asked them for help—not that you ever need it, since you're so perfect—but if you did, what do you want to bet they would do whatever kept them from being embarrassed?"

"I so don't believe that," I said. Darn my voice for quivering like that.

"You know I'm right," she said. "You're just too chicken to test it out."

I rolled over on my side away from her and closed my eyes. After a couple of minutes, she fired up her portable CD player, and some guy moaned in this raspy voice with stuff in the background that sounded like tin cans in a dryer. I was glad it covered up the words.

Obviously the music was good to clean out closets by because Caitlin went to it, muttering obscenities about the clothes my mother had hung there. I felt as if I were in a dark room with flashing lights and a bunch of empty-eyed people.

It wasn't loud enough to keep my thoughts out though. Or the Voice.

What if she's right, for once? I thought. *What if they really won't help me?*

With what? You don't need any help. You just need to get yourself down to seventy-five pounds, that's all.

But what if I do need help? What if I can't control it anymore, and I die?

Worse, what if you start eating and turn into a sow? Either way, nothing will be left of what was a pretty pathetic you in the first place.

I squeezed my eyes shut tight. Caitlin couldn't be right. She was the one who was so messed up nobody could control her. Why was I listening to her? I didn't need to prove it. I knew Mom and Dad would help me if I really pinned them down.

I spent the better part of an hour pretending to sleep and pretending I believed that. By after dinner, I was like a shaken-up soda, ready to explode if somebody flipped open my top. I had to check it out.

When Dad was in the den reading and Mom was in there, too, hemming a dress, I sidled in and cleared my throat and generally looked as awkward as it is possible for a human being to look.

Dad said, "Hon, you have something on your mind?"

I sat down on the plaid tweed couch next to Mom and fingered the dress. It was pastel flowers on polished cotton with a large square collar trimmed in ribbon. I hadn't seen her working on it before.

"What's this?" I said. "Is it for Caitlin?"

If it were, we might as well start mobilizing for Iwo Jima.

But Mom shook her head. "It's for you. To wear for your birthday dinner."

"Oh," I said.

She held it up, and I stifled a groan. Another puffy-sleeved, too-girly affair that looked like just about everything else I had in my closet. Plus it was miles too big—at least I hoped so. I hoped I wasn't as fat as *that* dress looked.

"What *is* it, Shannon?" Mom said. She thrust the dress impatiently back into her lap. "I get so annoyed when you pussyfoot around like this. Why can't you just come out and say what's on your mind?"

"Because so far nobody's given her a chance," Dad said from behind his book. He looked significantly at my mother over the top of the pages. I started to talk really fast before they launched into an argument and my chance was eradicated.

"Remember the other day, the day we went to Grass Valley, I was telling you guys that I thought I had a problem with eating? Then that doctor in the emergency room said he thought I did too?"

"Vaguely," Dad said dryly. But he did close the book on his lap to watch me.

"Well," I said, "I kind of think...I think I want to see a therapist."

Immediately they looked at each other, and one of those we've-been-married-so-long-we-don't-actually-have-to-use-words discussions took place. Nervously I pulled my hair up into a ponytail and let it fall. Strangely, I thought of that doctor at the hospital pulling out a handful of my hair. It did feel thin and dry and ugly.

"I just don't think it's necessary," Mom said finally. "I wouldn't even know which one to take you to. And it never did Caitlin one bit of good. How do you think we would pay for something like that? You know we've spent every dime we've saved on your sister's treatment—"

"Insurance would cover it," Dad said.

Both Mom and I looked at him, probably with identical expressions of disbelief.

"You don't mean to tell me you're agreeing to this?" Mom said.

Dad flicked an eyebrow. "We've met the deductible for this year. It isn't going to cost us anything."

"Except a lot of time," Mom said. "Unless you plan on finding one right down the street she can walk to."

I looked at my father, but he was already picking up his book. "But I think insurance will only pay if it's a medical necessity."

I passed out in church! I wanted to scream at him. *A doctor pulled out a bunch of my hair and said my fingernails were blue!*

So what? Caitlin was right; they're not going to stick out their necks for you, and why should they? What? You think you're worth it?

No, of course not. What a stupid question—even from me. I stood up and started out of the den.

"I'm sorry," I said. "I think I was overreacting."

"Please," Mom said, picking up her needle again. "One of those in this house is enough. Why don't you just stop thinking so much about it and spend a little more time on your music? Did you practice while I was gone?"

I was glad the phone rang, and I was really glad it was Marissa. I was starting to feel as if the whole world was crazy.

"Are you back from the meeting already?" I said.

"You know me; my parents want me in practically before dark." She giggled softly.

"So, how's Ira?" I whispered.

"He's hanging in there," Marissa said. "I would be so freaked out if I were him. But he has, like, this incredible faith. He just keeps saying if we all pray with him and for him, and if some of us show up the first day in court, he knows it's going to be all right."

"Oh," I said. "I can pray for him. But I can't go." Well, I could *try* to pray for him.

"I know you can't go to court. We're going to tell Doug tomorrow when the date is, though, because the three of us are going." She hesitated. "Your Dad was pretty set about that, right?"

"Yeah," I said. "And that isn't the only thing."

Why I let that slip out, I didn't know.

"What else?" she said. "Is it about your anorexia?"

I nodded—stupidly, since we were on the phone, for Pete's sake. But Marissa "heard" it. She knew me that well.

"I think I'm going to have to do something on my own," I said. "You know, like read a book on it or something."

"What about Ms. Race?'

"Huh?"

"Ms. Race. She says call her anytime. Didn't you used to talk to her a lot?"

I had. When Caitlin had first gone away, I had been in Ms. Race's office almost every day, and I had even been over to her apartment. It had been a while though...

"I don't want to bug her," I said. "She's getting ready to go on her trip and everything."

"She would be so upset if she found out you had a problem and she didn't know about it," Marissa said. "You know that."

"Who ripped off my Metallica CDs?"

I put my hand over the receiver, but I was sure Marissa had already heard an earful as Caitlin charged down the stairs, baying like some kind of wounded basset hound. "Why don't you guys just do a body cavity search on me, huh? Want me to strip down right here?"

"Caitlin Anne, don't you dare!"

"Well, what the—"

"Don't you swear or so help me I'll smack you right across the mouth!" Dad shouted.

"No hitting. We do not hit in this house," Mom instructed.

"And how else do you plan to get through to her, Bronwyn?"

"I have to go," I said into the phone. "I'll see you in the morning."

"I'm sorry, Shannon," Marissa said.

I was too. But at least Caitlin's pitching another fit made me sure about one thing—I was going to have to handle this without my parents.

CHAPTER FIVE

SO I CALLED MS. RACE THAT NIGHT AND I BASICALLY SAID, "I know I'm anorexic because this doctor already said so, and he says I need, like, a therapist and a bunch of other stuff, and my mother says she doesn't even know where to start, so Marissa said I should call you. Is that okay?"

All in about one breath.

I breathed a lot easier after she said, "Of course it is, Shannon. I've missed you. When do you want to get together?"

I just wanted to go over to her apartment right then. She said she would pick me up at the church the next day when our staff meeting was over.

I think that's how I made it through the next morning. Otherwise, I probably would have wrung one of my wrists right off.

Mom's attention to my eating was pretty short-lived, so that wasn't the problem. She was way more tangled up with Caitlin. She came into our bedroom at 7 A.M. and rolled up the shades till they flapped around at the top and left both of us squinting and going, "What?"

"Rise and shine, girls!" Mom sang out. "Breakfast is in twenty minutes, and I don't want any arguments."

We had none at that point. Who can argue when her brain isn't functioning yet? That would account for why Caitlin hauled herself out, stumbled to the bathroom, pulled on a pair of really baggy jeans and her black-and-red flannel, and made her way to the kitchen without a word.

Mom, of course, went into this long line of cross-examination about why Caitlin was wearing an outfit like that on a hot day, and why in the world she ever had her hair cut that way, and was she going to make sure nobody saw that tattoo on her right shoulder blade. Even I couldn't see how Caitlin was supposed to keep cool and keep her body art hidden at the same time, but I kept my mouth shut and concentrated on not eating the bowl of oatmeal in front of me.

I expected Caitlin to dig in her heels when Tobey came by to pick us up, but she followed me out to the car, eyes still at half-mast, and nodded numbly when Mom told her to behave herself at the church. Then Mom looked at me and started mouthing things, none of which I understood. But I knew she was telling me to include Caitlin in everything, introduce her to people, make her feel accepted…

So I did. When anyone came up and said, "Who's your friend?" I would answer, "Um, this is my sister Caitlin."

Mostly she shrugged, and so did I. I was thankful she wasn't curling her lip at everybody and throwing insulting remarks in people's faces. Until I introduced her to Adam.

Tobey had taken the comatose Caitlin over to meet Holly, when Adam said at my elbow, "So who's that?"

I looked up…and up…and up into his freckled face and gap-toothed smile.

"My sister Caitlin."

"Cool," he said. Then he left me standing there while he strode across the room in two long steps and said, "Hi. I'm Adam."

Caitlin took one look at him and stuck out her hand and shook his. You could see her face waking up.

Adam stuffed his hands into his pockets and curved his back over the way tall guys do when they're talking to short girls they really want to hear. I had a deep, green pang of envy.

Caitlin must have had some kind of pang too, because suddenly she was smiling, laughing, and dimpling. She pretty much had everybody charmed by the time we divided into teams for our small-group activity, which was to make collages around themes we were going to cover with the kids in the program.

I flipped through magazines for pictures of "letting go."

"What am I looking for anyway?" Cheyenne said. "'Letting go'; that's hard."

I glanced around at the other groups to see if anybody was yanking out photos of "self-discipline" and "sacred space" or whatever. My eyes snagged on Adam, sitting next to Caitlin and throwing back his red head to howl at something she had said. She poked him with her elbow and gestured toward a picture she was holding.

I turned around and impatiently grabbed the scissors.

What are you feeling so disappointed about? Did you think he even remembered your name? Get your body fat down, and then we'll talk...although about what I don't know since you can't carry on a decent conversation. Give it up.

I did. At least, I thought I did. In fact, all through putting together our giant collage, mopping up Cheyenne's overenthusiastic use of Elmer's glue, and helping Holly spread our finished product on the table with the others to dry, I was focusing on meeting Ms. Race for lunch. And wondering how to make it through a meal without having to pig out. It had been stupid of me to agree to *lunch.*

I was deep in reverie during our wrap-up session, when I realized somebody was saying my name.

"Yo, Shannon!"

I looked up from studying my kneecaps to find Doug—and everyone else—looking at me.

"Where were you?" Doug said, playfully rubbing his dark, freshly shaved chin.

Across from me, Caitlin rolled her eyes. Then she tilted back her head to look up at Adam, who was perched on the edge of a table behind her. She laughed up into his face. And he laughed back.

You see? He thinks you're a geek. He knows you're a geek.

"I was told this morning you play the piano like a mad dog," Doug was saying.

"How does a mad dog play the piano?" one of the Montana guys said. Randy, I remembered was his name.

"So," Doug said, "Shannon, would you play for the opening worship services when we get this thing rolling? Adam will join you on guitar from time to time."

"I still think you should let me play drums," Randy said.

Let him play drums! I thought. *Nobody wants to hear me play the piano.*

But I nodded dutifully at Doug.

"Great," he said. "I hear you can play just about anything."

"She can," Cheyenne said. Then she flung an arm around my neck and gave it a squeeze.

Marissa leaned in from the other side and whispered, "Are you okay with this?"

"Sure," I whispered back.

Of course, I wasn't. I hated playing the piano in front of people. The minute I knew somebody was listening, I developed six thumbs.

I checked across the circle to see if Caitlin was sneering, but she was busy sharing some private joke with Adam.

When Doug closed the meeting, Tobey said she would take Caitlin home.

I stood there while the three of them hugged me—and Caitlin curled her lip. Then I picked up the stack of sheet music Doug put in front of me.

It really doesn't look that hard.

Yeah, but you'll find some way to mess it up, Sweaty Palms.

"Psst, Shannon!"

I looked up. The room was empty except for Adam. He was still perched on the edge of the table with the collages, and his face was kind of blotchy, like he was blushing in stages.

"Could you stay a minute? I need your help," he said.

"Okay," I said. "What's wrong?"

"I'm stuck."

I looked at him stupidly. Stuck emotionally? Stuck on Caitlin? Stuck on Band-Aid brand?

"I don't think they're dry yet," he said.

"What?"

He nodded over his shoulder, and my gaze fell on the collage he was sitting on.

"That one's ours," I said. As much glue as Cheyenne had put on there, it might not dry until Halloween.

"Well, I think half of it's going to be on my rear end when I get up," Adam said. "I tried to stand up when the meeting was over, and the whole thing came with me."

I put my hand over my mouth. "What do you want me to do?" I said from behind it.

"If I raise up a little, maybe you could peel off what's stuck to my jeans and kind of stick it back onto the collage."

You want me to peel things off your fanny. Okay.

My previous most-embarrassing-thing-that-had-ever-happened-to-me was fast being replaced.

"Can you see the damage?" he said. He hoisted himself up on his hands. Staying about a foot from the table, I craned my neck around to see. One large square of glued-down magazine picture was clinging to the back pocket of his jeans.

"It's not that bad," I said.

"Can you get it?"

"Um, sure."

"Can you kind of hurry?" he said. "I can't hold myself up like this for too long."

"Um, sure." That was all I seemed to be able to say. I inched a little closer and reached out a hand. This was *so* the most embarrassing thing in life.

"Can you get it?" he said.

I slid my palm across the collage to his jeans and gently pushed away the paper. With only a small ripping sound, it came loose and swished back down to the tabletop. I surveyed the collage as Adam pushed himself off the table.

"How bad is it?" he said.

"Just one little piece. I can fix that," I said and started doing it.

"Aw, man." Adam gingerly fingered the back of his jeans. "See the part that tore off?"

I looked at the collage and nodded. About an inch of a picture of somebody in a hot air balloon was missing.

"It's now part of my Levi's," he said. "We have to take this off before somebody sees it. Man, I'll never live this down."

"We" have to take this off? I wanted to say. *What do you mean "we"?*

He turned around and pushed his backside toward me. "See it?"

It was hard to miss. A square of soggy magazine print was stuck on his left cheek.

"Quick, before somebody comes in," he said.

That was my motivation for sticking my hand right out there and prying.

"Are you getting it?" he said.

"Well, almost." I couldn't help but giggle.

He looked over his shoulder at me. "How much am I going to have to pay you not to tell anybody about this?"

"Nothing." I focused on scraping off the newsprint with my fingernail.

"Is it coming off?" he said.

"Yeah. Well, pretty much."

"'Pretty much' is not what I want to hear. 'Yes, Adam, you can't even tell it was ever there.' That's what I want to hear."

I pried off the last of it and said, "Yes, Adam, you can't even tell it was ever there."

He twisted his neck like a corkscrew trying to see, and I giggled again.

"It's not that I don't trust you," he said.

"Serious. It's gone."

He turned his whole body around then and grinned down at me. "Okay, so really, what do I have to do to buy your silence?"

"Nothing. Honest!" I put both hands over my mouth.

He smiled from one earlobe to the other, showing that adorable gap between his two front teeth. I wondered if he could tell I was smiling behind my hands.

I'm smiling! I thought suddenly. *I feel...weird.*

"I knew you would say that. That's why I waited for you. Anybody else would have it all over the church—all over town. They'd broadcast it in Montana."

I could feel my smile disappearing.

Why did you think he picked you, idiot? Because you have the personality of papier mâché?

I know, I know, I told myself.

But looking up at his dancing freckles and his gap-toothed smile, I wished he'd had a different reason.

Ms. Race was waiting for me in front when I came out, and she drove us down McCarran to the Five-and-Diner. It's this fifties-style restaurant where they have little jukeboxes at the tables and pictures all over the walls of Elvis and Buddy Holly. We slid into a red vinyl booth and ordered milkshakes. I got mine with yogurt; why I didn't know, since I probably wouldn't drink it anyway.

"The burgers here are incredible. Have you had the one with cheese and bacon?" Ms. Race looked up at me, and a soft furrow appeared in her forehead. "I'm sorry. Can you eat at all?"

I almost cried. She was the first person who had shown any kind of understanding, except for Marissa. I had done the right thing by coming to her.

"It's hard," I said.

"Do what you can," she said. "Will it bother you if I get a double bacon burger with fries?"

"No!" I said. "Their fries are great here. I remember that."

She reached across the table and squeezed my hand. "You'll have them again before you know it. I can practically guarantee it. Now, the lady who I—"

But the waitress came up then, flipping her ponytail around.

"Um, side salad for me, please," I said.

The chick stopped her ponytail in midswing. "That's it?"

"Yes, please."

"Are you at least going to have it with thousand?"

"No dressing," I said.

She looked at Ms. Race as if to say, "Is this girl weird or what?"

Ms. Race demurely ordered her lunch and handed back the menus. "That'll be it for now. Another person is joining us in a few minutes."

"Somebody else is coming?" I said when the waitress was gone.

Ms. Race nodded. "I can't believe I was able to set it up on this short notice, but Georgianna is a close friend of mine."

Well, she's not a close friend of mine! I wanted to yell. *I don't want everybody in Reno to know I'm a mental case!*

"I've never gone to her for therapy myself," Ms. Race was saying. "But several of my friends have. I met her at a women's conference through the church, and we just clicked. I think she's going to be perfect, but, of course, it's up to you. If you don't feel comfortable, all you have to do is—"

"Comfortable about what?" I said.

Ms. Race stopped with her last words still formed on her lips.

"About seeing her. It did happen faster than I thought it would, but God's timing is always so much better than ours."

"Timing for what?" I said. "I thought I was going to talk to you."

Her eyes got still, but I knew her mind was racing. She fingered her braid. "Shannon, were you thinking *I* was going to counsel you? I mean, long-term?"

"I know you're going away," I said. "I can wait until you come back, if that's the problem."

"No, honey, the problem is this is way beyond my level." She grabbed both of my hands just as I was about to drag them under the table so I could wring my wrists. "You told me a doctor said you have an eating disorder, and I agree with him. I've been worried about it for a while, but Marissa said you had gone to your parents—"

"Marissa told you?"

"Only because I asked her."

I didn't care whether I hurt her feelings or not. I wrenched my hands away and put them in my lap.

"I don't know enough about this to help you, Shannon. This is a life-threatening condition. You need a professional. Besides that, it needs to be someone who isn't emotionally involved with you. I think you'll love Georgianna."

I gnawed my lower lip as the waitress brought our milkshakes. I picked mine up and set it noisily at the far corner of our table. Ms. Race watched me, and the furrow in her forehead deepened.

"I don't have any money to pay for a therapist," I said, staring hard at the Formica tabletop until the red-and-gray design made me dizzy.

"We're talking about a real illness. Insurance will pay for it."

"My parents won't let me do it."

I could almost feel her hands tightening around her milkshake tumbler. "You've asked them?"

"Yes."

"And they said no?"

"They said no," I told her. "They have enough going on with my sister. I just wanted to handle this on my own so I didn't have to bother them."

"Bother them?" Her eyebrows shot up to her hairline, and she stared at me, eyes as wide as the coasters on the table.

"You don't know what dealing with Caitlin has done to our family," I said.

"Yes, I do," she said. "I can see it right in front of me, and you are every bit as important as Caitlin. Right now, you might even be in more trouble."

Her eyes flickered over my head, and she smiled. I could feel the swish and warmth of another person approaching our table and sliding into the booth beside Ms. Race.

"Hey, girlfriend!" Ms. Race said to her.

"Hey, you."

The woman kissed Ms. Race soundly on the cheek and then looked right at me. I didn't look down into my lap. I couldn't. I felt as if I were under inspection, and I might get demerits if I didn't pay attention.

"George, this is Shannon D'Angelo. Shannon, my friend Georgianna Diffie."

"Good to meet you, Shannon," Georgianna said. She put out her hand to me, and I put my palm against hers with the idea of pulling it right back. Her hands were warm. Strong.

"Strong" definitely was the word for this female. She was as tall as Ms. Race, I could tell even when she was sitting down. So that made her about five feet ten. She wasn't statuesque like Ms. Race though. She was more loosely put together, in every way. She had this straight hair about the color of maple furniture, streaked with gray, which made me decide she was about forty. Her hair hung to her shoulders, and it needed to be brushed big time.

She was wearing a lot of jewelry, and her clothes weren't any particular style. I mean, she wore a long skirt the way Ms. Race almost always did, but she didn't have Ms. Race's put-together look. This woman was slightly disheveled, rumpled, kind of careless looking.

The only things that didn't appear to be about to take flight from her were her eyes. They were blue. Very blue. Vivid blue. And she used them in a direct way. Even when she smiled at me, which she did as she finally let go of my hand, her eyes didn't waver.

Then the smile was gone, just like that, and we were back to that intense face. It scared the daylights out of me.

"Hi," I said. As soon as I could, I had my hands under the table, squeezing my wrists.

"Thanks for coming," Ms. Race said.

"Thanks for asking me," Georgianna said to both of us.

"Well, you might not say that after you hear what I did." Ms. Race said.

Georgianna pointed to a couple of things on the menu for the waitress while she simultaneously looked at Ms. Race and nodded.

"I misunderstood Shannon," Ms. Race said. "I thought she was looking for a therapist."

Georgianna looked at me. "You aren't?"

I shook my head.

"She thought I was going to counsel her."

"I can understand that," Georgianna said. "You're wonderful." She picked up a water glass and drank about half of it, her eyes still on me. That look was weirding me out.

"Well, it seems her parents aren't willing to foot the bill for therapy at this juncture," Ms. Race said.

At that, Georgianna set down the glass and, if possible, her face grew even more intense. She scoured my face with her eyes. "You've told them how you're feeling."

I nodded.

"Hmmm," she said.

"I'm sorry. I know you have such a busy schedule—" Ms. Race started to say.

But Georgianna waved her off. "I have to eat anyway. This beats cottage cheese in my office." She folded her hands in front of her. "Tell you what. Since I'm here, and you're here, and Enid is footing the bill for lunch—you are, aren't you?"

She turned her quick smile to Ms. Race, who wrinkled her nose. Then Georgianna turned back to me. "So what if I just ask you a few questions? Would you mind that?"

"I guess not," I said, though I would rather have danced on the table than tell this total stranger a single thing about my life over burgers and fries. I clutched my forearms and waited.

"This is hard, I know," Georgianna said. "In my office we

could take the time to get comfortable with each other. But let's just make the most of the moment."

"Sure," I said.

She gave me a look that clearly said, "I'm listening to you, and I'm hearing more than you're saying." And I had barely said anything.

Don't you dare say anything more than you have to either. You've answered all these questions before. Ms. Race already knows all this stuff; she could have helped you. She betrayed you.

"If you had a whole afternoon to yourself and money was no object, what would you do?"

I stared at Georgianna. "I don't know. I never had that."

"I'm not sure any of us has, but just use your imagination. What would you do?"

"I don't know," I said again. "I guess I'd..." Shoot, what was I supposed to say?

"First thing that comes into your head," she said briskly.

I didn't dare say "I don't know" again. "I'd...go running at Rancho San Rafael. Yeah, I hardly have time for that anymore."

"If you had to tell me the thing you've done that you're most proud of, what would you tell me?"

"Um, I got straight A's this time. But that wasn't the first time so, I mean, I'm not bragging—"

"You're supposed to brag; it's that kind of question."

"Um, okay, well, this other girl and I gave a recital, like, just the two of us on piano, way last summer, and my dad had the teacher present me with roses up on the stage because he was so proud. So I guess that's it."

"Your dad was proud."

"Was it supposed to just be me being proud? I could think of something else—not that I have a long list or anything."

"No, that's okay," Georgianna said. She looked up as the waitress approached with a tray held high over her head.

"One more question before the food comes," she said. "When was the last time you felt truly, genuinely happy?"

"Happy?" I said.

"Right. One of those crystal-clear moments when you just felt good."

The waitress didn't wait for me to answer. She dealt dishes onto the table, and I busied myself with shaking pepper and salt all over my salad so I wouldn't be tempted to eat the whole thing. When Ponytail-Flipper was finished delivering the ketchup, the relish, and refills on their milkshakes—not mine, I hadn't touched it—I thought maybe Georgianna would let the question drop. But she kept looking at me with that I'm-listening expression on her face. I stabbed a cucumber six times.

"You can't think of a time, can you?" she said.

I looked up and almost stabbed her.

"I know you can't," she said. "And that, my dear, is what you need to tell your parents."

"I've felt happy!" I knew my voice was quivering like some kind of wounded bird. "I felt happy just today, about an hour ago."

"How did it feel?" Georgianna said.

I cut up the cucumber, as if I were really going to eat it. Then I reached for the salt again. Georgianna caught my wrist in one hand.

"Try to remember," she said.

The only way to get her to back off was to answer. "I smiled without thinking about it. And I just felt...weird."

"Unfamiliar," Georgianna said.

"Yeah."

"Different than you've felt in a long time."

"Yes," I said viciously. *And please don't ask me what it was that made me feel that way because I'm not going to tell you! It's none of your business.*

"Shannon."

I looked at her. She was leaning toward me, her eyes going into me like examining hands.

"Just tell me one thing, and then I'll leave you alone."

"Okay," I said.

"Wouldn't you like to have that happy feeling more often?"

"I guess so."

She made a buzzing sound with her voice. "Wrong answer," she said.

"Yes," I said.

"Then you need to go home and do what you did when you were two years old."

"What?" I said.

"You need to whine and cry and stomp your feet until your parents give in. Because, Shannon, it doesn't matter if you see me or someone else, but I don't want that glimmer of happiness you had today to be the last of it you ever feel. And if you don't get help, it might be. It just might be."

CHAPTER SIX

MS. RACE DROVE ME HOME. BOTH OF US WERE SILENT. AS I was getting out of the car so I could escape into my house, she said, "I'm going to pray, Shannon. I know you will, too."

"Sure," I said. I slammed the car door.

Now she was telling me to pray.

Right. Like God listens to a person who is so stupid she puts herself in a situation like that. Lunch with a therapist you can't afford for a problem you could deal with yourself if you had any backbone. Not that it is a problem; it's just what you deserve.

Right. Pray. Talk to God. Like I used to, by myself and with my Flagpole Girls. Go to God and lay it all out.

It sounded so inviting I would have cried, if I hadn't been so busy trying to stuff the burning feeling back down my throat. And that was like trying to get your sleeping bag back into one of those nylon pouches.

The thought wouldn't leave me alone, though. I went up to "our" room where Caitlin was passed out on her bed. I tried to nap, but I couldn't rest. I had to force myself to lie there like a pole with my eyes closed. I kept picturing myself kneeling to pray.

No, just forget it, I told myself firmly. *Get hold of yourself. Then you get to go back to God. But not until you're a whole lot better person than you are right now. Right. And how do you intend to become that, Barney-Brain?*

I dropped off into a fitful sleep, only to be awakened by Caitlin rummaging through her drawers.

"What are you doing?" I said.

"What does it look like I'm doing? I'm getting dressed to go out."

I propped up on my elbow. "I didn't know they were letting you go out."

"They're not 'letting' me do anything," she said. "I'm just doing it."

So much for Caitlin having a good day. No trace of that morning's charm was visible anywhere on her person. She slipped on her plaid shirt and shoved her hands into the pockets of her baggy jeans. It was like watching a stranger walk out of our room.

But stranger or not, she could turn this whole house upside down if I wasn't careful. I went down to the kitchen where my mother was talking on the phone and motioned to her that I would help with dinner. She nodded gratefully as I chopped green peppers and minced garlic and sliced mushrooms.

We had dinner almost on the table before she said, "I'm going to wake up your sister. She is sleeping way too much…"

She was still talking as she went up the stairs. I cringed and dumped a box of pasta into a pot of boiling water.

Dad was coming in the back door when Mom charged back into the kitchen, hair falling down over her forehead as if she had just run a marathon.

"Now what?" Dad said.

"She's not here."

"Where did she go?"

"Now, if I knew that, would I be acting like a madwoman?"

"Did you check the backyard?"

"No! I just discovered she was missing."

"She isn't 'missing.'"

"Then what do you call it?"

"I call it going out for some air," said a voice from the doorway.

Caitlin rolled her eyes at both of them as she crossed the kitchen, Doc Martens wreaking havoc on my mother's linoleum.

"Where have you been?" Dad said.

"Why did you leave without asking me?" Mom said.

"Hi, Caitlin. How are you?" Caitlin said in mock falsetto. "Oh, I'm fine. Thanks for asking."

"Don't get smart, young lady," Dad said.

"Dad, I am not a lady, okay? As for young, I'm only as young as you two try to make me act. Which is, what? Three? Four, tops."

"Go to your room," Dad said.

"Gladly."

"No, now, John, we are not going to do it that way." Mom's voice was turning shrill.

"Look, I just walked in the door," Dad said. "I'd like to be able to take a breath before I have to start dealing with…this." He waved a hand toward Caitlin.

"You know, I really hate being referred to as 'this,'" Caitlin said. She turned on her heel. "Don't bother calling me for dinner. I'm not hungry." She looked at me and sneered. "Goody Two Shoes can have my share."

Mom started to go after her, but Dad grabbed her arm.

"Let go!" Mom said.

"You're the one who needs to let go," Dad said.

"Of what? Any chance we have of keeping her from going completely off the deep end?"

"Which one of you is going off the deep end?" Dad said. "You or your daughter?"

"How dare you—"

"Stop it! Stop it, please. Please. I can't stand this!"

My knees hit the floor before I realized I was the one sobbing those words, or that I had fallen, because suddenly I couldn't stand up. I careened forward and landed my forehead on my hands at Mom and Dad's feet. I kept crying, and I couldn't stop.

"Shannon, what are you doing?" Mom said. "Get hold of yourself now. We're just discussing—"

"Shannon?"

Dad was at my side, his hands on my shoulders. "What's wrong? What's going on?"

I cried and cried and shook my head. "Please," I said. "No more fighting. I hate this. I hate it!"

"Shannon, get up off the floor—"

"She can't!" Dad snapped at her. "Come on, baby, let Daddy carry you."

I could feel Dad's arms shifting me around and scooping me up.

"I don't want to go to the hospital!" I sobbed to him.

"I'm not taking you to the hospital," Dad said. "Bronwyn, bring her some water."

"I don't want any water!"

"Lie back now."

"I don't want to lie back!"

"What's going on?" I knew that was Caitlin asking, but I couldn't stop crying, not even for her benefit.

"Your sister is upset," Mom said to her as she hurried toward me. "Don't you see what you're doing to this entire family?"

"She's losing it, and that's my fault?" Caitlin said.

"You certainly don't help any—"

"Knock it off, both of you!" The living room grew quiet on the tail of Dad's bark. I heard Caitlin flop into a chair and felt Mom put a glass into my hand. I shoved it away from me. Dad pulled my other hand away from my face and made me look at him.

"Talk to me, Shannon," he said.

"I don't want to talk to you," I sobbed. I mean, I guess it was me. Shannon D'Angelo didn't say "I don't want to" to her parents.

"Who do you want to talk to then, honey?" Mom's voice was suddenly smooth. "Do you want me to phone Colleen for you?"

Across the room Caitlin grunted. I shook my head.

"Who, hon?" Dad said. "You're scaring me now."

"I want to talk to a therapist," I said.

I couldn't tell you where that came from. I just know it was out of my mouth along with the crying that I couldn't control.

I'm not sure I can even tell you what happened after that. Mostly Caitlin swore some and beat a hasty retreat with my mother yelling after her. I know Mom and Dad whispered for a while, and I remember being surprised they weren't screaming at each other. The only thing I remember clearly is that Dad finally sat on the coffee table looking down at me and said, "Okay, Shannon, we'll find you a therapist, and we'll see if we can straighten out this mess. You just need somebody to talk to."

"You know you can talk to me," Mom said over his shoulder.

"So I'll make some calls."

"I already know somebody," I said. "Can you call her?"

There was some real yelling then. I've purposely forgotten most of it. In fact, I curled up into a ball and covered my ears with my hands.

Two days later, I had my first appointment with Georgianna.

"I'm not riding home with you guys at lunch," I said to Tobey on that Thursday.

"How come?" Marissa said.

I wasn't sure I was speaking to her after she had blabbed to Ms. Race.

Caitlin answered for me from the backseat. "She's going to see her shrink."

A funny silence followed.

"Good for you, Shannon," Tobey said. "My dad says everybody could benefit from counseling at some point in life."

"Have you ever been to a therapist?" Caitlin said.

"No," Tobey said.

"Figures."

"But that doesn't mean I won't someday."

"If you're a preacher's kid, you probably will," Caitlin said. "Some of the girls at the school I went to were PKs. The most messed-up bunch of people I ever saw. They were worse than me."

"Tobey's not worse than you," Cheyenne said.

"Chey-enne!" Marissa hissed.

"Oh, I'm sure according to Shannon, nobody's worse than me," Caitlin said. She lapsed into sullen silence and looked out the window.

"I wish I could call my mom to pick her up at lunch," I whispered to Tobey as we walked up to the church.

Tobey put her arm around me. "She's no reflection on you, Shan. She's her and you're you; we don't blame you. "

Well, you ought to. If I weren't such a "nerd," like Caitlin says, I could do something about it. I could at least relate to her.

But that thought brightened me up actually. If I could get some directions from Georgianna today on how not to be anorexic anymore, then I could concentrate on Caitlin. So maybe it wasn't selfish to have pitched a fit to get a therapist after all. Yeah. That made it better.

At least until we walked into the waiting room at Georgianna's office. It was nice in there. Mom commented that she liked the way it was decorated, all Victorian furniture with bowls of pot-pourri and pots of geraniums. I thought it didn't look much like the Georgianna I had met. I was glad because I wasn't sure how Mom and Dad were going to take Georgianna, with her big, loose clothing and uncombed hair.

But when her door opened and a teenage girl with black lip-stick came out in front of her, the Georgianna who greeted us was a cleaned-up version. She still had on a long skirt, Birkenstocks, and a vest with geometric designs embroidered on it, but her hair was neatly sleeked back into a ponytail at her neck.

The I'm-listening-I'm-seeing look was firmly intact as she shook Mom and Dad's hands and then asked them to have a seat in the waiting room.

"Will we be talking out here?" Dad said.

"No, I'll have you come in, but I would like to chat with Shannon alone for a few minutes first. That will give you time to fill out forms."

Mom pursed her lips and made those lines between her eyes, and Dad's eyebrows began to take a dive. But none of that fazed Georgianna. She gave me her fast smile and ushered me into her office. I hoped my parents weren't going to "discuss" right out there in the waiting room.

"Welcome," Georgianna said as she closed the door. "Please sit on anything that calls your name."

I was pretty sure none of the stuff in there knew my name. It was a great room, don't get me wrong. It's just that it was all, like, low-to-the-ground, mushy chairs, pillows, and couches in earth tones. The room was clean and spare, inviting. But this was a therapist, and we had a lot to do in one hour. I picked the first low chair I came to and sat gingerly in it.

She selected a chair straight across from me, sank loosely into it, and surveyed me with her blue eyes. "Tell me why you're here."

"I'm here because I'm anorexic."

"That's the only reason?"

I nodded. "It isn't right to be this way. It's causing even more problems in my family."

"More problems? More than what?"

"Than what we already have."

I started to squirm. Time was going by. We couldn't waste any of it talking about Caitlin.

Then I felt guilty. That was the whole reason for all of this, really, to help Caitlin. She was the one who was in trouble.

"Shannon, if I'm going to help you, I need to know all about you—your family, everything. Do you feel comfortable telling me what problems you're talking about?"

"My younger sister, Caitlin," I said. "She's done marijuana. She's a real rebel. She's all messed up and driving my parents crazy."

"And you."

"It's not so much me. I'm mostly worried about her."

"Why?"

"Because she's already been in one car crash. I'm afraid something is going to happen to her."

"Are you afraid she's going to die?"

I hadn't really thought about that, but if that's where she was going with this, then, okay, yeah. Caitlin might just end up dead.

"Well," I said, "now that you mention it—"

Georgianna held up one finger, and I stopped.

"I have only a few rules for this room," she said. "The first one is the most important one: You never, ever say anything in here that you don't mean, nothing that isn't true for you. I don't care if it's true for anybody else. I want to hear what's true for you. Okay?"

"Sure," I said. But the Voice whispered in my ear, *What if what you think is true isn't really right?*

"So you're here because you don't want your problem to interfere with your parents dealing with Caitlin's problems, is that right?"

"Right," I said. "Serious. That's really it."

"I believe you." Georgianna smiled as she leaned back in her chair and folded her hands casually in her lap. "Then I guess we had better start right away. I have some questions for you."

"Okay." I sat up straight in the chair. Here we go: How much do you eat? How long has it been since you've eaten? How much do you weigh?

"Who's your best friend?" she said.

I tried not to look as if I were about to drop my teeth. "Um, Marissa, I guess."

"When was the last time you and Marissa did something to-gether?"

"This morning," I said. "We both work on the staff at church."

"I'm sorry; let me clarify. When was the last time you did something fun together?"

I flipped back through my mental calendar and shrugged. "It's been a while. Before school was out, like, in May."

"Have you spent time with any of your other friends?"

"You mean, for fun?"

She nodded.

"No, but we had finals, and then there was all this stuff with my sister."

"I see. How much do you weigh, Shannon?"

Here it came. "Ninety pounds," I said.

"How much did you weigh yesterday?"

"Last night?"

"Uh-huh."

"Ninety and a half."

"How about yesterday right after lunch?"

"Ninety and a half."

"And when you got up this morning?"

"Eight-nine."

I remembered how jazzed I'd felt when I'd seen that.

"So you could probably tell me what you weigh pretty much to the quarter of the pound any time of the day, right?"

"Right," I said. *Now she's going to tell you to stop weighing your-self, or that you have to get up to ninety-five pounds.*

"Okay, now let's go back to something you said. I'm a little for-getful sometimes, and I just want to be sure I'm clear." Georgianna seemed to sort back through my words. "You're here because you don't want to be anorexic anymore."

"I want to find out how to stop," I said. "Yes."

"Now, you realize that if you aren't anorexic anymore, you're going to gain some weight."

I didn't answer.

Of course you know that, idiot! What did you think she was going to try to do? If you're not anorexic, you're fat. Is this a big surprise to you?

"What are you thinking?" Georgianna said.

"Um..."

"Just say the first thing that comes into your head."

"Getting fat."

"Gaining weight means getting fat, right?"

I stiffened. "It does to me."

"It's okay, Shannon. I mean, in a way, that makes sense. It always did to me."

I blinked.

"I was anorexic for ten years. Got down to a mean, lean, seventy-five pounds."

Stop dreaming, Shannon. You'll never get to seventy-five, so give it up. You don't have what it takes.

"Would you like to weigh seventy-five?" Georgianna said.

She said you have to tell the truth. Call her bluff. See what she does with the truth.

"I'd like to weigh seventy-five, yes," I said.

"And then you'll stop."

"Uh-huh."

"Boy, you're better than I was. I started off thinking if I just got down to 110, I would be happy. But then I passed 110 and shot for 100. That still looked fat when I stood in front of the mirror, so I thought, okay, double digits—let's see how far down into the double digits I can get."

I sat very still. She was describing my thoughts, right down to the periods and commas.

"I don't know about you, Shannon," Georgianna said, "but when I reached double digits, I was scared to death to get fat."

All I could do was nod.

"But I found out even though not eating served a purpose for me, I didn't have to stay there. And I could get out of it without getting fat."

She looked down at herself and then up at me. "Do I look fat?"

"No!" I said. I squirmed again. "Can you tell me, like, how you did it?" I glanced at my watch.

Georgianna laughed. Her laugh was surprisingly silvery for someone who looked as if she could climb Mount Shasta in a single bound.

"In twenty-five words or less?" she said. "I don't think you're going to have to go through all I did, Shannon, and I'll tell you why I think that." She tucked one leg up under her. "In the first place, you're aware of your problem, and you know it's a problem. Most girls I see in your situation have to be dragged in here kicking and screaming by their parents. From what I can tell, it's your parents who are kicking and screaming."

I couldn't help but smile.

"In the second place, since you are here voluntarily, you aren't going to waste energy fighting the very people who are trying to help you. You can focus your energy on your real enemy."

"Who's my real enemy?" I said. Then I rolled my eyes. "Of course. It's me, right?"

"Oh, no, it isn't you at all," she said. "It's that somebody else who is living inside you, telling you what to do, how to think, what to eat, what not to eat. It's your anorexia."

This was weird. She was making it sound as if I were schizophrenic or something.

Maybe you are. You're wacko enough.

"Am I crazy?" I said.

"No," Georgianna said, "but this is a kind of illness, and it's curable. Don't let anybody tell you that you're going to have to live with this for the rest of your life and all you can do is control it. I don't believe that. Neither does God."

"God?" I said.

"Enid told me you were a Christian. We can talk freely about our Lord in here, can't we?"

"Sure," I said. Though I wasn't sure He wanted *me* talking about Him.

"The three of us can work this out, Shannon," Georgianna said. "God, you, and me. He and I are here to help you strengthen your Healthy Self so your Healthy Self can take care of your Eating Disorder Self."

I was confused. I had enough trouble keeping track of one Self.

Her face softened, and she leaned forward. "Is there any part of you that would like to eat like everybody else?"

I hesitated, and then I nodded.

"All right then. That's the part of you that we're going to get to know very, very well."

I squirmed yet again. This was sounding a lot different from what I had come here for.

"Now, I need to know one more thing before we go on. Tell me, Shannon, do you really want to get better?"

"Of course I do!"

"Now, listen to my question again," Georgianna said. "Do *you* really want to get better?"

"Me?" I said.

"Right. Do you want to recover because *you* want to, or because your mom wants you to, or because your dad is upset because you're not eating? Who is it for?"

Don't even think about telling her you're doing it for yourself. That's about the most selfish thing I've heard run through your mind. Don't even say it!

"I'm doing it mostly for my family," I said. "I just hate what's happening at home."

Georgianna nodded, but she didn't smile.

"What about God?" she said. "Would you consider doing it for Him?"

I shrugged. That was an honest answer. I truly didn't know.

"Then I have an assignment for you for next time," Georgianna said.

"Next time?" I said.

"I want you to say this to yourself out loud twenty times a day at least: 'I'm worth getting better because God loves me.'"

"Even if I don't believe it?" I said.

"Even if you don't believe it. Don't expect big results or big changes between now and the next time I see you. Try to eat what you can. You'll be surprised how much you can eat and still maintain your present weight. You're not in physical danger yet, I don't think, or the doctor you saw would have put you in the hospital. However, I do have to tell you, if you continue to lose weight, and I see you're in physical danger, I will ask that you be hospitalized. Deal?"

"You're not going to tell me how to start eating?" I said, voice quavering pretty nearly out of control.

"I can't do that," she said. "I can't take this away from you. I can't even *make* you give it up. But by working with me, I think you're going to *want* to give it up. Once you really want to, you'll be more than halfway there."

She gave me another smile and then went to the door. Mom and Dad came in, looking bristly and pushed out of shape. They were going to look worse than that when they found out there was going to be a "next time."

"Mr. and Mrs. D'Angelo," Georgianna said when they had heard their chairs calling their names, "we're in better shape than you might think."

Dad grinned, reached over, and squeezed my arm. "That's my girl."

"But we have a long way to go," Georgianna said. "We have early intervention, you are involved in her life, and Shannon is motivated to recover. Those things are all in our favor."

Dad was catching on, I could see. Mom was still reveling in the compliments.

"I'd like to see Shannon twice a week at first, until she's more stable, and I'm wondering if we could arrange for some family therapy as well. It seems some of the things going on at home may be contributing factors."

That was when my mother caught on. She drove a look through me that I could feel.

"If Shannon isn't comfortable with me, or you aren't comfortable, you could see other people in this office, and there are other good people in town. But I strongly urge you to make sure she gets this kind of help now."

"How long are we talking?" Dad said.

"I thought I would only have to come see you once," I said to Georgianna quickly. "That's what I told them. That's why they're surprised. Nobody's mad or anything."

"Shannon, please," Mom said. She gave me a this-is-adult-business look:

"Perfectly valid," Georgianna said. "That's a misconception a lot of people have. We like quick fixes these days. Unfortunately, this isn't one that can be repaired in short order."

"So what are we talking?" Dad said impatiently.

"We're talking therapy on an outpatient basis for at least a year, probably longer," Georgianna said.

I thought Dad was going to explode. Even Mom reached over and touched his arm. He held himself together, but his face was magenta and his eyebrows were about down to his upper lip. Meanwhile, Mom was pursing for all she was worth. I was so still I think my heart had stopped beating.

"All right," he said. "But I can't see a year—I'm going to be truthful with you."

"I wish you would be."

"Counseling never helped our Caitlin, and I can tell you we've spent some bucks on it."

"I know it's costly."

"So I'm putting a deadline on this. End of the summer, at the longest."

Georgianna surveyed him carefully. "What is it you want to see by the end of the summer?"

"I want to see her sitting down at the table and eating a meal without having to be coerced, that's what I want to see."

"I'm not sure I can guarantee that," Georgianna said. "But if until the end of the summer is all Shannon and I have, then let's start right away and see how much progress we can make. How about this Tuesday?"

"For all of us?" Mom said.

"No," Dad said. "That's the other thing. None of this family-therapy stuff. You deal with my daughter. I deal with my stuff the way I deal with it."

"Understood," Georgianna said. "I won't push it. So, Tuesday, Shannon?"

"Not Tuesday," Mom said.

I was about to fold into myself. Could they have made any more of a scene in front of this woman?

"What's the matter with Tuesday?" Dad said. He had said his piece, and he wanted out of there.

"Tuesday is her birthday," Mom said. "It's a family day."

"Oh, well, absolutely. Let's make it Monday, then, shall we?" Georgianna said. "And, Shannon, if you need to talk to me before then, feel free to call."

"I don't think that will be necessary," Mom said.

After nods and stiff good-byes, finally, finally, we got out of there.

Too bad I left without a spark of the hope that had started to ignite somewhere inside.

CHAPTER SEVEN

I REALLY *HAD* FELT HOPE WHILE I SAT THERE WITH Georgianna. It was just for a minute or two, but it was like I felt when I was talking to Adam. I had a glimmer of something weird and unfamiliar and realized it was happiness. They were just flashes, but all the way home I kept thinking, *I want more of that.*

Yeah, like you deserve more. What did you do that spells out anything but guilt?

Okay, maybe not happiness yet. But what about hope? Why can't I dream that maybe I can get out of this mess?

Go ahead; dream on. See how far it gets you.

As it turned out, I was put to the test not long after that. A few days later, when we were having our final staff meeting before the program started with the kids on Monday, Doug said, "You guys have been superhuman this week."

"Yeah!" Randy said in this voice that sounded like an entire football team in a huddle.

"So I've decided to throw a bash for you."

I could almost see Caitlin's antennae go up. "You mean, like a party?"

"Not 'like' a party," Doug said. "An actual stuff-your-face, laugh-your-buns-off shindig."

Caitlin smirked. "Oh. I can't wait to laugh my buns off."

If anybody else caught the sarcastic edge on that remark, no one showed it. "Tomorrow night," Doug said. "Six o'clock, right here. Pizza and ice-cream sundaes."

"With whipped cream?" Cheyenne said.

"Would I serve sundaes without whipped cream?" Doug said.

"Nuts," Randy said. "I want mine loaded with nuts."

"Can you get butterscotch sauce, too?" Holly put in.

A pang like a tongue of flame licked at my insides.

Forget it, Thunder Thighs. If you get within two feet of hot fudge, you'll put your fat face right in the middle of it, and they'll have to surgically remove you. Start oinking now 'cause we're talking Porky Pig.

With that shouting in my head, it was hard to do my "assignment" from Georgianna twenty times a day. I did keep track on a little notepad in my purse how many times I said, "I'm worth getting better because God loves me." Actually *saying* it was a lot like throwing up; I practically had to gag to get it out.

"I'm...I'm...I'm worth..." I would croak as I was in the shower taking stock of how far my ribs and hipbones stuck out.

"God loves...God loves," I would hiss during my power walks at Rancho San Rafael to work off the salad my mother forced me to eat for lunch.

"...getting better...getting better," I would whisper while I practiced the summer program music on the piano in the living room.

But it was never as convincing as the Voice that said, *Are you actually considering going to this major food party? Do you want to turn into the Pillsbury Doughboy? What about your sister, you self-serving little wench? She can only have so many good days before she blows this whole thing. You need to get your mind off food and concentrate on her.*

I compromised. I did my twenty times a day like Georgianna told me, and I marked them down in my little book. But I didn't believe a word of what I said. Not a word.

I couldn't get out of going to the party though. I drank a whole bunch of water before we went so my stomach wouldn't growl.

The party started out with pizza—every kind anybody could dream up. Adam was passing it out when we arrived. I sat in the circle on the floor with everybody else and accepted the slab of pineapple-with-Canadian-bacon he gave me on a paper plate. I picked off the pineapple and chewed on it awhile and spit it into my napkin.

"Aren't you going to eat the meat?" Cheyenne said to me.

"You want it?" I said.

"Shannon, nothing personal," Tobey said, eyes twinkling, "but that is a really lame question."

Cheyenne grinned and proceeded to pull off the bacon.

"Take the whole thing," I said. "Really, I'm done with it."

"Hey!" somebody said.

I looked up at Adam's tall frame. He was standing right over me, two greasy-bottomed boxes in hand.

"Me?" I said.

He squatted down. The odor of pepperoni assaulted my nostrils. "Your plate's empty," he said.

"Yeah, I'm through."

"No way," he said. "One piece of pizza? That's un-American! Which kind you want?"

"Neither really," I said.

"You're hurting his feelings," Adam said.

My eyes darted back up to him in spite of me. "Whose feelings?"

"The pizza's! Come on, pepperoni has feelings too!"

"Nuh-uh!" I said.

He set the sausage-and-mushroom in front of Cheyenne, who helped herself to two wedges. Adam scooped up a piece of pepperoni and cupped it in his palm.

"Take me!" he said in a high-pitched voice. "I always get picked last."

I realized I was smiling. I let my smile stay there. I let myself think, *I'm happy again! It's another glimmer.*

"Uh, is it just me or are you talking to that slice of pizza?"

I looked up at Caitlin, who was standing beside Adam. He stood up and grinned, gap-toothed, down at her.

"Like I would carry on a conversation with an inanimate object."

"So you were talking to Shannon," Caitlin said.

"Yeah."

"Then you *were* talking to an inanimate object." Caitlin was so delighted with herself, she let out this big old snort that brought all other discussion in the room to a halt.

"What was that?" Holly said.

"It sounded like Babe," somebody else said.

Caitlin proudly raised her hand. "It was me. Want me to belch for you?"

"Yeah!" Randy was using his jocks-in-a-huddle voice again. I, in the meantime, was trying to run from the Voice in my head.

Happy? Right. What were you thinking of? Like you're really going to compete for a guy with Caitlin. She's got you in every department. Besides, what are you going to do with him? Bore him to death?

I scrambled up and dumped my plate in the trash and started to collect other people's.

"Shannon's tidying," Doug said. "Must be time for the next course."

The pizza boxes were abandoned in a chorus of shouts, and from somewhere tubs of ice cream and squirt bottles of syrups appeared on the table. I made a beeline for the bathroom where I threw up.

Then I dug my notepad out of my purse, said my assigned thing twice in my head while I was rinsing out my mouth, and went back to the party room.

I barely got to the doorway when a hulking form appeared in front of me, carrying a bowl that was oozing whipped cream, chocolate sauce, and about a half-pound of walnuts. I crossed both arms over my middle.

"Are you really going to eat all that?" I managed to say into the maraschino cherry.

"No," Adam said. "You are."

I shook my head, but he pushed it closer to me.

"You have to," he said. He leaned down and pulled his voice to a whisper. "It's for not narking on me for that toilet thing and the collage-on-the-rear-end deal."

By then the sundae was so close to my nose I almost inhaled whipped cream. The ice cream was puddling around the plate's edges and mixing in with the hot fudge to form swirls. It tried to pull me into a trance, tried to magnetize my hand and let it glom right onto that spoon that stuck so invitingly toward me...

Touch it, and you draw back a nub, D'Angelo.

I snatched my right hand behind my back. With the other one I gave the sundae a shove that sent the cherry sideways.

"I don't want it," I said. "Please. Just...I don't want it."

I sidestepped him and retreated to my spot in the circle. Behind me, I heard Randy say, "Dude, that looks good. Let me have a bite."

"You can have the whole thing," Adam said. His voice was like a thud in my stomach. I knew I could never look at him again.

And wouldn't you know it, who should have the wrap-up pep talk at the end of the party but Adam? When he perched himself on the edge of the now-cleared sundae table, I stared at the nail-polish chip on one of my toenails and didn't look up.

Very smooth indeed. What's your next demonstration of poise? A swift kick in the shins?

You didn't want me to eat it!

No, but did you have to throw it in his face? Although, it's really okay. Now you've blown it so you don't have to worry about keeping him from Caitlin. Check it out, check it out, she has the dimples in overdrive. Can you do that?

No.

Then give it up.

I had no idea what Adam said. The Voice was keeping me too busy listening to it. Next thing I knew, Adam was suggesting we close in prayer.

Heads bobbed and bowed. I waited just long enough for all eyes to shut before I took off for the door. The hallway was a blur as I tore down it for the bathroom again. I just flung myself at the sink and held on to it while I cried.

"I just want to be friends with him, that's all," I whispered. My voice echoed in hisses against the tiles. "Why can't I even have that?"

Because you would be his little charity case, that's why. Is that what you want?

I shook my head and kept crying.

What else would you be? You have nothing to offer in return, that's for sure. You're lucky he doesn't tell Doug you're too unstable to even be on this staff. Which you are, or you wouldn't be seeing a shrink. Wait till Caitlin gives him that little piece of information.

"No!" I said.

I looked up at my blotchy, swelling face in the mirror. Wild eyes stared back at me. Over my shoulder, the door sighed open, and Caitlin's dark head poked in. I bent my face toward the sink and turned on the water.

She was in midlaugh until she saw me. Then the giggle twisted into a sneer. "I bet you came in here to make yourself puke. Am I right?"

She observed me as I tore frantically through my head for an answer. I didn't need one. She curled her lip and strolled into a stall. "I'm right," she said.

I left the rest room.

I didn't say a word all the way home, and when we got there I went straight up to our room and put on my pajamas. When I came back from brushing my teeth, Caitlin was sitting cross-legged on her bed. She looked up at me and dimpled.

"Hi, sis," she said.

I could feel my eyes narrowing, but I tried to keep them from sweeping the room. I thought she looked as guilty as sin itself, but I didn't want her to know I thought that.

Though why I should care, I have no idea, I thought. *She doesn't give a flip about my feelings.*

Your feelings don't count, remember? Just keep your mind on everybody else and quit worrying so much about yourself. Man, you're self-centered.

Caitlin stretched herself out on the bed and propped up on one elbow. "You know, it's a good feeling to finally have stuff on you."

I froze with my hand on the closet doorknob. "I don't know what you're talking about." I forced myself to let go of the knob and walked stiffly to my bed. I sat on it like a wooden puppet and watched her roll over snakelike and curl toward me.

"I walk in the bathroom, and there you are, looking like you just hurled. I'm sure Mom and Dad would love to hear that little tidbit."

"I'm working on *my* problem."

She laughed that unfunny snicker. "By seeing a shrink?"

"She's a therapist."

"She's a moneygrubbing busybody is what she is. I know; I've been there, remember?"

"You didn't go to Georgianna."

"Oh, man, are you hooked!" Caitlin bent her index finger and hung it inside her mouth like a fishhook. "One session, and she has already reeled you in."

"Why did you hate your psychiatrist?"

"It was because of him they sent me away. A Christian boarding school was the best marijuana rehab they could think of, they said." Caitlin gave another hard snort. "It was punishment, that's all it was."

"Was it really that bad?"

She turned her head to look at me. "You probably would have loved it. There were enough Little Miss Perfects for you to fit right in."

I inched up to the headboard and leaned against it. I felt as if I were being backed into a corner at gunpoint.

"Mom and Dad's little plan backfired on them. At first, I was glad just to be away from them, but that passed, and then I felt like I was locked up. That was before I discovered Farrell."

"Who?"

"Farrell Cunningham. One night I went out on the fire escape to smoke a whole cigarette I had found on the ground, and she was there with a lighter and a pack of Virginia Slims. We smoked the pack, and bingo, we were best buds."

The thought of it made me gag. I was sure my face turned green.

"Anyway, she invited me to go home with her for a weekend, and after I went through all these hassles getting permission from the 'rents and the administration and everybody but Bill and Hillary, I went." Caitlin dimpled, though it wasn't cute. She looked like some kind of vixen. "They put us on a bus to Chico, and I felt like I had been let out of a cage, I'm not kidding you. Then we got there, and her parents weren't home. I don't know how she pulled it off, but anyway, some other kids were there she knew in her public school before they shipped her off to Nevada City. They brought, like, a quarter pound of pot and all this booze." Caitlin shook her head. "Dude, I was like a dog that had been tied up in front of a roast I couldn't reach. Once I was let go, I went nuts. I got sick all over everything."

She said it the way somebody else might say, "I had the best time of my life." She had her eyes closed, obviously reviewing each and every wonderful retch.

Say something, Stupid.

I hugged harder on the pillow. "Couldn't you have, like, gotten *really* sick? I know you think I'm, like, this social moron…" *You are. Cut to the chase already.* "But I've read about that stuff. That much marijuana, that could make your heart go too fast or let you do something really weird or fall down or something—"

"Ooh, devil weed!" Caitlin gave the loudest snort yet. "I know more about the 'teen drug problem' than you do, Shannon." Caitlin hooked her fingers into quotation marks. "I've read what they don't hand out in school. Like, did you know it takes fewer puffs to get high than it did on the marijuana our parents' generation smoked? So that cuts down on the damage to your lungs. And—get this—a fatal overdose would take, like, forty pounds of grass smoked over a half-hour period. Like anybody's going to do that. If marijuana were dangerous, it wouldn't be so cheap. Besides, everything is okay when I'm high, you know?"

I shook my head. I knew nothing about everything being "okay."

"I can be so ticked off at Mom and Dad. Then I take a few drags on a joint, and all the anger goes away. I think this is the way it works," she went on. "Mom and Dad have all these rules for us, right?"

"Yeah."

"I can't follow them all. I mean, I can't. According to them, that makes me a bad person. And I *feel* like a bad person. So why not just enjoy myself? When I'm on dope, I don't worry about how bad I am."

Try something else. Think, Lard-Brain!

"So, is that why your grades were, like, pretty awful?" I said.

"Nah." Caitlin waved me off. "They stunk because I didn't study. Marijuana actually increases your thinking ability."

"Nuh-uh!" I said. "It keeps you from thinking."

"How do you know? Because you read it someplace? Who do you think wrote that? Some high-school administrator or something. I've done my own research."

"Yeah?" I said.

Caitlin nodded smugly. "Yeah. Everybody who actually does dope says being clean and sober is a block for creative people, and they're right. Aerosmith and Red Hot Chili Peppers? They totally *bit* after they got sober!" She turned suddenly toward me. "You don't really need a shrink. What you need is a good party."

"You mean, smoke pot?"

"Yeah." She rolled her eyes. "'Course, you wouldn't do it because you're afraid God will send you to hell."

"Don't you think that?" I said.

"No."

"Why? Because you don't believe in God?"

Caitlin's look was unmistakably defensive. "Who said I didn't believe in God?"

"Then you do?"

"Sure I do."

"I don't get it. If you believe in God, how come—"

"How come I misbehave?" She rolled her eyes again. "I think just about everybody believes in God, okay? I've had Him shoved down my throat all my life so it's a little hard not to. But I've also been told about 750 times that God loves me. If God loves me, why would He send me to hell, no matter what I did?"

"I don't think it's like that," I said feebly.

"Let me tell you what it *is* like," Caitlin said. She sat up cross-legged and talked with her hands. "You light up, okay? And first everything, like, slows down, and you relax. Then everything everybody says seems funny, and you start hootin'. And then, you know, if you keep smoking, you can barely feel your feet touch the ground. That's when the good part kicks in for me. I just want to be alone so I can think and dream and create—which they do *not* let you do in school."

"What have you created?" I said.

"Huh?"

"Do you, like, paint or something?"

"Dude, you've bought the whole thing, haven't you?"

I squirmed. "What whole thing?"

"The whole Mom-and-Dad thing. They are so achievement oriented. You're nothing unless you have some kind of product to show off—a piano recital or a 4.0." She gave a disgusted grunt and flopped over onto her back again. "It's enough to just sit and *think*, have decent ideas. It's just this painless state. I'm into that. I'm sick of pain."

"What pain?" I said.

She didn't answer. She just lay there, staring harder and harder at the ceiling. Her face became so stiff I felt uneasy. She looked as if all the life had gone out of her.

"Caitlin?" I said.

"What?" Her lip curled. Her eyes hardened into slits.

I shrugged. "Nothing."

She rolled away from me and pulled the pillow over her head. "Turn the light out." Her voice was wooden.

I did. Miserably, I closed my eyes. The room became still, and the Voice started in.

Great job, Marble Mouth. You really convinced her to lay off the pot. Wow, miraculous rehab. What a joke. Another five minutes, and she would have had you smoking the stuff! Which is no big surprise. You have the self-control of a mosquito.

I tried. I really tried!

Uh-huh. Is that what you're going to say at her funeral—"I tried"?

Her funeral!

You heard what that Georgianna woman said. You're freaked out that Caitlin's going to do something stupid and die. She just might, and whose fault would that be?

I can't blame it all on myself.

Enough of it's your fault. You better pray you can get through to her somehow.

Pray?

I sighed deep into the pillow. It would be so good to pray, to spill my guts to God, as Norie always put it. But I couldn't go to God in the shape I was in. I had to get it together some before I could go back.

CHAPTER EIGHT

SOMETHING STRANGE HAPPENED OVER THE NEXT COUPLE of days. Caitlin behaved like the model child—going to church without a battle, wearing the green-print skirt my mother made for her, and clearing the table without being asked. I pretty much figured she was up to something. Mom, on the other hand, was about beside herself.

When Tobey beeped her horn Monday morning and Caitlin went running down the driveway, Mom pulled me into this major mother-hug. "I'm so pleased, Shannon," she whispered into my hair. "I think this was the right thing to do, bringing her home. Look at how well she's doing."

"Yeah," I said. "I have to go, Mom."

"Let me know how she does, okay? I'm not going to ask her. I don't want her to think I'm being pushy."

It occurred to me as I hurried toward Tobey's car that Caitlin would have outdone herself snorting if she had heard that. She definitely was up to something.

Real nice, Shannon. The chick starts to shape up, and you're all suspicious. Shows what kind of person you are.

Sorry! It's just...she's so...

So what? So worse-than-you-are? Have you looked at yourself lately? You stop looking like the Sta-Puf Marshmallow Man, and then maybe you can judge her, okay?

I climbed in the car still trying to shake the Voice out of my head.

"This is going to be so rad," Cheyenne said.

"What is?" Caitlin said.

"Our VBS."

"Oh. Yeah."

"Are you nervous, Shannon?" Marissa said.

Her eyes were pleading with me, "Are we still best friends?" I felt a stab of guilt.

What are you stressing for? She's the one who blabbed your condition all over Reno, for Pete's sake. Who needs her?

"I'm not that nervous," I said.

"Oh, for sure," Caitlin said. She grabbed my hand and turned it palm upward for Cheyenne and Marissa to see. "Notice the sweat beads. Feel the rapid pulse. Stick out your tongue, Shannon. Let us see your cotton mouth."

I actually almost did it. I would have, if Tobey hadn't said, "You don't have anything to be nervous about, Shan. You play great. Do you want to pray before we go in?"

"Uh, no thanks," Caitlin said, as Tobey pulled into the church parking lot. "Let me out, Shannon."

I did and miserably followed her across the parking lot. I didn't hear any doors slamming behind me. When I looked back, the three of them were still in the car, heads together in intimate conversation.

Forget it. When you have your act together—if you ever get your act together—you can be buddy-buddy with the Flagpole Girls again. Until then, you have stuff to do.

I wasn't sure how I was going to concentrate on playing the piano while the kids trailed in, much less fumble through the songs Adam was going to teach them. The shouting in my head was louder than ever as I settled myself at the piano in the church.

Just try not to mess this up, okay? the Voice said.

"Hey!" Adam was suddenly looming over the music rack on his elbows, grinning.

"Hi," I said. My eyes flicked to the sheet music, where the image of my shoving a hot fudge sundae into his face obliterated the notes.

"You okay?" he said.

"Yeah."

"You ready to kick tail for the Lord?"

I had to smile. "I guess so."

"You only guess so? You don't know?"

"Well, I mean, I've been practicing…I'm going to try…"

"We have to pray. Come on."

Adam moved his tall self around the piano and suddenly was on the bench next to me. He picked up my right hand, swallowed it into his two freckled paws, and bowed his head. I didn't get mine lowered until he was four words into the prayer. I stared at his freckled nose. He had a great profile, kind of unexpectedly chiseled.

It wasn't until he paused that I realized I hadn't heard a thing he had said. Then it took me a second or two to realize he was waiting for me to say something. When he figured out I wasn't going to, he said, "We've done our homework; now we need You. Help us to belt it out for You. Amen."

"Amen," I murmured.

He gave my hand a squeeze and then let go. He was already grinning.

"I'm going to get you a Kleenex, girl," he said. "I thought *my* hands were sweating!"

I wanted to crawl into the piano. He just lumbered over to some mother who was ushering her kids into the front row and bummed a tissue off her. When he came back and handed it to me, he grinned and did one of his suddenly-I'm-not-here-I'm-someplace-else moves, over to where Doug was adjusting the microphone. I recognized the glimmer inside me right away.

Back off, Juliet. He's everybody's Romeo. Look at that; he's about to do the jitterbug with that chickie from the Montana staff. What's her name? Kyla?

I know.

Oh, and here comes Caitlin. Look at his eyes light up.

Caitlin was headed right for him, arms filled with song sheets to be passed out.

I opened a songbook and plunked out "Celebrate You."

Then something weird happened. Kids who were already scattered around the church started to clap in time. My eyes darted above the music to see if I was hearing things, but the slapping together of hands was unmistakable. Adam looked up from his obviously hilarious conversation with Caitlin and joined them.

The second time through, he leaped over to the piano and whispered, "All right, Shannon!"

The whole opening went pretty much like that. The kids—all 150 of them—loved everything. They laughed at Doug's jokes. They about lost it every time Adam did bunny ears behind Holly's head or vaulted over a pew to drag some kid up front to "volunteer" for a skit.

And every time I started to play, they started to clap. I was pretty sure nobody heard any of my mistakes because they were singing so loud. Adam was glowing with excitement and sweat as they all filed out to their first activity and he came over to the piano. I was still playing going-out music, but he talked anyway.

"You are awesome!" he said.

"I made a bunch of mistakes," I said.

"No way."

"Yes, way." Seven mistakes, to be exact.

"Nobody heard them. Anyway, it was cool."

"They're off to a great start," Doug said from behind him. "Come on, let's hustle to our places. They're expecting more!"

I was supposed to "hustle" to the kindergarten room where the plan was to keep the four- and five-year-olds moving from one activity to the next so they wouldn't have time to think about stuffing clay up each other's noses. I had to be ready when it was song time for them. I had been practicing "Father Abraham" all weekend.

The little kids loved "Father Abraham." Making masks from paper plates, listening to a story about some little kid who pretended to be a gorilla, and eating nauseating amounts of vanilla wafers and Kool-Aid also did it for them. There didn't seem to be anything they didn't like—except going home.

"I don't want to!" this little red-headed kid squalled the minute his mom darkened the door. It was the first time all morning he had taken his finger out of his nose.

"You can come back tomorrow," Holly told him.

That didn't console him or any of the rest of them, who all took up the cry, like dogs howling at a siren. The red-headed kid wrapped himself around my leg, and I could feel soggy vanilla wafer being smeared across the back of my right knee.

"I want to stay here!" he screamed.

"Looks like you're doing something right," his mom said to me. To him, she said, "You can tell me what you learned about Jesus today while I buy you a Happy Meal."

McDonald's seemed to be the key. Red let go of my leg and halfheartedly trailed off with her, finger back up into his right nostril.

That must have been what Adam was like when he was a little boy, I thought.

Get over it, would you?

I did, for the moment, because it was time to think about the next thing: my session with Georgianna. Armed with my little notepad, my twenty-times-a-day dutifully marked down on its pages, I rode in silence with Mom, who pursed her lips the whole way. I was glad to leave the chill of her company for the squishy futons of Georgianna's office.

Georgianna looked intently at me as I sat on my cushion trying not to squirm. I made a dive for my purse and pulled out the notepad.

"I did my assignment," I said.

Georgianna eyed the pad curiously. "Did I ask you to write something? I don't remember that."

"No," I said. "I just kept track of how many times I said my thing you told me to say. Wasn't I supposed to?"

"That's fine," Georgianna said. "May I see? Do you mind?"

I shook my head and handed it to her. She looked at it, and then she stared up at me, her face in its serious mode.

"You certainly did the quantity," she said. "How about the quality?"

I panicked. "Quality?" I said. "I don't know what you mean."

"You said your 'thing,' let's see, 120 times. Do you believe it yet?"

I started to nod automatically. Her left eyebrow went up. I looked at my knees.

"Not yet, huh?" she said.

"No," I said. "I'm sorry."

"Why be sorry? 'Not yet' is a perfectly reasonable answer. If you had said yes, I'd have been suspicious."

I looked up in surprise. "Can you, like, read my mind?"

"No, but I can read your face. Don't ever try to play poker, Shannon. You'll go bankrupt."

"Okay," I said.

She handed me back the pad, and I resisted the urge to jot that "assignment" down.

"Since you like to keep track of things," Georgianna said, "as you continue that affirmation, write down what you think about right after you say it."

"Like, what kinds of things?" I said.

"Well, let's take this morning. What did the affirmation make you think about? First thing that came into your head; see if you can remember."

"Um, I thought about how my sister said the other night she didn't think God was going to send her to hell for smoking marijuana because He couldn't do that if He loved her."

"Ah," Georgianna said. She squinted her eyes. "What do you think about that? Does God love Caitlin?"

"Yeah!"

"No hesitation there; you're absolutely sure."

"Yes."

"Why?"

"Because God loves us all."

"Even you?"

Man, she had me cornered. I pulled up my knees and hugged them and inspected my toenail.

"Shannon?" Georgianna said.

"I guess," I said.

Georgianna made her game-show buzzing sound. "Don't you remember the rule? I had you pegged as a rule-keeper."

"I am. I'm sorry. I'm not supposed to say anything I don't really believe."

"Right. So let's try that question again. Does God even love *you*?"

"I..." I jiggled my legs and looked up at the ceiling.

She didn't prompt me. She just waited.

"I don't think so," I said finally.

"Can you tell me why?"

"Because I'm not...I'm not a good enough Christian."

Both of Georgianna's eyebrows went up this time. "And Caitlin is?"

"Well, no, but she has problems."

"Oh, so God has compassion for her. What about *your* problem? You've already admitted you have one. You have an eating disorder, and that's why you're here, right?"

"Right. But see..." I squirmed.

Georgianna sat with her hands folded, completely relaxed while I writhed like I was in labor.

"It's different. I, like, *know* better, you know? I have the Flagpole Girls—"

"You're talking about the girls that Enid is involved with."

"Right."

"Okay, go on."

"Well, so I have, like, this Christian place to belong. And I haven't gotten involved with, like, really bad kids so nobody's steered me the wrong way. I've been really involved in the church. So I should know better. I shouldn't mess up the way I do."

"So you've had all these opportunities and you've blown them and so you're out of chances, is that what you're saying?"

"Yes. Is that stupid?"

"No. Definitely not stupid. I promise you I'll tell you if something is stupid." She actually smiled at me. "And I can guarantee you, you will probably never hear those words cross my lips. You are obviously anything but stupid."

She just doesn't know you yet. Give her time.

"Right now, Shannon," Georgianna said, "what's important to you?"

I shrugged. "I don't know. I guess—"

She buzzed. I giggled. Then I told her my parents, the church, making good grades, playing the piano.

When I mentioned that last one, Georgianna's antenna-eyebrow went up. I was beginning to figure out that meant she was about to challenge me.

"You play the piano," she said slowly. "Is that really important to you?"

"It's important to me not to mess it all up when I play," I said.

"Do you enjoy it?"

"What?"

Georgianna couldn't smother a smile. "Do you enjoy it? You know, does it give you a peaceful feeling? Does the time fly by when you're doing it?"

"I have to practice at least an hour a day," I said. "Is that what you mean?"

"No, here's what I mean." She scratched the side of her head. "If you were a song to be played on the piano, what song would you be?"

"I don't know," I said.

I waited for the buzz, but Georgianna was nodding.

"I think that's true," she said. "I don't think you do know. All right. Anything else?"

I shook my head. That was more than I had known I had to say in the first place.

"Now, what you've told me, Shannon," she said, "are your values. Do you know what I mean by that?"

"Yes," I said.

"What do I mean?"

"Um, what's important to me. What I live by."

"Right. Now, there are no wrong answers to this, but I do want to ask you one question. Why didn't you mention God?"

"I did!" I said.

"No, you mentioned your Christian friends and church, but you didn't say anything about your relationship with the Lord."

"Um, I guess…I mean, I don't think I really have a relationship with God. "

"And why is that? I'm not challenging you now. I just need you to tell me. Dig down in there and see if you can tell me exactly why."

Think fast, D'Angelo, or you're going to end up telling her the truth, which is basically that you aren't good enough!

Isn't that what I'm here for?

No, you're here to get fixed so you can help somebody else for a change. And don't you forget it.

"There's a pretty big battle going on in there!" Georgianna said.

"I'm just trying to—"

"Trying to decide what I want to hear, perhaps?" Georgianna said.

"Yeah," I said.

"Rule number two, which is an addendum to rule number one: You must only tell me what you really think and feel, not what you think I want to hear. What I want to hear is what you really think and feel!" She took a big, comical breath, and I smiled.

"You have a beautiful smile, Shannon," Georgianna said. "You really do. Now, tell me, if you can—no pressure, just if you can—tell me why you don't have a relationship with our Lord."

"Because I'm not good enough." There it was, spilled out between us like an overturned glass of milk.

"Shannon," Georgianna said, "that is probably the most honest thing you have said to me yet. Now," she rubbed her palms together, "we can get some work done."

I was confused, but I nodded. I didn't mind discussing this stuff, but when was she going to give me instructions for getting over anorexia? We only had until the end of the summer.

"Guess what I'm going to ask you next."

"Um, why I don't think I'm good enough?"

"Bingo."

"Because…you know all that stuff I just told you, about what's important?"

"Yes."

"I don't do any of that."

The eyebrows did their thing.

"I don't!" I said.

"Okay, let's start with…what was it? Your parents. What is it you do that keeps you off the I-please-my-parents list?"

"I don't like some of the things they do, and I think bad stuff about them."

"Can you give me an example?"

Great. Now you're parent-bashing. You better shut up, Cavern Mouth.

"First thing that comes to you," Georgianna said.

"I don't like some of the clothes my mother makes for me."

"Do you tell her?"

"No! I just think some of them are too little-girlish, and I feel like a geek wearing them."

"Do you make ugly faces when she shows them to you?"

"No."

"Do you go to your room and slam the door?"

"No."

"Do you just not wear them?"

"Oh, I wear them."

"Why?"

"Because her feelings would get all hurt if I didn't."

"So what you're saying is that it's just *thinking* the dresses are geeky that makes you a bad person. Right?"

"Right," I said.

She let that hang in the air for a minute. I felt myself looking up as if I could see it now that it was out there. It sure *sounded* lame. How did it look?

"Let's change that list around a little bit," Georgianna said. "Let's take that first one, about your parents, and let's talk not about what you think you should do, but about what you need."

"What I need?" I said.

"What a concept, huh?" she said. The corners of her mouth tilted elfishly up. "Let's just take your mother. What do you need from your mother when it comes to these clothes she makes for you?"

"I don't need anything," I said. "I have more clothes than anybody I know."

"You aren't answering the question," Georgianna said. "Take a minute to think about it this time."

I didn't dare. The Voice was screaming in my ears. Any minute, I was going to be screamed to death.

She isn't going to let anything happen to me if I say it.

What control does she have over Me?

I shook my head. Georgianna was watching me, but she didn't question me. She just kept waiting.

I shook my head once more, shook the Voice away in mid-word, and said, "I need...I mean, if I could have anything I wanted..." I stopped. "Isn't that selfish?"

"No. Just say what you need, even if you think it's bad."

"Okay then. I need her to ask me what I want to wear before she goes and makes me something."

There. It was out. I had never said it to another human being. I waited for the Voice to break my eardrum. Nothing happened.

"That's it?" Georgianna said.

"Yes. Really it is."

"You know, Shannon, that sounds perfectly reasonable to me."

"It wouldn't to my mother," I said.

That—and the sudden flare of my voice—surprised both of us. I could tell by the flicker in Georgianna's eyes.

"Your mother wouldn't like it if you said, 'Gee, you make me beautiful things, Mom, but they just aren't me. Could we go together and pick out some fabric and a pattern?' She wouldn't like that?"

I shook my head. "She likes to surprise us."

"Ah. That's what *she* needs—to see your delighted face when she presents you with her latest project?"

"Right," I said.

"So what she needs conflicts with what you need."

"Yes!"

She grinned. "Did a light just come on in your head?"

"Yes." I sagged. "But what good does that do me? I can't change that. My mom is my mom. That's just the way she is."

"And wanting to have some say in how you dress is who you are."

"But it seems so selfish to say, 'This is what I want, and that's the way I'm going to have it.' That's what Caitlin does."

"Does Caitlin go to your mother and say in a reasonable voice, 'Mom, this isn't me. Could we go together next time...'"

"No!" I laughed aloud. "That is so not even close!"

"Uh-huh, but you figure just because your mother cries when Caitlin tells her in her way, she's going to cry when you do it your way."

"Yeah, and then she won't talk for days. She says if we aren't going to be grateful for what she does for us, she is going to stop making our clothes and we can just go naked."

"Does Caitlin go naked?"

"No, she buys her own stuff."

"This is big," Georgianna said. She glanced at the round redwood clock on the wall. "Unfortunately, our time is up, but I want to give you another assignment."

I flipped open the pad, pencil poised. She leaned toward me and smiled. "I don't think you're going to need to write this down; I don't think you'll forget it."

"What is it?" I said.

"Has your mother made a dress for you recently you don't care for?"

"Yes," I said. "The one she's doing for my birthday tomorrow."

"All right. Now, I only want you to do this if you can. I don't want you to come in here next time feeling like a failure if you haven't been able to pull if off. Just think about doing it. Imagine yourself doing it."

"Doing what?" I said.

"Telling your mother you would rather not wear that dress for your birthday. That you would rather wear something else that looks more like you."

I practically bored another hole in my toenail polish with my eyes. "Why? What does that have to do with...I mean, my anorexia? I mean, is that okay to ask?"

"Yes, it is, and here's why: I think—and I'm not sure yet because it's different for every person—but I think you are refusing to eat because that's something you can control. What you can't control is what's really hurting you. I have a hunch it might have something to do with Mama, but let's just find out. And this is going to help you see that you've given up what you really long for, for the sake of avoiding this very real hurt."

"What if I can't?" I said.

"There is no 'can't,' Shannon. There may be 'not yet,' but there is no can't."

I held on to that like a life preserver as I walked out of her office—and saw my mother attaching the last of the lace to my puffy-sleeved birthday dress.

YOU'VE PROBABLY GUESSED I DIDN'T RUSH RIGHT UP TO my mother and tell her the dress had to go. In fact, I tried it on like a good little girl when we got home and showed the appropriate amount of appreciation while she tucked, poked, and pulled until I wanted to throw a pincushion.

Don't do it, the Voice told me. *I don't care what that Georgianna woman says; just don't even think about it.*

But I *did* think about it. I even had a nightmare about it. Toward dawn I was dreaming I had thrown the dress straight into my mother's face. She was screaming hysterically, and the paramedics were coming in to take her away. Tobey and Adam were the two people carrying the stretcher, and they both were looking at me like I was Jack the Ripper or somebody.

In the dream, Tobey grabbed my arm and I kept yelling "No! No!"

Only I opened my eyes, and it wasn't a dream. Tobey *was* standing there holding on to my arm, and judging from the way her eyes were twinkling in the glare of our overhead light, I hadn't actually yelled "no!" At least one thing was going my way.

"Tobey?" I said sleepily. "Are you taking my mom?"

"No, Bright Eyes, we're taking you!"

My head swiveled to the other side, where Norie was standing, face puffy with sleep, but smug. And beside her were Cheyenne and Marissa.

"I'm not talkin' trash about your momma or anything," somebody else said next to Tobey. "But I am *not* takin' that woman out to breakfast." Brianna, of course.

"But we're taking *you* to breakfast, so get up," Tobey said.

Before any of it had a chance to sink in, Cheyenne was pulling the covers off me, and Norie was shoving a sweatshirt over my head.

"Where do you keep your shorts?" Tobey was saying from the direction of my dresser.

"Bottom drawer," I said. I was coming to life now. Obviously they were kidnapping me and taking me out of the house.

"Hey, we didn't sing!" Cheyenne said.

"Go for it," Tobey said, tossing me a pair of freshly ironed white shorts.

Cheyenne immediately launched into a raucous chorus of "Happy Birthday" while I turned pale and pulled on the shorts. When I stood up, my nightgown hung out of the bottom of the sweatshirt.

Brianna shook her head. "None of us looks like Christie Brinkley at this hour, but, girl, you are not leavin' this house with your shirttail hanging down to your knees."

She took one side of the sweatshirt, and Norie took the other, and before I could even open my mouth, they had pulled it off and the nightgown with it. There I sat in the middle of my bed, bare-chested with the five of them around me.

"Dude, Shannon," Cheyenne said. "You better eat about two stacks of pancakes. You are *skinny!*"

"You have such tact, Jackson," Norie said dryly.

"But you can totally see her ribs!"

"And I can totally see your tonsils because your mouth is so big. Come on. Somebody haul D'Angelo out of that bed and let's get going."

With a little too much laughter, Tobey and Marissa stuffed me into my sweatshirt, and each grabbed an arm and peeled me up off my mattress.

"Get her feet, Brianna!" Tobey said.

"I can walk!" I said.

They ignored me and carried me, going in four different directions but essentially toward the door.

Suddenly a stream of out-of-a-dead-sleep cussing erupted from under the pillow on the other bed. For about a second, the

Girls slowed down and gave it a glance. But then, like one person, they moved on. They were getting really good at pretending they didn't hear things I wished they hadn't heard.

But that was the last wrinkle in the next hour and a half. Things began to smooth out as soon as we piled into Norie's father's new Suburban. Amid everybody's personal rendition of "Happy Birthday," Norie drove us to the WestSide Cafe in the shopping center. Then they did the let's-carry-Shannon-but-which-way-are-we-actually-going thing again and got me—all of us shrieking and howling—inside the place, where a booth in the back was decorated with balloons and streamers. A party hat was at each place, and Cheyenne was the first one to demonstrate that we also had those blow-it-and-unroll-it horn things—right in my face.

But by then I was awake enough to laugh, and to keep saying over and over, "You guys shouldn't have done this. This is so neat. You shouldn't have done this."

"We wouldn't have actually," Norie said. "We really wanted to take you to lunch."

"Yeah, my breath isn't as bad at noon," Cheyenne put in.

"But your mother said it was family day," Marissa said. She glanced around the group, and each Girl seemed to pull a zipper across her own lips.

"The only time your mom didn't have something planned was breakfast," Tobey said. "I guess birthdays are a big deal at your house, huh?"

"Mmm-*mmm*," Brianna said. I never had been able to figure out exactly what that meant, but I knew it wasn't approval, for sure.

"Yeah, she has something going throughout the day," I said.

"I bet that was great when you were five," Norie said.

"I bet it's still great," Tobey said. Her voice was pointy.

"So, do you think they have our waffles ready?" Marissa said.

I started to inwardly freak.

Oh, come on, don't wig out. You know the drill. Just cut them up and push them around the plate. Take a bite and spit it into your napkin if you have to, but if you swallow one mouthful, you might as well kiss the rest of the day good-bye.

It's my birthday! They went to all this trouble!

Since when do you deserve some major feast just for being born?

I felt a soft breath in my ear.

"You don't have to eat them all," Marissa whispered. "Nobody's going to be mad at you."

When the waffles, whipped cream, and strawberries arrived, the happy chatter covered up the fact I didn't eat a single mouthful. I did drink a whole glass of water and gave Marissa my orange juice.

When the plates were finally whisked away, and I didn't have to look at those oozing-with-syrup, soggy pieces of ironed dough, Tobey and Brianna disappeared under the table. They surfaced holding a huge box wrapped in paper that was decorated with pictures of female faces. I stared at them.

"That's you guys!" I said.

"Dude, you got it right away!" Cheyenne said. "I told them if it was me, I'd have it half torn open before I figured that out."

"Brianna painted it," Marissa said.

"Wow," I said. "You're so talented, Brianna. I never could even think about doing something like that."

I examined the paper closely, but my eyes blurred the water-colored likenesses of Marissa, Norie, Tobey, Cheyenne, and Brianna, and I realized I was about to cry.

Dry up, D'Angelo. They do something like this for everybody's birthday.

"Open it," Tobey said. "I'm dying here!"

They evidently all were because I had a lot of help tearing off the paper and opening the box. Inside, all I could see was tissue paper, which I peeled away sheet by sheet until Norie reached in and pulled out the whole wad.

Underneath was a pile of fabric, filmy material in deep, rich colors I could almost feel as I put my hand in. I wasn't touching the silkiness but the autumn-oak-leaf rust, the Tahoe-pine-tree green, the whisper of aspen-gold. I gasped.

"She likes it," Cheyenne whispered.

"Take it out; hold it up to you," Norie said.

At her command, I took it gently in my hands and pulled it out. It unfurled like a flag across the table, a long, sleek, sophisticated dress with thin straps, long, princess lines, and a flare at the bottom that fell gracefully down over the edge of the tabletop.

"There's more," Cheyenne said. The poor kid was having a

hard time keeping herself from jumping right into the box, I could tell. "Take out the other piece!"

The Girls all grinned and craned their necks as, still holding my breath, I reached in again. Texture rubbed against my fingertips. I pulled out a mass of deep green lace, a jacket with short sleeves that would go over the dress and come just above my waist.

"This is gorgeous," I whispered. "Is it really...it's for me?"

"Uh, yeah," Norie said.

But she didn't add her usual sarcastic tag. She just grinned along with everybody else as I gazed down at the dress. It was the most beautiful piece of clothing I had ever owned.

I draped it across me as if I would actually wear it, as if I really could pull off that sophisticated look, those clinging lines...

You can just dream on. You wear this, and everybody's going to say, "Why are you wearing Colleen's dress? Aren't you a little old for playing dress up?"

"I thought you liked it," Cheyenne said.

I looked up to catch the droop in her big brown eyes.

"I do!" I said. "It's...it's incredible!"

"It's from all of us," Marissa said.

"We each had a part in picking it out," Tobey said.

"Well, you saw it first," Norie said. "And I just said, 'That's it; that thing makes a statement.'"

"And I go, 'Oh yeah, can you see a necklace and earrings with that?'" Cheyenne said.

"Cheyenne has an eye for line, we found out," Tobey said.

Marissa nudged me. "Brianna was the color person."

"I looked at that and I said, 'Oh, honey, those colors are going to bring out a whole other side of Shannon—mmm-hmmm.'"

"A whole other side?" I said.

Don't fish for compliments, D'Angelo.

"Not that you don't look real sweet in those pastels you always wear," Brianna said. "But you have a vivid side we hardly ever see, you know what I'm sayin'?"

Evidently everybody else did, because a unanimous nod followed.

"And you were right," Marissa said. "See how gorgeous that is next to her face?"

The minute she said that, I pulled down the dress and pretended to want to look at it out in front of me, at arm's length.

"The lace jacket was Marissa's idea," Brianna said. "She said you had to have it."

"'Cause you're so feminine," Marissa said.

"Not ruffled feminine," Cheyenne put in.

"Sophisticated feminine," Tobey said. "This was the perfect touch."

"I…it's so…wonderful."

"Go try it on!" Cheyenne said. "Go in the bathroom!"

Norie glanced at her watch. "Don't have time. That's why we came here instead of going all the way over to Pneumatic. I promised your mother I would have you back in time to do your thing this morning."

When the Girls dropped me off, I hugged everyone good-bye and ran into the house and up the stairs to stow my present in the back of the closet before my mother could see it. I knew what her reaction would be.

She was already reacting, though, to something else. She stalked into my room, hands on hips, lips pursed so tight her eyes were bulging.

"They took me to breakfast," I said breathlessly.

"I know. I told them they could. But I thought Caitlin would be invited."

"Why?" I said.

It slipped out before I had a chance to think about it. My mother's eyes flamed. "Because she was lying right here in her bed when they came in and dragged you out. You don't think that hurt her feelings, seeing you all go out of here laughing and her being left out?"

Uh, no. It hadn't occurred to me for a moment. All I could do was look at my mother and blink.

"I knew I should have just said no when they asked me," Mom went on. "You were no sooner out of here than the phone rang, and it was Colleen, calling to wish you a happy birthday. You missed that completely."

"I'm sorry," I said.

"Birthdays are family days, Shannon," she said. "They always have been."

"But I didn't know they were taking me out for breakfast," I said. "I couldn't very well—"

"Just wear something nice. Your father is picking you up at lunch. He has a surprise for you."

"Do you want me to wear the dress you made?" I said. I hoped it wasn't too obvious I was begging for a no.

"Oh no, that's for tonight. You don't want to wear that to crawl around on the floor with children. Although you had better not be crawling around in whatever you do wear. They're just going to have to understand it's your birthday and you have family commitments."

Mom drove Caitlin and me to the church, giving me the silent treatment but chattering away to Caitlin, who was answering in grunts and eye rolls. Mom pretended not to notice.

We barely arrived in time for me to play one warmup song. When the last little chirp faded out, Doug held up his hand and told the kids it was a special day. Somebody was having a birthday. Adam struck a chord on his guitar, and everybody launched into a serenade of "Happy Birthday." I was trying to duck behind the music rack when they finished, but Holly and Randy dragged me off the piano bench, and Adam and Kyla were on me with this card as big as a billboard that they and all the kids had signed.

"That's mine; that's where I wrote my name!" Red shouted from the first pew. He was standing up on the seat, pointing a chubby finger at the huge, crooked letters, S-A-M, on the back.

"I see that!" I said. "You write so well!"

He beamed, baby teeth gleaming like little pearls. I had a glimmer.

And then I had another one. After the opening service was over and the kids were running—they always ran everywhere—to their next activity, Adam came over and leaned on the piano, chin resting on his folded arms. For a minute, he looked just like Red Sam.

"I'm sorry about that bad chord in the first song," I said.

"Oh yeah. Twenty lashes," he said. Then he stuck a white envelope over the top of the piano.

"Is that for me?" I said.

No, stupid. He's handing it to you so you can run it out to the White House.

"It *is* your birthday, right?" Adam said. "That's why we sang the song that makes you feel like a geek and gave you the big ol' honkin' card."

"Oh, yeah!" I said. "I just...never mind." I practically snatched the card from him. "Thanks. Can I open it later? I have to get to class."

"Sure," he said. "You can't leave those kindergartners without armed guards."

I tucked the card in my bag and took off. As soon as I was out of the sanctuary and around the corner, though, I whipped it out. I couldn't wait.

The front looked like a scene from *Fantasia,* with gold musical notes floating around with stars. *Really* schmaltzy. But I smiled to myself as I opened it.

It started to play "Happy Birthday"—classical style—in that loud, obnoxious, robotic sound like those musical socks you wear at Christmastime. I mean, *really* loud. So loud two kids who were headed down the hall stopped to stare at me.

"Happy birthday to you!" Piano arpeggio. "Happy birthday to you!" Major glissando. "Happy birthday, dear friend of mine!" Dramatic chord progression. "Happy birthday to you!"

I had to giggle. This was so incredibly cheesy only Adam could pull it off.

It kept playing over and over. I giggled harder. One more time—

"Pretty lame, huh?"

I jerked my head around to see Adam lurking at the corner.

"Um, no, it's—"

"Hey, it was the only thing I could find that had music on it." He grinned, but he didn't look at all as though he had just given me something so cheesy you could have served it on a cracker. He definitely didn't look as embarrassed as I felt.

"How do I get it to stop?" I said.

"I think you close it," he said.

I did, and it shut up, and Adam chuckled.

"Open it," he said.

I did. Grand introduction up and down the tinny keyboard.

I slammed it shut, and it cut off. Adam laughed and took it

from me, opening and closing it half a dozen more times. It sounded like a spastic concerto. I started to giggle uncontrollably.

"She likes it! Hey, Mikey!" Adam said. He looked at me, face suddenly sober. "You do like it, don't you?"

"Yeah, yeah, it's the best. Thanks!"

"Hey, D'Angelo." Caitlin was leaning around the corner with her lip curled.

I deflated like a popped balloon. "What?"

"That Holly chick is looking for you."

I turned away from Caitlin, but I didn't look up at Adam. "I have to go." I took the card carefully from him and put it into my bag still without looking at him. Then I took off around the corner. Caitlin was right on my heels.

"Oh, Adam!" she said in a high-pitched, Marilyn-Monroe voice. "It's the best. Thanks ever so much!"

"I didn't say that!" I spat at her.

For a second her eyes opened big, her lip uncurled, and she looked genuinely stunned. Just as quickly, she re-sneered. "Oh, is Miss Butter-Wouldn't-Melt-in-Your-Mouth going to say something nasty? Dare I say it...God forbid...actually get mad?"

"Shut up," I muttered.

When is it going to happen, D'Angelo? When are you going to lose control with her, huh? Man, you better rein yourself in, because you cannot—I repeat—you cannot lose your cool.

So much for the at-least-three-minute-long glimmer I had felt out in the hall with Adam. Even the nonstop birthday cards little Red Sam finger-painted for me for the next hour didn't bring it back.

At lunchtime, I had to go in the bathroom and paste a smile on my face before I went out front to wait for Dad. I saw the car coming around the far street corner when I remembered Caitlin, and the chewing-out I'd already received that morning for neglecting her.

I put my head inside the door and saw her standing in the hall.

"Caitlin," I said, "do you want to go with Dad and me? I don't know where we're going, but you could come."

"Why?" she said, as if I had just asked her to join me at the county dump.

"I just thought you would want to—"

"I'm going to lunch with Adam and them. I was invited."

She smiled about as sweetly as a crunched-up aspirin. I went back out and once again tried to plaster on a smile for my dad.

He, on the other hand, was grinning from ear to ear when I climbed into the car. "You look like my little princess," he said.

I mumbled "Thanks" and nodded amiably when he said he was taking me "someplace special."

He wasn't lying. Adelle's is pretty special. It's probably the most expensive restaurant in Reno. Dad swung open the door for me like Prince Charming himself and asked for "a nice table for the lady." A waiter led us to a plush booth in a brocaded corner and brought water in crystal goblets with slices of lemon suspended gracefully amid the ice chips.

As I opened the menu and stared at the lavish descriptions of gourmet lunches—with bile coming up my esophagus—Dad said, "At least you're eating now so you can enjoy this."

I'm eating? When did you see me eat?

You make it look like you eat, Dumbo. Just like you're going to do today!

I ordered a crab salad that I could push around and make it look eaten. Dad added a bowl of the lobster bisque for me, as well as shrimp cocktails for us both. I could feel myself turning green.

As soon as the waiter had whisked away our menus with a promise to be right back with those cocktails, Dad dug into his pocket and pulled out a small, velvet-covered box, which he set on the table between us. Then he reached for my hands and held them tight as he looked into my eyes.

"I think it's time that, if you want to go out on a date with a boy, I think that would be all right," Dad said. "Not single car dates, now, but if you want to double with another couple—as long as your mother and I meet the boy and we know he's a decent sort for you to be going out with—I think it's time you had that privilege. You've earned it."

"Thanks," I said.

Wow. You get to date. And who, pray tell, is going to ask you out?

"Now." Dad cleared his throat and let go of my hands. He

picked up the box and toyed with it. "With that privilege comes responsibility. I'm going to ask you to make a promise, not just to me, but to yourself and to God."

"Okay," I said automatically.

He lifted up the box. "This one is hard for some young women to keep. I think you're the exception, but I still think you need me to back you up. Anyway, I want you to promise that you are going to wait…until marriage."

I almost said, "For what?" But I didn't. At least I had *some* class. As soon as he opened the box and faced it toward me, I knew. A shiny gold ring winked out at me. I recognized it from *Brio* magazine. It was a True Love Waits ring.

Dad took my left hand and slid the ring onto my second finger. It slipped right on over my knuckle and hung limply. I pulled it toward me and pretended to admire it under the light.

"Is it too big?" he said.

"No," I lied. "It's perfect. Thank you."

Somehow I swallowed several shrimp and begged off the other three because the soup came, and I told Dad I didn't want to get too full. Actually, I did have a major lump in my throat. It was sweet—it really was—Dad wanting to protect me, giving me a beautiful ring, bringing me to this fabulous restaurant. I found myself wishing I were wearing my sophisticated dress, the one that was still in the box in the back of the closet. You would have to call what I felt at that moment a mixed glimmer.

I gagged down some of the crab salad and ate the whipped cream off the top of the dessert the waiter brought in flames. They didn't sing "Happy Birthday" at Adelle's—far too classy. For that I was grateful.

My plan was to throw up the minute I reached the house, but Mom met me at the door. Unfortunately she was in a much better mood and wanted to chat. I evidently was back in favor.

"Did you have a good time, honey?" she said.

"I did." I edged toward the stairs.

"Let me see your ring. Oh, isn't that precious."

She squeezed my hand and kissed it and then gave me a hug, which she ended by patting me on the rear.

"Caitlin is upstairs," she said, holding me out at arm's length.

"I want you two girls to spend some time getting ready for your birthday dinner."

"I just had lunch!" I said. And then I remembered to laugh. It didn't sound so much like arguing that way.

"This is a special dinner, and it warrants some primping," she said. "You two will have fun curling each other's hair and all."

"So she's back?" I said.

"Well, yes, what did you think?"

"Nothing," I said hurriedly and tried not to look relieved as I went upstairs. If she was back already, her lunch with "Adam and them" couldn't have been that big a deal.

Real nice. Begrudge her any fun at all, especially with Adam. Give that up!

I opened the door to my room. Caitlin was on her bed, painting her toenails black.

"Happy birthday to you!" she sang in a Janis-Joplin-times-ten voice. "Happy birthday to you!"

"Could we skip it?" I said.

"Ooh, the birthday girl is in a foul mood!"

"I am not," I said. "I'm just...full."

"So go puke."

I didn't respond but tossed my purse over the chair and went to the closet.

"We're supposed to get ready for dinner," I said.

"Yeah. I'm painting my toenails in your honor. Don't expect much more than that."

I reached into the closet, pulled out the dress Mom had made for me, and hung it up on the door. Behind me, Caitlin snorted.

"You aren't actually going to wear that, are you?"

"I'm supposed to."

"So what happens if you don't? Will Mom take away your birthday?"

I hesitated. In a skewed kind of way, Caitlin sounded like Georgianna. What *would* happen if I had it my way instead of Mom's? If I came down to dinner in that beautiful dress with the lace jacket that my friends had picked out for me, bought with their own money, and presented to me over breakfast at six in the morning because they wanted that much to be with me.

"What? No Shannon to Mom's rescue?" Caitlin said.

I looked at her. She was sitting with the nail polish brush suspended in midair, her eyes in scrutinizing slits.

"I don't know," I said.

"You are so totally...smashed," Caitlin said.

"What do you mean, 'smashed'?"

"Smashed," she said. "Squashed. Oppressed, repressed, suppressed. Every kind of pressed you can name except impressed. That's why I smoke dope."

I looked at her sharply. "What?"

"I smoke dope because I don't want to be smashed. It's the only way I can get away from them doing this..." She drove her thumb into the bedspread. "...to me all the time. I get so sick of them telling me who to be, what to say, who to talk to, and what to like that I want to scream. Only we aren't allowed to scream. I screamed, and they sent me to boarding school. So I get away. Unlike you, I refuse to be squished like some ant on the counter. What are you staring at?"

I shuddered. I *had* been staring at her—in rapt attention, as if she had just pulled a veil off the answer to the ultimate question or something.

I went to my bed and lay down and stared up at the lace, the buttons, and the ruffles on the pink dress that signaled my sixteenth birthday. Even as I fumbled with the ring on my left hand, I knew more clearly than I had known anything else in my whole life: Caitlin did dope for the same reason—the very same reason—that I couldn't bring myself to eat.

CHAPTER TEN

IF I THOUGHT THE WHOLE WEAR-THE-FLUFFY-DRESS, EAT-the-disgusting-roast-beef birthday dinner was bad, I hadn't seen anything until the next morning.

At 6 A.M. I woke up for the fifteenth time since two, as usual, and stayed awake. I could hear the shower in my parents' bathroom below, the gurgling of the coffeepot in the kitchen, and the deep, even breathing in the other bed. It was safe to get up, dress, and creep down to the hall bathroom to try to get rid of the roasted potatoes and carrots and the sickeningly sweet double-chocolate cake my mother had monitored the eating of.

You were a total hog, putting away all that food, the Voice said as I made my way soundlessly down the hall.

What was I supposed to do? They were all watching me. I couldn't even spit anything out into the napkin.

Yeah, well, you're going to pay for it today. Nothing. No water, nothing.

But does that really keep them from controlling me? I mean, really?

What? What did you say?

Well…

Are you really buying into that dog food? You're a bigger idiot than I thought.

I closed myself into the peach-toweled bathroom, pulled my hair back with one hand and stuck my finger down my throat with the other, but nothing happened. I coughed. I gagged. I thought my esophagus was going to turn inside out, but I couldn't make myself throw up. I gripped the toilet seat with both hands and clenched my throat muscles, but only a thin trickle of saliva splashed into the water. And a tear.

Oh, get over it. Accept it. You can't do anything right. You disgust me.

Letting the lid fall angrily, I went to the sink and snatched up my toothbrush. When I looked up into the mirror, my eyes were wide and terrified.

An abrupt banging on the door set them bulging.

"Are you making a career out of it?" Caitlin's gravelly, waking-up voice rasped. "Hurry up. I gotta take a leak!"

"Caitlin, since when do we talk like that in this house?" I heard Mom say.

"What did I say? Geez!"

"And we don't say that either."

"You people all have something permanently inserted up your anal cavities. I mean it."

"Caitlin!"

"Mother!" Caitlin's voice matched Mom's so exactly I would have laughed, if I hadn't felt like I wanted to go right down the drain of the sink I was clinging to.

"Go to your room," Dad said. Both his Brut cologne and his barely controlled voice filled the hall.

"No. I want to settle this right now!" Mom said. Her voice was already going off the shrill scale.

"What are you going to 'settle,' *Mom?*" Caitlin said.

"That you will *not* talk like some street child in this house!"

"So what kind of 'child' do you want me to talk like?"

"You can start by getting that tone out of your voice."

"What 'tone'? The one that shows I might have a brain cell in my head—unlike Shannon who sounds like your little robot."

"At least Shannon shows some respect—"

"Respect? She's a freakin' hypocrite!"

"What?"

"Do you know what she's doing in there right now? She's cramming her finger down her throat. She's freakin' *purging*. At least I do my vomiting right in your face!"

I definitely felt like throwing up now, but I stood frozen at the sink, unable to tear my eyes from the mirror where my reflection was slowly turning gray.

There was a different banging on the door. Sharper, more parental.

"Shannon," Mom said, "what are you doing in there?"

"Bronwyn, this is not about Shannon. Caitlin, get to that room *now!*"

"Oh, Father, please, not the room, not exile from the arms of my family!"

"John, no!"

There was a stabbed silence, as if someone had just run all three of them through with the same butcher knife.

Caitlin's rough voice broke it off. "You were going to hit me, weren't you, Dad?"

"No, he wasn't," Mom said. "Don't be ridiculous."

"He holds his hand like this, but he's not going to hit me. What was he winding up for then?"

"Go!" Dad's voice rattled the family pictures on the hall walls. I could hear them shivering against the wallpaper. I could hear Caitlin swearing under her breath and stomping back up to our room. I could hear the door slamming, and one of the pictures sliding down the wall and crashing to the floor. And I could hear my mother rushing to it, already sniffling.

"That was completely unnecessary," she said, heading back toward shrill.

Dad didn't answer. There was only the most deadly kind of silence, followed by my father trying to punch holes in the hardwood floor with his feet as he marched down the stairs, flung open the front door, and slammed it behind him. The doorbell gave a faint and startled ring.

I could hear Mom straightening the fallen picture, and at that point something unfamiliar soared up my esophagus. It wasn't nausea. It was something that burned and made me squeeze the sink until my knuckles went white.

She is straightening a picture. Our whole family is ripping itself apart from the inside out, and she's straightening a picture!

Cool your jets, D'Angelo. She's your mother. Get out there and fix her.

I opened the door and peeked out. Mom was digging tears out from under her eyes as if they were lice. The lips had gone beyond pursing. She was about to draw blood.

"Are you okay, Mom?" I whispered.

"Do you *think* I'm okay?" She stood back and surveyed the picture, then directed her eyes at me. "Go have some breakfast."

"Is Dad gone?" Caitlin yelled through the door.

"Yes," Mom answered.

"Great. When are *you* leaving?"

Mom's face crumpled, and she headed upstairs for our room. "Caitlin, I will not have this!"

While she was screaming that and a whole lot of other things at the immovable door, I slapped my hair into a ponytail and rushed downstairs just in time for Tobey to drive up.

"I'm going!" I called out, and then I did. The only good thing about the whole ordeal was I didn't have to eat breakfast.

"How was your birthday?" Cheyenne said when I joined her in the backseat.

"Fine," I said.

Nobody said anything, but the way they all smiled sympathetically, it was like I had just told them the whole thing.

"You got presents, right?" Cheyenne said. Sympathy or no sympathy, she couldn't leave that part alone.

"Yeah," I said. "My mom made me a dress, and my dad gave me a—"

I looked down at my hand. The ring wasn't there. It was sitting on my dresser, locked in the room with Caitlin. It was safe, I knew. She had announced at the dinner table the night before that Dad shouldn't bother getting one for her sixteenth birthday because she had no intention of waiting for sex or anything else. That was when her fall from the good-girl stool she had been sitting on had started.

"Gave you a what?" Cheyenne said. "I don't see anything."

"It's a ring," I said. "I just didn't wear it today."

Tobey changed the subject. I looked out the window and let the Voice shout in my head.

What now, D'Angelo? How are you going to put your family back together, huh?

I don't know!

Of course you don't know. You can't even control yourself, much less Caitlin. But you better get hot before your dad breaks her nose or something. The dude's practically out of control. Guess it runs in the family, doesn't it?

Tobey pulled the car up to the front of the church and stopped. Nobody made a move to get out.

"Aren't you going to park?" I said.

"No," she said. "Remember? We're going to court for Ira's first day. We're just dropping you off."

That was about all I needed to make the morning as perfectly awful as it knew how to be.

"Oh yeah," I said. "Well, you guys have a good time. I mean… well, not a good time, but—"

"You want us to pray for Ira for you?" Cheyenne said.

"Do," I said. "Pray for him for me."

Good idea. You know about how much your prayers are worth.

The Voice didn't stop as Tobey pulled away and I watched the three of them go off to join Norie and Brianna at the courthouse, without me. It didn't stop even while I mechanically played the morning's songs, helped Red Sam with his Popsicle-stick sculpture, and held little Tiffany on my lap during the story. By the time we reached snack time, I was exhausted. One look at the orange Kool-Aid, and I knew I would lose it right there in the kindergarten room if I stayed another minute.

"I don't feel so good," I said to Holly.

"I believe it. You look awful," Holly said, mahogany ponytail falling to the side of her head as she plopped Dixie cups on the table. "Get out of here. Go get some air or something."

I pushed my way into the empty room where we had our staff meetings and retreated to the piano, which was almost against the wall. I sat at it, but I couldn't bring myself to take my hands off my ears to even touch the keyboard. If I did, I knew the Voice would scream me right into the corner.

I went cold all over. I had to get away from everything.

Looking wildly around, I saw only one hiding place. My heart assaulted my chest as I wriggled between the back of the piano and the wall and curled up like an unborn baby.

Well, well, I didn't think you actually could fit back here with all that roast beef on your backside.

Stop it!

Excuse me?

Stop it!

Honey, if I "stop it," what's going to happen to you? You might as well hang it up.

Then I heard a swishing sound. My mind lurched to a stop, and I listened. The door was opening and closing. Somebody had come into the room, was walking on rubber soles across the floor, was whistling under his breath—her breath?

I *stopped* breathing and strained to hear.

To my horror, the piano bench scraped back over the floor, and the piano keys started to plunk, vibrating right up my spinal cord.

Plunk—a chord here. Plink—another chord there.

No, that didn't make the player happy. Try a different combination...there we go.

It wasn't a tune I recognized. Matter of fact, it sounded like somebody was making it up as he or she went along. My mind started to race again. What if whoever it was realized some nut case was curled up behind the piano?

"She smi-i-iles when she's supposed to—"

I couldn't help cringing. Whoever this poor person was, he sure couldn't sing.

"The kind of girl...you'd give a rosé to..." Plunk. "Aw, man, could you *get* any more lame?"

Those last words were spoken, and I had to slap my hand over my mouth to keep from gasping. It was Adam.

"But her eyes don't have a gleam..." he sang haltingly. "Not even when you..."

He attempted several more chords, then "erased" them with a palm-crunch on the keys and started over.

"She smi-i-iles when she's supposed to..."

So he already had a girlfriend. Probably back home in Montana.

I was ready to start chewing on that while Adam went on playing, but the door swished open again, and Holly's voice said, "Have you seen Shannon?"

"No, not since this morning. Why? She didn't ditch you, did she?"

"No, are you kidding? She's more conscientious than Gandhi,

who probably ate more than she does. What are you doing anyway?"

I groaned inwardly as the door swished closed and Holly's sandals tapped across the floor toward the piano.

"Messing around," Adam said.

"Writing another song?"

"Yeah."

"For VBS?"

"Uh, no."

There was a rich silence.

"What?" Adam said.

"You have it bad for some chick, don't you? I can see it all over your face."

"No. Those are freckles."

"You are such a liar! You have a crush on somebody."

"Yeah, Hol, I've been meaning to say something. It's you, babe."

There was a smacking sound, and Holly laughed.

Okay, so cross her off the list. Obviously it wasn't somebody he had been going with for a while. This was a new love, a secret one.

"So," Adam said, "if you're not in there and Shannon's not in there, who's keeping the ceiling on in the kindergarten room?"

"The kids are gone," Holly said. "It's lunchtime, pal. What are we eating today?"

"Yesterday Caitlin said something about wanting tacos, but she didn't come today."

"Caitlin. So she's the one!"

"No, don't even think about it!"

"Oh, I'm going to think about it. It's Caitlin, isn't it? Adam, you cradle robber! What is she...three years younger than you?"

By then, their voices were fading toward the door. One more time it opened, and the conversation was lost out in the hall.

I, on the other hand, was lost behind the piano.

I walked home that day, and when I got there Caitlin was, miraculously, out of our room. She was sitting in the swing on the front porch with her portable CD player in her lap. Even with the headphones firmly planted in her ears, I could hear the vibrations of Nine-Inch Nails, that song she always listened to with the cans in the dryer. Good thing Mom couldn't hear the words.

"Hi," I said. "Are you okay?"

She gave me a withering look as she mashed a button on the CD player and reluctantly pulled out one earpiece.

"What?" she said.

"I said, 'Are you all right?'"

"Why wouldn't I be? I did my own kind of purging. I feel fine now."

"I don't purge," I said. "I mean, just for your information. I'm not bulimic."

"Only because you don't binge first."

I blinked.

"You're not the only one who can read," she said. "Every time you open a magazine there's an article about some chick's eating disorder. It's enough to make *me* puke. Personally, I could never starve myself. Pot gives me the munchies, you know what I mean?"

Stupidly, I shook my head.

"Of course you don't," she said. And she snapped the earpiece back over her ear and shut me out.

That unfamiliar burning feeling came up my pipes again. It took every ounce of control I had to smile and say, "See you later," and go inside the house.

"Hi, sweetie," Mom sang out from the kitchen. "I have lunch ready."

"I ate at the church," I said.

Great. Now I'm lying.

I slipped up to my room. I just needed a few minutes alone before I had to fix on a plastic smile and say all the right things. I went over to the dresser and picked up my brush. My face in the mirror was not a pretty sight. Under my eyes dark, smudgy-looking rings went halfway down my cheeks, and the whites of my eyes were this putrid yellow color. I kept brushing and looked down at the dresser top. Might as well put my needless True Love Waits ring on. That would make Daddy happy.

But it wasn't there, at least not where I had left it last night when I went to bed. I yanked out the top drawer and pawed through it, but it hadn't fallen in there either. I crawled around to the side of the bureau and peeked behind it. Nothing.

Maybe I hadn't put it there. Maybe it was on the bedside table.

That revealed only that my Bible had been gone through, because the marker was askew, and that somebody had rifled through the little drawer.

Caitlin had gone through my stuff.

I dove for the closet and frantically swept aside the rack of flowered, ruffled skirts to get to the back corner. The box was still there. It hadn't been opened. The dress was still safely folded inside. Its wonderful newness wafted out to me as I peeked in, relieved.

The ring was one thing. I liked it, and it had been sweet of my dad and all that, but the dress, that was something else. What it was I couldn't name, but I had to keep my dress where I could look at it and smell it.

"You just get weirder by the minute."

I backed out of the closet like something was after me and stood up, hair in static wisps over my face. Caitlin was standing there with her arms folded just above her exposed belly button with its little gold ring.

"Has Mom seen you in that?" I said, nodding to the low-slung, cutoff shorts and the halter top that barely would have covered *my* chest.

"Not yet. You might want to take cover before she does."

Caitlin gave me one more suspicious look before she flopped, face first, onto her bed.

Grasping for a way to distract her from the contents of my side of the closet, I shut the door behind me and said, "Why do you do that?"

"Do what?" she said, voice muffled in the pillows.

"Bait Mom."

"Because I don't have anything else to do." She came up on one elbow and watched me go to my desk and start tidying. "Did they miss me at church?"

"Yes," I said.

"Did Adam ask about me?"

"I don't know."

"You hate it that he likes me, don't you?"

I didn't mean to look over my shoulder at her, but I couldn't help it. She was lying on her back now, hands behind her head, watching me with her lip curled and her eyes gleaming. I opened the desk drawer and straightened pens.

"Man, I can't even get you into a good fight," Caitlin said. "No wonder I'm so *bored!*" She shouted the last word as if she were riling up a crowd at a rock concert. I forced myself not to jump. "You know, you get more like Mom every day."

"I do not," I said stiffly.

"Yes, you do. Look at you; you're *cleaning*, for Pete's sake. And you're trying to give me the old silent treatment. You need more practice though. You haven't learned how to frost the room yet."

I took a deep breath. The burning in my chest didn't stop.

"I think she just does that because she's afraid she's going to say something she'll be sorry for," I said.

"Ba-loney! She's trying to punish us, trying to make us feel guilty and horrible, which you end up doing, which is why she keeps doing it. If something works for her, she sticks with it."

"Is that what you do, stick with what works for you?" I said. I shoved the drawer closed and started in on the stationery section.

"Mostly. Although I do try new techniques once in a while."

"Is your latest one stealing?" I said.

Her silence stabbed me between the shoulder blades.

"Stealing?" she said finally.

"Yeah. Taking stuff."

"What stuff? Can you ever just come out and *say* something?"

"You took my ring," I said. I was still facing away from her.

Before I could take the next breath, she was in front of me, leaning across my desk, lip curled and eyes narrowed.

"Did you just accuse me of stealing that cheesy little piece of jewelry that's supposed to keep you from having sex until you're forty?"

My momentary glimmer of courage died, right there in front of her. And I knew she could see it going.

"It's missing," I said. "Who else—"

"Anybody else! I told you I have no intention of 'waiting.' In fact, the first chance I get, I'm going for it, man. Who knows? Maybe it'll be Adam."

I knew my face was absolutely stricken. I could hear it in the laugh that burst from her like car exhaust.

She went back to the bed, still forcing laughter out of herself over and over until I couldn't stand it any longer. Without even knowing I was thinking at all, I went down to the second floor and picked up the phone. I dialed Marissa's number. She answered on the second ring.

"Um, remember the other night, when you asked me to stay over?" I said.

"Yeah, I really want us to get together."

"How about tonight?"

"Yeah, that'd be a blast! I want to tell you all about Ira's first day in court. I practically took notes because I knew you would want to know. Plus, I'm making carne asada, which you don't have to eat if you don't want, only—"

"I already ate," I said.

"This is for dinner."

"I had a big lunch. But Marissa, can I bring my dress, the one you guys bought me?"

"Well, sure."

"I want to show you how it looks on me."

"That would be so cool! Yeah, bring it. I can't wait. See you in ten?"

It took me three to throw some pajamas, my toothbrush, and tomorrow's clothes into a bag. Another five went to waiting for Caitlin to fall asleep so I could take my dress out of the closet and smuggle it out to Marissa's house, where I intended it to stay.

Over at Marissa's, I put the dress on for her and pretended I had tried it on before. She oohed and aahed and did my hair, and we played around with some makeup.

"Look in the mirror!" she said.

I stood in front of the mirror, but I closed my eyes. Seeing my own reflection was never a good thing for me. All I ever saw was how fat I was.

How thin do I have to be? I thought.

A lot thinner than this, the Voice answered.

That was why I closed my eyes and just felt the dress, sliding against my skin in all its silken elegance. It was one of the longest glimmers I had had yet.

But at dinnertime, the glimmer winked out, and I begged off, saying I had a headache. While I listened to the clink of forks against plates, I lay on Marissa's bed and looked up at the poems she had pinned to her wall.

She's so good, I thought. *I wish I were more like her.*

Yeah, well, you're not, and you never will be if you don't keep it together. You almost blew it with Caitlin this afternoon.

I won't do that again. I'm really going to try not to tick her off. Mom and Dad don't need that. Neither do I.

And what you need matters because…?

Because God loves me?

Okay, do the rest of the assignment. How does it make you feel to say that?

I turned on my side, closed my eyes, and felt a hot tear splash down onto my nose. It made me feel empty and horrible.

THE NEXT MORNING, I ASKED MARISSA IF I COULD LEAVE
my dress with her for a while.

"Sure, if you trust me," she said.

Seems to me you're taking a pretty big chance, D'Angelo, the
Voice hissed at me. *Isn't she the one who blabbed to Ms. Race about
your "problem"? Isn't she the reason you ended up with a shrink?*

I shook my head and smiled at Marissa. "You can wear it, if
you want. I bet it would look fabulous on you."

"If I could get my big toe into it." Marissa looked down at the
figure that, in my view, was like this perfect hourglass. "You just
don't know how thin you really are. Is it helping, seeing somebody?"

"I'm great," I said. "I think a few more sessions, and I'll be
cured. In fact, I may just not even go back."

There you go. Now you're talkin'.

I had no idea where that came from. Marissa looked as surprised as I felt.

"Really?" she said.

"Yeah."

Tobey's horn blew out front. I was relieved when we got in the
car, and the talk was all about Ira's first day in court.

Marissa had told me some of the highlights the night before:
How vulnerable Ira looked sitting there in his wheelchair in that
big courtroom and how the guy from the district attorney's office—the "DA dude," she said Cheyenne called him—had made
it sound as if Ira had been planning to off Dillon Wassen for
months.

I had stopped listening to Marissa after a while. It hurt too much to think what Ira must be thinking about me—that I didn't even have the guts to show up for his first day in court. But in the car, there was no getting away from it. Tobey and Cheyenne were overflowing with stuff to tell me.

"Ira was so cool the whole time that DA dude was talking," Cheyenne said. "I would have either been bawlin' my eyes out or trying to take him out at the knees with my wheelchair."

"That's an attractive image," Tobey said.

"I mean it. That guy was just pacing back and forth up there, lying about Ira!"

"The jury will figure that out," Tobey said. "Did you see those people? They were so into it. Ira's lawyer told him he thinks the jury will really be sympathetic."

"Besides, they had to be impressed by all of us sitting there rooting for Ira," Cheyenne said. "It was like we had a cheering squad—only silent."

"It was awesome," Tobey said. "I don't know about you two, but I could just feel God when we were all sitting there."

I sagged down into the seat and tried to be invisible for the rest of the ride. When everybody got out of the car, suddenly all these black spots were in front of my eyes.

"Are you okay?" Tobey said.

I fumbled for the door handle. "Yeah, I'm fine. I have to get in there and set up my music."

I pushed open the door and held on to it while I steadied myself on my feet. For a minute I thought the ground was coming up to meet me.

"Shannon?"

"What's wrong?"

"Dude, she's going to keel over!"

Hands were all over me. Another second, and the ground receded, and my eyes cleared. I shook them all off.

"I'm *fine!*" I said.

"All *right* then!" Cheyenne said. She tossed her fringed bangs and walked off.

"She's touchy this morning," Tobey said a little too cheerfully. "Come on, Shan', we'll walk you in."

"I said I'm *fine!*"

Tobey kept her smile in place. Marissa lost hers and took a step backward.

"Okay," Tobey said. "We'll see you at break then?"

I nodded. Tobey took Marissa's elbow and ushered her toward the church. Marissa glanced at me over her shoulder, but Tobey kept talking and waving her arms until they were out of earshot. Then their heads bent together, and I knew I had just become the topic of conversation.

What's the matter with *her?* they were probably saying. We were just trying to be nice.

Just remember this, the Voice said. *Not a one of them could do what you're doing. They wouldn't be able to stand to miss one meal, much less go without for two days. You might be a loser in most departments, but you have it all over them when it comes to food.*

Yeah, but—

No buts. Just keep remembering what you said this morning, about how you don't need therapy after all.

But I don't know why I said that.

Between the Voice and the black spots and the way the floor kept rushing up to me, the morning went by in pretty much of a blur. I did notice that Caitlin showed up. Mom must have brought her. And I also noticed that she was in Adam's space every chance she had. He didn't seem to mind it. Now he was calling her "Cait-lou." I was finding it pretty hard to remember to say "God loves me."

At noon Tobey said, "Come to lunch with us, Shannon."

I was surprised—too surprised to make up an excuse. "Sure. But I kind of have to ask Caitlin to come too."

Cheyenne was going to say "No way!" I could tell. Marissa jabbed her a good one in the ribs while Tobey coughed and said, "Sure. But I think she would be bored. We're just going to talk about Flagpole stuff."

"I promised my mom I would include her in everything."

As it turned out, I should have saved myself the trouble. When I finally found Caitlin, "helping" Adam mop Kool-Aid off the linoleum in the kitchen, she greeted me with an upper lip curled practically all the way up her nostrils.

"You want to go to lunch with us?" I said.

"Nah, I'm doing tacos with Adam."

For the first time I looked at Adam. He was focused on the mop like it was an AK-47 he had to keep control of. He wasn't even aware I was in the room.

"Okay," I said to Caitlin. "Have fun."

"Oh, no doubt. You too. What are you guys going to do? Pray?" She sneered.

I did the dishrag thing with my hands. "No. Well, I don't know—"

"Well, whatever it is, go do it," she said.

So I did. I wasn't even worried about how I was going to get away without eating. I could honestly say my esophagus was burning so bad I *couldn't* eat.

Besides, we didn't head for a restaurant. We ended up in front of Ms. Race's apartment house. The doors to Tobey's car came open, and everybody got out.

"Do you just want me to wait here while you get her?" I said.

Tobey stuck a hand in for me to grab. "No, we're having lunch here."

"She's a great cook," Cheyenne said. "Even *you* will want to eat her stuff."

"*Chey-enne*," Marissa said. It was the most exasperated I had ever heard her sound.

Another surprise was waiting for me when Ms. Race opened her door to us. Norie and Brianna were there too.

"Hey, you beat us," Cheyenne said to them. "Is any food left?"

"Don't worry, Garbage Gut," Norie said, grinning. "We haven't even touched it."

So Cheyenne, Tobey, and Marissa had known everyone was going to be there. Everybody seemed to know about this meeting except me.

You were an afterthought, D'Angelo, face it. If you hadn't been at church, they would have done this without you. This group is only for people who have their act together, remember?

"Chips and things are over there," Ms. Race said as she closed the door behind us. "Let's talk first, and then we'll have lunch."

Cheyenne complained, but somebody shut her up as we all

formed a circle on Ms. Race's floor. I had been at her place before, and I loved the fat cushions, the bright wall hangings, the carved wooden animals she had brought back from her mission trips all over the world. But today the place felt strange and cold. I shivered and pulled my long-sleeved shirt down over my hands.

Once everybody—except me, of course—had stuffed a few salsa-dripping tortilla chips into her mouth, it grew quiet. Everybody seemed to be looking at Ms. Race.

"Shannon," she said, "we're all concerned about you."

I stared at her.

"So we thought the best thing to do would be to just gather around you and show you that we love you and that we want to help you."

I was feeling a lot of things just then, but "helped" and "loved" weren't on the list. "Cornered," "trapped," "betrayed"—now, those were right up there, along with "pitied," "humiliated," and "about to die of heartburn."

With all that going on, a feeble, "Me? Why?" was all I could get out.

Ms. Race looked around at the group. Next to me, Tobey put her hand on my leg. I wanted to shake it off, but I sat there, stiff and frozen.

"We know you're seeing a therapist," Tobey said, "and we think that's totally brave."

I shrugged. "So what is there to talk about?"

"Marissa said you were thinking about quitting," Cheyenne said.

I couldn't keep my eyes from honing in on Marissa. She was looking at me, but as soon as my eyes met hers, she dropped them to the Bolivian rug we were sitting on.

"Do you have to tell everybody everything I say to you?" I said.

If I had hauled off and slapped her, I don't think it would have flabbergasted them more. Marissa didn't answer, but I sure had gotten Norie's hackles up. Across from me, she sat up ramrod straight and narrowed her small eyes at me.

"We would have to be completely blind not to know you're hurting, Shannon," she said. "We happen to care about you, and none of us does more than Marissa. It wasn't like she was gossiping."

I shrugged again.

"What is that?" Norie said.

"May I say something here?" Ms. Race placed a restraining hand on Norie's shoulder. "Shannon, Marissa did tell us that you mentioned not seeing your therapist for much longer, and that concerned all of us."

I hugged my knees. I felt as if I had to hold on to them tight, right up against me, or I was going to fly apart and be splattered all over Ms. Race's apartment.

"We know things are really hard at home for you," Tobey said. "A lot is going on, and so you might not be getting the support Ms. Race was talking about."

"Even if you are," Ms. Race put in, "you can use all the love and encouragement you can get. We just want you to know we're here to give you that."

"We're behind you totally," Marissa said. Her voice was trembling.

I hugged my knees harder.

"The other thing is the work you have to do," Norie said. "I've read about this stuff. We did an article in the paper on it last winter. I don't know if you saw it—"

"Anyway," Tobey said pointedly, "you have, like, this gargantuan job to do, and it isn't going to happen if your heart isn't totally in it, and that's what we're worried about—that you're not really convinced you want to get better."

Like it's any of their business.

The Voice surprised me. Not because it spoke, but because it hadn't up to that point. I wanted to throw my arms around it.

"I'm trying," I said. My own voice quavered defensively. "I do all my assignments. At least I try to—"

They all waited. But there was nothing else I could say. I planted my forehead on my knees.

"We can't begin to comprehend how hard this must be," Ms. Race said. "But we can pray. Let us just put our hands on you, Shannon, and go to God for you."

I shook my head.

Then another voice that had been quiet drove itself in, right at my heart. "Girl, you mean to say you are turning down *prayer?*"

It was Brianna. I couldn't answer her.

"Look at me, girl, right here."

I had no choice but to raise my head. She was pointing to her eyes. Her face was as firm and smooth as a muscle.

"I know how it is when you're hurtin' so bad you can't think straight," she said. "About the first thing to go is the praying. You have so much goin' on inside you, the last thing you think you can do is go to the Lord. Do I have that right?"

I had to nod. If I didn't, I knew my eyes would give me away anyway. Brianna came across the circle on her knees and took my face in both of her long, cool hands. "That's when you need your friends the most, girl, and here we are. Don't you dare refuse our prayers. Don't you dare."

"It won't do any good," I said. "You can pray, but it will be a waste of your time."

"Why?" Tobey squeezed my leg hard. "Why do you say that?"

"Because…I'm not…I'm not…"

You're not actually considering letting them do this prayer thing, are you?

Why not? What's it going to hurt?

It's going to hurt every chance I have of keeping you from blowing up like a balloon because you're such a selfish pig!

"I'm a selfish pig!"

I didn't realize I had actually said it until Cheyenne's arms were around my neck from behind, and she was saying, "You are not either. You're the best. You're totally the best!"

"We love you, Shannon."

"Don't ever say that about yourself."

"God doesn't make selfish pigs."

Their voices, their hugs, their hands on me, it was all so loud, so clear I couldn't hear the Voice. I put my forehead back on my knees and nodded my head. "Okay then," I said. "You can pray."

They didn't give me a chance to change my mind. Within seconds the room was filled with their voices, soft and husky and reverent, taking my miserable mess to God. I don't remember much of what they said. I don't think I actually even heard it at the time. But one thing stood out for me, and it's still sparkling clear in my mind. Tobey picked up my right hand in both of hers, and she kissed it and said, "Please let Shannon know that she has power, power that can come only from You. The power to change and heal."

Those were the words that made me cry. It was quiet crying, coming from down in my gut and releasing me the way throwing up did. I cried and I cried while they stroked my back and my hair and rubbed my feet. It was like a long, long amen.

Somehow everybody got different rides home, and only Tobey and I were in her car. That was good, because I actually had something to say.

"You know that power you were talking about," I said. "Do you, like, have that?"

"Sometimes," she said. "Like last fall when all that stuff went down with Coach, remember?"

I nodded.

"I couldn't have done that without the power—and all of you guys."

"Yeah, but you're so strong anyway."

"Oh right. I couldn't eat. I couldn't sleep. I was throwing up all the time. If it had gone on any longer I probably would have flunked every class. Don't think you're the only one who doesn't always know what to do."

"I never know what to do."

"Isn't that why you're in therapy?"

"I don't know," I said. "I'm supposed to try to figure out why I'm doing it—and I don't know."

"Then can I say something, as long as you're kind of asking?"

"Okay."

Tobey pulled up to a red light and scanned the windshield thoughtfully. "I think you have to do it for you. And maybe not just you but because it's what Jesus would want you to do."

"How do I know that though?" I said.

"Well…" She pulled away from the stoplight and cocked her head at the road ahead. "You pray, and you wait; that's what I do. But you have to think about it too. And I can tell you something I've come up with."

"Okay." I could hear my voice quivering—with eagerness.

We were at my house by this time. Tobey parked and turned to look at me with the eyes of a woman way older, way wiser than I was.

"God gave us a will, right?" she said. "So anything that takes away your will, that makes you stuck or immobile or whatever, that isn't right. God wants things for you that will make you strong."

"I don't understand," I said.

She laughed. "I'm not sure I do either! It just came to me so I'm passing it on." She touched my arm, really gently. "You'll figure it out, you and God. I know it. He isn't going to let you go. You're just too special. Believe that."

Of course I didn't. Nor was I so sure I had all those choices she was telling me about. But as I went up the front walk to our house, I did know one thing. Tomorrow when I saw Georgianna, I was going to tell her I really wanted to go for it.

"Why?" she asked me when I told her.

"Because I need to be healed," I said. "That's all I know."

"Shannon, I'm pleased," she said. "Giving someone permission to help you out of a trap is the ultimate act of courage. This is the beginning of so many good things."

Yeah. Well, I didn't set my hopes too high. I went back to crackers and water instead of just water though. And I didn't have that burning thing in my chest for a while.

At least, not until Sunday. And it happened, of all places, in church.

When I arrived there I walked between my parents, and Caitlin dragged behind as if we were taking her in for a root canal or something. Adam was standing on the front steps with a fake walkie-talkie in his hand and a pair of sunglasses on his face. He brought the radio up to his mouth and said, "Yes, Lord, the D'Angelo family has arrived. I repeat, the D'Angelos have arrived."

Dad grinned and stuck out his hand. "John D'Angelo."

Adam nodded solemnly. "It's a pleasure, sir. Unfortunately, I'm on duty so I'm not at liberty to chat. I will ask you to hand over custody of your two daughters, however."

Dad chuckled. "Gladly. What do I owe you for them?"

"Don't give yourself tendinitis whipping out your checkbook, Dad," Caitlin said.

"I guess you two are sitting with this young man," Dad said to me. "No carrying on in there."

"Group all present and accounted for," Adam said into the toy radio. "Ready to enter the building."

Caitlin flashed him her dimples, tucked her arm into his, and steered him toward the door, but not before glancing over her shoulder at me and saying, "You coming or what?"

As if he had just been given a cue, Adam stuck out his other elbow and said to me, "Come on, Shannon!"

That obviously wasn't what Caitlin had in mind because her smile curled itself up under her nose. Then she flipped her face away from me with a toss of her one-sided curls that said, "Touch him, and you'll live to regret it."

Since I had regret in me I hadn't even gotten to yet, I just followed them with my eyes on the ground. That is, until we got inside and somebody whispered, "Psst! Shannon! Sit here!"

I looked up to see Cheyenne pounding the seat next to her. As I slid obediently in beside her, she moved over one space and said, "Sit there, Adam!"

Adam was scanning the congregation from behind his shades, still totally in character. He nodded to Cheyenne as if she were Command Central and dropped into the seat beside me. That left Caitlin standing in the aisle. Cheyenne smiled up at her and whispered, in a sweeter voice than I'd ever known the girl to use, "Caitlin, there's a place at the other end."

Caitlin gave her a dark look, but she took herself down the pew behind us, and I wasn't sure where she ended up. No way was she going to make a scene about sitting next to Adam. That definitely wasn't her style.

Nor was it my style to gloat. Not with the Voice winding up in my head.

Now that was considerate. So much for including her in everything.

It wasn't my fault! What was I supposed to do?

You could get up and give her your seat.

I didn't. It felt too cozy there in the shadow of Adam's big shoulders. He had a nice smell, too, that I had never noticed before. It was like a combination of Salon Selectives shampoo, Old Spice deodorant, and Kids' Crest toothpaste—as if he had forgotten to bring his shaving kit on the trip and was borrowing everybody else's stuff.

The organ crescendoed, and we all stood up, hymn books in hand. Only one was available for Adam and me, and he already had the page open. He stuck it toward me, and I grabbed my half.

We're holding the same book!

Wow! Start planning the wedding!

"Let us break bread together on our knees," Adam sang.

I joined him under my breath, partly because I hate for anybody to hear me sing and partly because I wanted to hear Adam.

Not a wise move on my part. I had forgotten how bad Adam's voice was when I had gotten an earful of it that day behind the piano. With his voice coming out in squeaks and croaks, I had to bite my lips to keep from smiling.

Every time I did open my mouth to join in, my face twisted itself into a giggle. I put my hand over my mouth. Adam gave me a sideways glance, still singing. I could hear the laugh in his voice.

I tried to stiffen my mouth. I tried to sing. But the louder he held forth, the more I wanted to laugh, and the harder I pressed my hand over the whole lower half of my face. Adam's next note came out a guffaw, and I lost it.

My shoulders shook, and my mouth refused to close. I had tears forming at the corners of my eyes. Adam kept on singing, but his whole face was one big grin. Even the freckles seemed to smile individually. He made it impossible to stop laughing. The more I tried to stifle it, the worse he sang, big blue eyes egging me on the whole time. I finally turned my head away from him, and the hymn ended before I burst a blood vessel.

He was still chuckling as we sat down for the sermon. Dad would definitely have considered this "carrying on."

It gave me a glimmer, which lasted until Cheyenne poked me in the rib. "Give this to Adam," she whispered and shoved a folded-up piece of paper at me.

I passed it on and focused on Reverend Winston, who was already in the middle of his sermon. "This is Communion Sunday for us. Now, Jesus could have chosen any number of occasions to prepare His disciples for what was about to happen. But I'm convinced that even if Jesus had waited until today to appear, He would still have gotten his disciples around him at a table—maybe in a back room at Columbo's."

"Or Pneumatic Diner," Cheyenne hissed to me.

"He said, 'Do this in remembrance of Me.' And we do, over and over again, because Jesus is waiting for us to join Him at His table. I want you to picture yourself walking down the street, so hungry, empty, and yearning for nourishment you don't know which way to turn. I don't think any of us has to stretch his imagination too far to think of a time when we felt that way."

Um, you got that right, I thought.

"There you are—broke, busted, disgusted—and suddenly a door opens just ahead of you. It's the door to Adelle's, and out steps Jesus Christ Himself. He's dressed in His crisp, black cummerbund and His white shirt with the starched tucks in the front, as if He's been expecting you. He even calls your name and says, 'Come on in! I've been waiting for you. Your table is ready.' And so it is. It has a big 'reserved' sign on it, and the table is heaped with your favorite culinary delights."

"Cheeseburger," Cheyenne hissed.

"Lobster," Adam hissed back over his shoulder. He was leaning forward, slurping up the images.

"Now," the preacher said, "let's suppose your stomach is gurgling so loud they can hear it out in Lyon County, but you feel like you can't possibly sit down at that table and let Him wait on you. In the first place, you aren't dressed right. You don't have any cash on you, and your credit cards are maxed out. How are you going to pay for this? Besides, the Lord waiting on *you*? How could you do that? I mean, He's so…Him…and you're so…you."

Reverend Winston's pained expression brought out congregational chuckling. I didn't join in.

"But you see? That's the very time, the instant when Jesus wants you at His table the most. He wants to feed you, nourish you, and fill you up—and not with the mesquite-broiled swordfish. He wants to feed you and fill you up with Himself. Why is it we forget that?"

He went on to answer the question, I guess. I stopped listening and pulled my hands together and clenched them in my lap. Was that true? Was Jesus waiting for *me*? Was He the only one in the world not trying to make me eat pizza and tuna casserole? Did He really want me to have…Him?

He's talking about the rest of them. Jesus doesn't want you.

But why? Why am I so different from everybody else?

You just are. I know what I'm talking about.

Then how come Reverend Winston is saying something different?

He doesn't know you.

But he says everybody has felt like I do sometimes.

He doesn't know everything.

But he's supposed to know stuff like that. Why do you know more than he does?

There was silence inside my head. I was so startled I looked around to see if anyone else noticed it. Everyone was staring, spellbound, at Reverend Winston.

"Today, as we celebrate our Eucharist, I want you to know that Jesus is waiting at this very table. He doesn't care how you're dressed, what baggage you're dragging behind you, or how much junk food you've already consumed. He wants to feed you. It's free—and there's plenty of it. That all-you-can-eat buffet at the Peppermill has nothing on this. Let us pray."

Heads bowed. Mine went down too.

Don't even think about it, D'Angelo. You'll get one bite of that little cracker they're going to give you, and you're going to want to grab the box and consume the entire thing.

I just want my piece!

Do you think you're supposed to have everything you want? What you want is to be pure and perfect, and you'll never get there by—

Going to Jesus? Really?

Once again there was silence in my head. Adam nudged my elbow.

"You coming?" he whispered.

An usher was standing at the end of the pew looking at us expectantly. I got up like somebody else was moving my body, and I moved to the front where all of us in the first few pews stood and waited for the plate of crackers and the tray of tiny containers of grape juice to make their way to us.

Suddenly the plate was there, and I was reaching down and taking a tiny piece, and hearing the words, "Take, eat, this is My body, which was given for you."

I took the juice, too, and it drained easily down my dry throat. I closed my eyes as the tray passed.

Thank You, Jesus, I thought. *I don't deserve it, but thank You anyway.*

A happiness-glimmer rippled through me. I had just prayed.

But it may have been the shortest entry yet on my personal glimmer-record. When I turned around to follow Adam back to our pew, I was just in time to see him smiling down at Caitlin, and tucking a folded-up piece of paper into her hand.

CAITLIN COULDN'T SEEM TO WAIT TO OPEN THAT PUPPY up. I couldn't wait for church to be over so I could get out of there. I was pretty much convinced the entire staff in the first two rows had watched me make a fool of myself, laughing and "carrying on" with Adam while he was passing notes right under my nose to my sister, the Professional Flirt.

Don't say I didn't warn you, the Voice said.

I couldn't deny it. But one thing was different this time. Even though I still agreed I was the worst loser who had ever drawn breath, I kept telling myself, *Tomorrow I'm going to see Georgianna. What she's going to help me with is more important than Adam.*

My work with Georgianna really started to move then. She was like a whole other person after I told her I was ready to go for it. I would show up for my appointment, and as soon as she had said hi to Mom, who always treated her the way she did a sales-clerk she didn't approve of, Georgianna would close the door and lean toward me with her very blue eyes on fire. She acted like what we were going to "discover" that day, as she put it, was going to change all of life as we knew it.

I myself wasn't too sure at first. The term "go for it" suggests you're going to break out in a sweat tearing after something. The only thing I learned fast was that therapy doesn't work that way. It's more like you plod along as if you have this big pack on your back that's so heavy you can barely move, plus you don't really know where you're going. But then you turn a bend, and what you've been looking for is just standing there in front of you.

The first time that happened was when Georgianna asked me

for what seemed like the forty-fifth time what I did for fun and how I got what I needed. I kept telling her stuff, and she kept saying, "That's for your mother, Shannon," or "That sounds like something you do to make your father happy," or "What about you?" It was like walking with the backpack *while* pushing a Chevy Blazer uphill. I kept trying, and I kept feeling my esophagus growing hotter and hotter. Just when I thought I was about to explode, I kind of did. I said, "I don't know! I don't do anything for myself! I don't have time!"

But did she back off and give me the keys to the Blazer? No way. She loaded it with rocks. She said, "If you did have time, what would you do?"

I basically couldn't push any farther. I said, "I...don't...know! You can fire me or whatever you want, but I don't know!"

She smiled that sudden flash-thing that went across her face, and she sat back and nodded until her earrings swayed. "That was the answer I was waiting for. Do you know what, Shannon?"

I shook my head stubbornly.

"In trying to be everything for everyone else, you've become disconnected from yourself. That's why it was so easy for anorexia to take over. Do you ever feel as if somebody else is inside you running your show?"

There I was, standing in the path, the Chevy Blazer off to one side, the backpack on the ground, looking an answer straight in the face.

"Yeah," I said.

"You just got something. What was it?"

"It's that Voice," I said.

Then I shrank back onto the cushion. My hands clenched together. I was going to catch it for sure. I had just exposed the Voice. It would never let up on me now.

"It's all right, Shannon," Georgianna's voice was husky and soft. "It can't hurt you."

"Yes, it can. It says horrible things to me!"

"You can learn to turn that down so you won't have to hear it most of the time."

"How?" I said.

"That's what we're here to find out."

A ray of hope, only as big around as a pencil and about that long, shafted through. I went to it like a moth to the light.

"Would you teach me?" I said.

"You'll need to tell me what you can about the Voice. What's her name?"

I squinted my eyes at Georgianna. "Her name? I don't think she has one."

"Maybe you should give her one."

"Edith," I said. "I hate the name Edith." My heart, for some reason, was pounding like I was about to bust somebody's chops—I guess. I had never busted anybody's chops before now.

"You hate that Voice then."

"Yes."

"Because…"

"Because it doesn't matter what I do or think or say, she tells me it's wrong, and it's bad, and I'm evil! Maybe she's right, but I am so sick of it. I keep trying and trying, and I'm never good enough."

"What happens when you aren't good enough?"

"I feel guilty."

"But what happens?"

"I hate myself."

"What else?"

"Nothing else; I just hate myself."

"So do you take a switch to yourself, pull out your nose hairs one by one with red-hot tweezers…"

"No!"

"What do you do then? What do you do when you hate yourself?"

"Nothing. I just try harder."

"Shannon."

She was looking at me dead center, seeing more than I was telling. I tried to look down at my lap, but I couldn't. I could only look back at her.

"You can say you're not ready to talk about it yet. You can tell me it's none of my business. You can tell me to get out, if you want to. But don't lie to me."

I wanted to shake my head. I wanted to say, "I'm not lying! This is the truth!" But her eyes wouldn't let me.

"I don't want to say it," I said finally.

"Why?"

"Because she'll say awful things, and I can't forget them. They drive me crazy!"

She waited. She didn't point out I was now crying and hadn't bothered to wipe the snot off my upper lip. She didn't push me on. She just waited.

And while she waited, nothing happened. The Voice was strangely silent, as if it, too, were waiting.

"Why isn't it screaming at me now?" I said.

"Because right now, somebody else is in charge."

"You?" I said.

"No." Georgianna cocked an eyebrow. "You."

"Not me!" I said. "I've never been able to shut it up."

"But right now you're very strong."

Then it was a cinch I better say what I had to say before I wimped out. "When I mess up, she—Edith—she won't let me eat."

Before I knew what was happening Georgianna had grabbed my hands in hers and was smiling into my face. "My dear, you are now on your way."

Of course, we weren't done.

"I wonder if you could talk back to Edith," Georgianna said to me another day.

"I do. I argue with her all the time."

"No, I mean, engage her in discussion. Get her to explain herself. We could find out why she thinks she has to have control and try to make you be perfect. Is there anything good about having Edith in there?"

I thought about that. "She tells me what to do when I don't know."

"And that happens often?"

"All the time! If my mother isn't there to tell me, then Edith tells me."

Georgianna's eyebrows went all the way up, I think past her hairline. I was a little surprised myself.

"Are you amazed you said that?" Georgianna said.

"Yeah!"

"I think it's wonderful! What that says to me is you've just figured out you've never had the chance to make decisions for yourself, so you sort of carry a tape of your mother's voice around with
you. Only I think Edith has distorted her somehow. What do you
think, honestly?"

I nodded slowly. It made sense to me.

Georgianna fingered one of her earrings. "Now, knowing that,
anytime Edith tells you to do something and you don't want to,
maybe you could tell her 'No, I don't think so. I can think for
myself.'"

"I can't."

"Don't rush it," Georgianna said. "Just think about it. Whenever
you're ready. Even though your father gave us a deadline, I don't
have one."

"No, he means it," I said.

"I know he does, and I respect that."

My stomach went into knots and stayed that way for quite
some time.

What if I haven't discovered everything by September? I would
ask myself while I lay awake at four in the morning.

Then you know you haven't worked hard enough, Edith answered one day.

How come you say stuff like that to me? I said.

Oh no, you're not going to pull your junior therapist routine on me.
That was as far as we got.

As if that weren't enough, still another day, Georgianna
brought up something else. "What are the Girls up to these days?"

"You mean, the Flagpole Girls?" I said.

"Right. They're your best friends, aren't they?"

"Uh-huh."

"Well, so what are they up to?"

"I don't know," I said. That was always a safe answer.

Both eyebrows went up. She wasn't buying it. "Why don't you
know?"

"I'm really busy with Bible school. It's a long program."

She sat back, folded her arms over the muslin-with-beads top
she was wearing, and waited.

"They're all wrapped up in Ira's trial," I said.

She gave a quick smile, and the arms came unfolded. "Okay. Tell me about the trial."

"I only know what they've told me, " I said "I can't go to court or any of the meetings over at Ira's where they pray with him and stuff. My dad won't let me."

"Ah."

"He doesn't want me getting mixed up in it."

"Very protective, your father."

Again, she waited. How she always knew when I was leaving something out is still beyond me.

"Last spring, when the skinheads were out to get Brianna, because of her art, and Ira challenged them to an off-road race and a white guy was killed, everybody else helped her, except me."

Georgianna wasn't watching my face anymore. Her eyes were on my hands in my lap. I was clenching them in a death grip.

"Are you angry with your father about that?"

"I don't like it."

"That's what you *think*. I want to know how you *feel*. Can you tell me that?"

"No."

"That's okay. Your hands have already given you away."

I unclenched them and wiped their sweat off on my skirt. That didn't do much for the burning in my esophagus though.

"What does Edith say when you think about how much you would like to help Ira?"

"She says I can't. She says I have to do what my dad says, and so I might as well forget it and try to just obey for a change. I ought to appreciate what he's trying to do." I wrapped my hands around each other, and then I flung them from me and looked up. The ceiling blurred. "Brianna and Ira are African-American, that's why my dad won't let me go."

"Aren't you angry with him for trying to foist his prejudices off on you?"

"I can't be angry with him."

"Why not?"

"Because he's my father!"

Georgianna gave me a blank look. "I never heard that rule."

"Well, in the Bible. You know, honor your father and mother."

"That doesn't mean it isn't okay to be angry with them."

I looked down at my hands.

"If you disagree with me, Shannon, say so," Georgianna said.

I spoke slowly down at my palms. "I always thought it meant you were supposed to agree with them and obey them and stuff. Isn't that what it means?"

"Are you asking for my interpretation?"

"I'm asking you what's right."

"I'll give you my opinion, and you decide what's right, okay?"

I nodded, and she went on.

"I think that commandment means you obey your parents and follow their rules while you're living in their house. And I think it's telling you to treat them with the respect they deserve. I don't think it's telling you that you can't have your own feelings. It's what you do with those feelings that makes the difference."

"Okay."

Her eyebrow went up suspiciously. "Do you want me to give you an example?"

"Yes," I said.

"Let's say you're as angry as you know how to be at your father for not letting you help your friends just because they're black. So you walk up to him, slap him across the face, and say, 'You're a big, fat bigot, and I hate your guts.' You aren't honoring your father then."

I giggled. I had a life-size picture of me doing that.

"But," Georgianna continued, "let's say you write about how mad you are in your journal, or you say, 'Dad, I think this is so unfair and I hate it,' you are still honoring him."

"He wouldn't think so," I said.

"Ah," Georgianna said. She looked sad. "There isn't much we can do about that. But you are still entitled to your own feelings, and the worst thing you can do is stuff them down someplace where even you can't find them."

I shrugged and looked at my lap. "I just wish he wouldn't be like that."

"I know of only two things you could do that would help even a little bit. One, you can pray for your father. Ask God to work on this issue. He likes to be asked too."

My heart sank. Why did her suggestions always have to be so hard? "What else?"

"Don't allow your father's prejudices to isolate you from all your friends. You may not be able to hang out with Brianna or go to court for Ira, but you can still spend time with the others. If you're honest with them, they'll understand."

"I want to get my act together first," I said. "I want to be all better before I go back and hang with them again."

Georgianna leaned forward, hand on her chest. "You know what, Shannon? If I waited until I was all put together, every piece perfectly in place, before I hung out with my friends, I would spend every single day by myself. And I certainly wouldn't be here talking to you."

Something about the expression on my face cracked her up. She threw her head back and howled. Then she grabbed my hands and looked right into my eyes, her face still shimmering with laughter.

"I love that face of yours," she said. "Whatever you don't want to say is broadcast live right there in your eyes. You just looked at me like you want out of here bad! 'What was I thinking? Get me somebody who has it together!'"

"I just—"

"It's all right. I put a big hole in something you've probably believed since you were old enough to believe anything. You don't have to accept that today. It takes time."

"But I don't *have* time! I only have until the end of the summer!"

"No, Shannon," she said. "You have the rest of your life."

CHAPTER THIRTEEN

I STARTED THE REST OF MY LIFE BY CALLING MARISSA and asking her if we could do something after VBS the next day. She said she would take care of it. I didn't even bother to invite Caitlin. From the time I went up to our room that night until the Girls and I left the church the next afternoon, her sole purpose in life seemed to have changed from tormenting my parents to torturing me.

While I was trying to sleep, she played that Nine-Inch Nails song, the one with the twisted electric sounds and the angry, heavy beat in the background, about twenty times.

When I went to the bathroom in the middle of the night, she rolled over and said, "Are you going to puke?"

The minute she came back from taking a shower the next morning and found me on my bed, trying to read my Bible, she gave her hoarse, too-many-cigarettes laugh and said, "You are such a freak show."

Then we arrived at the church, and she really turned ugly.

We had to be there early for a special staff meeting, and everybody was standing around looking puffy-eyed and eating glazed donuts when we arrived. Caitlin immediately went for my jugular vein.

"Eat," she whispered to me, "or I'll have to report you."

"I don't do donuts," I said.

"You are such a freak show sometimes!"

Then Adam walked up, and she moved on to her second form of terrorism. "Hey," she said to him. "What's up?"

Her lip had magically uncurled, and she was doing the flip-the-hair, bring-out-the-dimples thing. I could feel myself fading into nothingness beside her.

"Nothing," he said, grinning back at her. "I just thought I would come over here to harass you two. But if you're having an actual conversation…"

"Shannon was just jacking her jaws at me," Caitlin said. "You know she can talk the ears off a mule."

Adam looked a little confused. I spared him and hurried away.

"Was it something I said?" I heard Adam say.

"Nah," Caitlin told him. "She just does that sometimes. Her therapist says to humor her."

In spite of myself I glanced over my shoulder. She managed to look up, starry-eyed, at Adam and give me a smug glance at the same time.

I hate her. Sometimes I just hate her.

You aren't allowed to hate her. She's your sister.

Would Georgianna say that?

Fabulous. Run to your therapist like the loony tune you are.

I let that sink in.

I'm going to ask Georgianna, I thought finally. *I just am.*

When the donuts had just about all been scarfed down, Doug called us to attention and said that on Saturday he wanted to take us on a picnic to Lake Tahoe.

"I've reserved a pavilion at Sand Harbor," he said. "You don't have to bring anything. We'll provide burgers, dogs, some beans—"

"S'mores!" Randy said. He turned to the rest of us and garnered support with his hands.

"I just smell those things, and I gain five pounds," Holly said, looking at her thighs.

I managed to slip out and head for the church. My head was spinning.

A picnic? How am I going to deal with that? Food will be every-where. Everybody will be stuffing their faces all day. I wish I could.

What did you say?

Nothing.

Liar. You said you wished you could pig out, right?

I just want to be normal.

Well, give it up. For once Caitlin is right. You are a freak show.

I'm going to talk to Georgianna about it.

You're beyond neurotic.

Shut up!

But she didn't. Edith drilled on in my head as I entered the empty sanctuary. The piano was waiting for me, cold to my touch and already full of the mistakes I was going to pull out of it in a few minutes.

What did you expect? You don't practice enough. You have the focus of a four-year-old. Red Sam has a longer attention span.

I punched my bottom down on the bench and flattened a book open on the music rack. The notes seemed to be sticking their tongues out at me, daring me to play them correctly. I banged out the first two chords on the keys, then two louder, then another so hard it hurt the tips of my fingers.

The chords came down like wooden puzzle pieces, fitting in where they were supposed to, and if one wouldn't go, I pushed it, forced it, then went on to the next one.

What do you enjoy doing? I could imagine Georgianna saying. *Playing the piano?*

No! I hate playing the piano! I hate practicing an hour every day. I hate memorizing pieces and playing them for people who couldn't care less. I hate that my palms sweat all over the place and that I make mistakes that go up people's backbones like fingernails on chalkboards.

"Wow," said a little voice. "You're playing loud!"

I spasmed about a foot off the bench. Red Sam was standing at my elbow, gazing wide-eyed at my hands. He had even taken his finger out of his nose.

"I am?" I said.

"Yeah," he said. "I could hear you all the way out there. You were playing mad."

"I'm sorry," I said.

He grinned, showing his tiny pearl-teeth. "I liked it! Do it some more."

"Um, I can't right now, Sam," I said. I looked around the church. Little heads were beginning to appear above the pew backs. "I have to play the right way now."

"Oh," he said. His face drooped. He shrugged, sighed, and

went off to his seat, going for his nostrils with his index finger again. I stared down at the piano keys.

It was like I had been trying to kill them. I had never liked playing—not the way Adam seemed to relish playing his guitar or even plunking clumsily on the piano. It had never occurred to me to just sit down and mess around at the keyboard. Write a song? Forget it! How would I know if it were right?

Matter of fact, I didn't enjoy anything.

That thought came to me in a glimmer, another one of those clear moments when everything seemed real. Only it wasn't a glimmer of happiness this time. It was pure sadness.

"Shannon?"

I spasmed. The book tumbled off the rack and hit the keys, banging out several disjointed notes on its way to the floor. Giggles erupted from the front row.

"Hey, if you don't like that song, we can sing something else. I can take a hint."

Adam. Was it just me, or was he always there when I was acting like a spastic?

"Here you go." Adam set the songbook back on the rack. "If it jumps off again, just wing it. That's what I do half the time."

"Okay," I said.

He smiled a gap-toothed grin, and he ran a hand through his color-of-sweet-potatoes hair and shrugged his big, lanky shoulders, but he didn't leave. I looked from him to the music and back to him again so many times I was getting dizzy.

Finally he hunched down a little and said, "You know, if you ever need to talk, I'm around. You have the number on the staff phone list, right?"

"Uh-huh," I said.

"You can call me anytime," he said.

Doug appeared just then, pointing to the watch on his hairy arm in exaggerated fashion. "Are we going to do this before the Second Coming?" he said.

"Yeah, yeah, yeah," Adam said cheerfully. He ambled off to his guitar, but he looked over his shoulder, rolled his eyes at me, and grinned. I grinned back. It was like we were suddenly on the same side or something.

But that only lasted until lunchtime when Cheyenne and I were out in the entryway waiting for Marissa and Tobey. Caitlin went by—with Adam in tow. I mean, physically in tow. She had hold of his hand, and she was pulling him toward the door, her head thrown back in...okay, it looked like ecstasy to me.

"You promised me tacos," she was saying so the entire city of Reno could hear. Especially me.

"Not that place you dragged me to last time," Adam said. "I think they were chasing kitties all night to make those tacos."

"No, this is a good place," she said. "Me and my friends used to go there all the time..."

The glass door sighed closed behind them.

"My friends and *I*," Cheyenne mumbled beside me. "Even I know that." She poked me with her elbow. "She was making him go. Anybody could see that."

I shrugged.

"You don't have to act like you don't care for my benefit." Cheyenne gave her bangs a toss. "She's being really evil about this. I bet she doesn't even like him that much. I bet she's just trying to get him away from you. Which is totally hateful. But then, what did I expect? I mean, no offense, I know she's your sister and all that, but she might as well just go 'Nah, nah, nah, nah, na-a-ah.'" Cheyenne stretched out her mouth with both hands and stuck her tongue straight out.

"Cheyenne, what the Sam Hill are you doing?" Tobey came up to us grinning. She looked back over her shoulder at Marissa. "She's regressing."

"No, I was just imitating Demon Seed Child," Cheyenne said. I giggled.

All three of them suddenly grew quiet and stared at me. I looked down to be sure my shirt wasn't unbuttoned or something.

"What's wrong?" I said.

"Nothing," Tobey said. She shook her head like she was clearing out cobwebs. "It just struck me."

"What?" I said.

"That you laughed," Cheyenne said. "Dude, I thought you had forgotten how."

"Oh," I said.

Marissa had arranged for us to go to the park near the high school where we sometimes held Flagpole meetings. Everybody was there: Norie and Wyatt, Fletcher, and Diesel, who was on his lunch hour. Even Brianna showed up with Ira. Everybody tore over to Ira's van and helped get him out and into his wheelchair.

"What are you guys doing here?" Norie said.

"Court's in recess until tomorrow morning," Brianna said. Her eyes went down into slits. "Good thing, too, because I was about to jump up and smack somebody in there this morning."

Ira eased himself down into his wheelchair and looked up at all of us. His usually confident face looked pinched and tight. "I need you to pray for me," he said.

"What's going on?" Tobey said. "You're scaring me."

"Yeah, well, you aren't the only one scared," Ira said. He looked down at the cream-colored palms of his hands. "I think I might end up going to prison after all."

"I don't get it," Wyatt said, looking in that intense way he had from behind his glasses. "I thought everything was going our way."

"It was," Brianna said, "until the prosecution brought in all these people who got up there and talked this trash about Dillon Wassen. Made him sound like he was snatched right up out of the church choir."

"Nuh-uh!" Cheyenne said.

"Yeah-uh," Ira said.

"They're just trying to get jury sympathy," Norie said. "That isn't proof. If the jury has their act together at all, they'll know they can't convict on that—"

"Even if it were true," Tobey said. "Which we all know it's not."

"Ain't nobody called *us* to the stand though, have they?" Brianna said. Her voice was so bitter it made me shiver.

"I'll get up on the stand!" Norie said.

A chorus of agreement arose from everyone but me, of course. While they hunkered down over the table and launched into the testimonies they were going to give, as if Ira's lawyer already had them on the stand, I sat on the end of the bench and clenched my hands and hoped nobody noticed I was acting like I had laryngitis.

Please don't ask me, I thought as I dug my fingernails into my palms. *Please don't make me say in front of everybody that my father won't let me.*

Like you would do it anyway. Your father's just an excuse. You would be so freaked out up there...

"You know what though?" Norie was saying. "The burden of proof is on the D.A."

"Oh yeah," Cheyenne said. "I remember that."

"From what?" Tobey nudged her playfully. *"Law and Order?"*

Cheyenne shook her head. "No, I think it was *The Practice.*"

"Moving on," Norie said pointedly. And she did—right to me. "So, Shannon, how's it going with your therapist?"

My heart started to hammer. This was so not what I wanted. It was time to make a break for the rest room.

But Marissa slid her arm around my shoulders, and everybody leaned from Ira to me. All these pairs of eyes softened down around me. I would have had to make a scene to get out of there.

Tobey cleared her throat. "Um, Shannon, do you want to tell us how you're doing in therapy or not? Either way it's fine with us, right?"

Everybody nodded. No one pushed me, poked me, or begged me with their eyes. They just nodded and waited, like it really was my choice. Of course, I had no idea what to do, but I could hear Georgianna now, *"Just say the first thing that comes into your head."*

"I feel like I have to tell you," I said. "I kind of had a break-through yesterday."

"That's incredible!" Tobey said. It came out with a little more enthusiasm than I think she intended, but it gave Marissa permission to chime in with "That's great, Shannon."

"What was it?" Norie said.

Diesel grunted.

"Girl, do you have to push it?" Brianna said to Norie.

"A breakthrough; that's good, right?" Cheyenne said.

I nodded. "I just discovered something that's going to help me get better."

"What's wrong with you?" Fletcher said.

As Cheyenne gave him the inevitable smack, Tobey turned to me grinning. "There's only one thing to do. We have to celebrate."

Everybody grabbed on to that idea like it was the last lifeboat off the *Titanic*. Marissa peeled off the lid of some Tupperware, revealing her taco dip, and Tobey said, "Let's go for it!"

Fletcher looked at me, his chip already poised over the dip. "You want to go first? It's your party."

"Go ahead," I said. "Do you have any plates, Marissa? I could serve everybody."

That's how I got out of eating, although I still felt like I was part of the party—maybe for the first time in months. But it wasn't quite right, not inside me. I was thinking about it on the way home after Tobey dropped Marissa off. Cheyenne and Fletcher had decided to walk home.

"You want to talk about it?" Tobey said. "You don't have to. It's just, you look tense."

I shrugged.

"Tell me for real, did you want to answer all Norie's questions?"

I started to shrug again. Instead, I shook my head.

"That's really hard for you, huh?" she said. "Telling people to get out of your face."

"I've never done it!" I said.

"I hate doing it too. I get freaked out and sick to my stomach."

"You do?"

"Oh yeah. I'm so neurotic."

"But do you do it anyway?"

"Well, I don't actually do it. It's more like God does it."

"Oh," I said. I had thought I was onto something there. But God? Nah. He wouldn't do it for me—would He?

"I have to ask Him, of course," she went on. "And a lot of times it doesn't seem like He's listening just then. But when I really need to do something hard, it always works out. And I get this feeling like I didn't do it. So it had to be God." She tucked her hair behind her ear. "I guess that sounds weird."

"No," I said.

"You just looked like you didn't believe it."

"I believe it!" I could feel my face losing color. "I'm just not sure it would work for me."

"Why not?"

I looked down at my lap. I watched Tobey's hand cover my hands, which were clenched together like teeth.

"You don't have to answer that," she said. "You have so much going on. Why don't you just let me pray for you?"

"That's okay," I said. "I should do my own praying."

"But I really want to. Would you mind?"

I shrugged and saw my hands and hers disappearing in a blur. "If you want to."

On Friday, I asked Georgianna, "Is it okay to have other people pray for me when I can't? Or is that copping out?"

"Prayer of any kind could never be a cop-out," Georgianna said. "Besides, it doesn't surprise me you can't pray for yourself. If I had somebody in my head telling me I was worthless, I might not bother either!"

"Am I crazy?" I said.

"Why do you ask?"

"When we talk about Edith, it's like we're talking about somebody else, like a real person."

"We are talking about something real," she said. "Don't ever forget that. She's a very real force we have to contend with. Otherwise she wouldn't have such a hold on you." She shook her head firmly. "No, Shannon, you are not crazy. If you were crazy, you wouldn't be here. You would be listening to Edith and believing everything she told you."

"I believe most of it," I said.

"But not all of it."

"No."

"You're trying, and that's all God asks." Then she smiled the longest smile I had ever seen on her face. "I've been praying for you myself. And I think it's working already."

WHEN SATURDAY STARTED, HOWEVER, I WASN'T SO SURE Georgianna was right.

We hadn't been sitting at the breakfast table two minutes when Dad gave one of those significant sniffs from behind his newspaper.

"What?" Mom said and then peered over my shoulder. "Shannon, don't think I haven't noticed you're just playing with those eggs."

I poked a forkful into my mouth.

"Here's an article about that colored kid who killed the white boy up by Peavine," Dad said.

He directed a look at me over the top of the paper, as if I had somehow been in collusion with Ira. I gagged on the egg.

"Doesn't look like things are going too well," Dad said. "Turns out the boy he killed wasn't the hood the coon made him out to be."

"Careful, Dad, your bigot's hanging out," Caitlin said.

Dad glared at her. "You don't know anything about it, Caitlin."

"Then ask Little Miss Perfect. She hangs out with his girl-friend."

Dad's glare shifted to me. I didn't actually see it; I was busy staring at my fork, but I could feel it. I could also feel Mom hurrying back over to the table.

"I thought I told you to stay out of that," Dad said.

"At least twenty times," Mom put in.

"I'm not involved in it," I said. "I only know what the Girls have told me."

"Just don't even discuss it with them," Dad said.

"While you're at it, don't think about it either, Shannon," Caitlin said. I could *hear* her lip curling.

"Watch that mouth, or you won't go to any picnic," Dad said. He folded the newspaper with a snap. "If it were up to me, Caitlin, I wouldn't have given you permission in the first place, but since your mother already—"

"It's a church function, John," Mom said. "I doubt there will be too many temptations."

Caitlin gave an evil laugh. "You obviously haven't seen Adam."

She wiggled her eyebrows and pushed herself away from the table. I couldn't even look at her, so I watched my mother. Bad move. An expression of motherly pride crossed her face.

"So," she said to Caitlin, eyes shining, "you have a crush on a boy at church?"

Dad groaned, but even he sounded like Caitlin had just brought home a straight-A report card.

"A 'crush'?" Caitlin said. "No, Mom, I don't get crushes. Shannon gets crushes. I just go after what I want."

"Define 'go after,'" Dad said.

Before Caitlin could start defining, I left the room.

However, after that, things started to look up. For openers, Caitlin got out of the car the minute we reached the church and made it her business to avoid me. She did immediately attach herself to Adam like a piece of lint.

Edith started in on me. *Just give it up. You get what you deserve if you keep torturing yourself…blah, blah, blah.*

Somebody touched my elbow and said, "You want us to pray with you before we go?"

It was Tobey. I looked up at her and nodded. She, Marissa, and Cheyenne gathered around me, and we held hands, and they talked to God for me. When Cheyenne said, "Please, God, let Adam like Shannon instead of Caitlin," I laughed. I wasn't sure why; it was just that for a minute there, it felt good.

I felt that way over and over in little bursts as the day went on. When we all climbed into two vans to make the trek up to Sand Harbor, Adam commandeered the front seat of ours so he could ride shotgun. I was in the second seat, catty-cornered from him. I wondered how he had gotten away from Caitlin, but Cheyenne didn't. She smiled smugly at me and pointed upward. I smothered a giggle.

The trip took about an hour, and everybody sang and told jokes. Adam did his impressions of Doug, Reverend Winston, and little Red Sam. When he started to pick his nose, though, we all shouted him down.

Then, when we arrived at the picnic site, I expected Caitlin to grab Adam in a half nelson. But she didn't look at either of us, and I sure wasn't going to say to her, "Everything all right, sis?"

To tell you the truth, in about two minutes, I forgot all about her. Like about when Adam said to me, "A bunch of us are going to climb those rocks. You guys want to come?"

I looked at Tobey. She had one arm around Cheyenne, hand poised to clap it over the poor kid's mouth if she opened it.

"Not me," Tobey said "I get really weirded out by heights."

"You do?" Cheyenne said. "I never knew—"

The hand fell neatly into place, and Tobey steered Cheyenne away, still talking through Tobey's fingers. Marissa laughed and followed them. "Have fun," she said over her shoulder.

"Lightweights," Adam said. He looked at me. "You up for it?"

I looked around to make sure Caitlin wasn't one of "a bunch of us," but I didn't see her anywhere. "Sure, I'll go."

I had grown up coming to Sand Harbor in the summer, and Caitlin, Colleen, and I had spidered our way up those rocks more times than I could count. That day, though, it was a whole other thing. It may sound cheesy, but I don't think my feet ever touched the rocks. I kind of floated up that cliff.

Randy, Holly, and Kyla headed up first, and Adam and I brought up the rear. There was a bunch of hooting and hollering and stuff as we stopped every couple of feet to look out over Lake Tahoe, sparkling clear blue in the bowl the Sierras formed for it. All I really heard was Adam saying, "You okay, Shannon?" "Be really careful here." "Why don't you let me go ahead of you, and I'll grab your hand?...There you go."

He would do this for anybody, Edith said in a particularly nasty tone.

"Let me just give you a boost," Adam said. His voice drowned out hers.

"This is as far as I go," Holly said. She plopped down on a flat rock that jutted out a few yards from the top and readjusted her ponytail. Randy and Kyla joined her on the rock.

"You want to go to the top?" Adam said to me.

"Yeah," I said. "It's not that hard."

Adam stuck out his hand. "You're not going to let me fall, are you?" He waggled his fingers several more times before I caught on that he wanted me to grab on. Duh.

So I did, and we finished the climb together. It was a little awkward with me tugging at him the whole way, but I could do awkward. Awkward was suddenly right up there with ecstasy.

"Whoa!" Adam said. "Dude, that is awesome!"

I turned to follow his gaze out over the water and up to the tips of the mountains. The fluffy pines, the majestic rocks, the sun sizzling its patterns across the lake had never looked more vivid to me.

He moved as close to the edge as he could and stood there gazing out. I sat on a rock and leaned back to soak the warmth in through my back. Even in July it was cool up here, and when the wind kicked up, it could swish your breath away. Mine, at least. It was feeling a little thin at the moment.

I hugged my knees to my chest and closed my eyes. I had a strange, shaky feeling—not like relief, and not even like I hadn't eaten much. It was a Jell-O sensation in my legs and arms.

You're out of shape, loser. That's what you get for showing off.

I closed my eyes. *Make her go away,* I thought.

Then, with the sun-hot rocks warming my back and the Tahoe breeze teasing my face, I fell asleep.

When I woke up, it was strangely still. For a second I wasn't sure where I was—it was that kind of nap—and I sat up almost in a panic. Something slid off my arm, and I jumped. A freckled hand reached down and picked it up.

Only then did I realize I was covered in an assortment of clothing that somebody had laid over me like unattached quilt squares. There was Adam's T-shirt, the towel Randy had had around his neck, and Holly's beach cover-up. I looked blankly at Adam, who was sitting beside me.

"I was afraid you were going to be burnt to a crisp," he said.

He shrugged his big shoulders, and I noticed the goose flesh on them.

"You're freezing," I said. "Here, put on your shirt."

He shook his head dolefully. "Story of my life," he said.

"What?" I said.

"Girls telling me to put *on* my shirt. I don't get it, Shannon. Nobody wants to look at my pectorals, you know?"

I laughed. I wanted to say, "I'll look at them all day!" but of course I didn't. Instead I glanced down the slope and said, "Where did everybody go?"

"They got hungry and went back down," Adam said. "I told them I'd stay here till you woke up."

"You must be hungry. We better go down and get you something."

"Too late," Adam said. "They put the food away an hour ago."

I could feel my eyes getting wider. "How long was I asleep?"

"About two hours."

"You sat here all that time? I am so sorry..."

I started to scramble up, but Adam caught my arm. Like always, his hand was warm and strong, and I liked the feel of it—almost as much as I liked his smell, his freckles, the space between his teeth.

"I didn't have to do it," he said. "I wanted to. I was sick of performing."

"I thought you liked performing," I said.

"I do sometimes." Adam picked up a rock and poked at the dirt with its point. "But then people expect me to be, like, this riot all the time, and sometimes I just don't want to be center stage, you know?"

"I never want to be center stage! Which is probably fine. I mean, they're not, like, begging me to perform the way they do with you."

"Yeah, but people like having you around," he said.

"Nuh-uh," I said.

"How do you know? You're not other people. It's nice to be with somebody who doesn't jack her jaws all the time." He stopped himself. "I've been hanging out with your sister too much; I'm starting to talk like her."

I craned my neck guiltily over the side, down to our group's spot. "I'm surprised Caitlin didn't climb up here. She can do it way faster than I can."

"I haven't seen her all day," Adam said. "Not since she went back to the van."

"Back to the van?" I said.

"Yeah. I was sitting up here just watching everybody, which was cool because they didn't, like, know anybody was looking at them. God must have a blast, you know?"

I laughed.

"Anyway, I guess it was right after we got up here, she took off across the parking lot and disappeared into those trees. She must have forgotten something in the van."

Probably her cigarettes, I thought.

"Never did see her come back," Adam said, "but then I wasn't looking for her."

"I hope she found somebody to hang out with," I said.

"That's cool. Most sisters could care less about each other."

"It isn't that cool," I said. "It's just my mom's going to kill me if Caitlin doesn't have a good time."

"Wait, let me get this straight," Adam said. "Your mom is going to kill you if Caitlin doesn't have fun? Why is that your responsibility?"

"Because Caitlin has a lot of problems."

"I know about her problems. She's told me. I've been talking to her and praying for her and all. But she never said she expects you to live her life for her."

I could feel myself caving in. Adam had been talking to Caitlin about her personal problems, praying for her. He also had told me I could call him anytime…

Duh, Clueless. You're just another charity case for him. I tried to tell you.

"I didn't mean to badmouth Caitlin," I blurted out. "If you like her—"

"You couldn't badmouth somebody if you tried." He was studying the design he had created in the dirt with his rock. Then he looked up at me and smiled. It was almost shy, the kind of look that, for some reason no girl will probably ever be able to explain, goes right through you.

What would have happened after that, I'll never know. Adam's eyes flickered out over the beach, and he shaded his brows with his hand. "Are they calling us?"

I leaned over to look too. Doug was out on the beach, waving a red towel. When Adam waved back, Doug made a huge beckoning motion with his arm.

"Um, I think so," I said.

Adam gave me half a grin. "I guess the party's over."

For me it wasn't. Adam had hold of me practically the whole way down, and I know my body was white from toenails to hair roots with embarrassment mixed with ecstasy. The feeling disappeared the minute we hit the beach.

Doug ran toward us through the sand with Cheyenne, Marissa, and Tobey on his heels. His usually dark face was in a hard, white knot.

"What's going on?" Adam said.

My throat went dry. It already felt all wrong.

Doug put out his hand and smothered my shoulder with it. "Now don't get upset. But we can't locate Caitlin."

"She's been gone for about two hours!" Cheyenne said. "Nobody's seen her!"

"We're not going to jump to conclusions," he said. "We have the park people looking, and we've broken up into small groups."

"I saw her about two hours ago from up there," Adam said. His face was white too. "She was headed off that way."

"You go there then," Doug said. "And stay together; we don't want anybody else lost."

"She isn't lost," I muttered under my breath, as we took off at a trot up the beach toward the parking lot.

Adam looked at me sharply. "What?"

"Nothing." I clamped my mouth shut, but my mind went right on shouting.

She isn't lost; she just took off. I bet she might even have run away again.

A lot you care. You would love it if they found her at the bottom of the lake.

I would not! I just hate that she gets everybody all stirred up all the time.

You just wish she hadn't spoiled your little tryst with Adam, and you know it. She probably looked up there, saw you two together, and got so upset she couldn't stand it.

"This is where I lost sight of her," Adam said. We had stopped in a stand of trees that went on to surround the parking lot. "I thought she was going back to the van."

"We checked there," Tobey said. "Besides, Doug said he's had the keys all day, and nobody has asked for them."

"Could she have jimmied a lock?" Cheyenne said.

"She has her problems, but she's not a crook, Cheyenne," Tobey said.

Something burned through me, and I felt my empty ring finger. It was all I could do not to say, "You better check those locks."

"Is there, like, a store anywhere close by?" Adam said.

"Up the road about a half mile," Tobey said. "Why don't you two keep searching this area, and we'll go back to tell Doug to drive to the store. Come on, you guys."

She, Marissa, and Cheyenne took off toward the beach. Adam grabbed my hand, swallowing it up in his big one, and pulled me across the parking lot. He tugged at it a little as he looked down at me.

"Any ideas?" he said. "You know her better than anybody."

"I know her, all right." I wanted to bite off my tongue, but Adam didn't look surprised.

"She's definitely a trip," he said. "I thought she was coming around though. I thought I was getting through to her."

"Good luck," I said. It was like a dam had opened, and the words were rushing out of control. I looked up at him quickly. "But I guess if anybody could get through to her, you could."

"Yeah right. That's why she took off."

"You think that too?"

"I guess I got too cocky. I should have—" But he cut himself off and for some reason squeezed my hand. If I hadn't thought I would hurt his feelings, I would have pulled away. After all, what was the point? He wasn't with me because he liked me. He was the knight in shining armor, looking for damsels to rescue. I was just the latest maiden screaming "help" from some tower. Now Caitlin was his mission.

Well, aren't you bright? You wouldn't have had to go through this humiliation if you had listened to me. The only good thing that's come out of this day is that you didn't eat.

Adam stopped at the far edge of the parking lot. A fence was hidden discreetly in the trees but high enough to deter anybody except the most determined from climbing it.

"Could she climb this?" Adam said.

"Yeah."

I barely had it out before Adam had hurled himself at the chain link and started up, hand over hand. His lanky legs flailed for a second, and then his feet caught hold, and he hoisted himself up farther.

"Um, what are you doing?" I asked stupidly.

"I have no idea. Maybe I can see her from up here, or at least be able to tell whether somebody else has tried to do something this idiotic."

He tried to laugh, but it just came out like the rest of the huge breaths he was sucking in. He hadn't breathed that hard going up the cliff. He was scared—for Caitlin.

I told you!

"Shannon!"

I jumped and called out, "We're back here!"

Cheyenne broke through the trees, red-faced and out of breath. She stared up at Adam. "Dude, you two got serious."

"What's going on?" Adam called down to her. "Did they find her at the store?"

"No," Cheyenne said. Then turning to me, she rolled her eyes. "Right after Doug got back, she came strolling up the beach. We're all freaking out, and she just goes, 'Can't a person even take a walk?'" Cheyenne's dark eyes grew darker. "Like she couldn't have told somebody where she was going—"

I didn't hear the rest. I just took off, out of the trees and across the parking lot toward the beach. I think Adam yelled my name a couple of times. I'm not sure. The burning in my chest was the only thing driving me. I knew if I didn't run, it was going to consume me.

Just like Cheyenne said, Caitlin was standing there in the middle of everybody, arms folded in that red-and-black-checkered flannel across her chest, looking like the questions they were asking her were an extreme imposition on her precious time. With no clue to what I intended to do when I reached her, I hurled myself into the circle and faced her. Her eyes only flashed surprise for a second before she recovered.

"What, Freak Show?" she said.

I couldn't answer. My esophagus was on fire.

"Since you asked," Caitlin said, "I went for a walk and lost track of time. I didn't know everybody was going to assume I had run away. I guess I have you to thank for that."

Holly tugged at her ponytail. "Who said anything about running away? We thought you drowned or something."

"I thought somebody snatched you up and kidnapped you," Kyla said.

Caitlin snorted. "They would have brought me back before this."

She led the group in laughter while I fumed. Leave it to her to turn the whole thing into a joke.

"Cait-Lou, what were you thinking?" Adam broke through the circle and brought his big self nose-to-nose with Caitlin. When she looked up at him, it was the first glimpse of remorse I had seen in her since she was about five years old.

"I took a walk." She tossed her black curls, but she couldn't quite meet his eyes.

"I think we've established that she took a walk," Randy said to the group.

Doug chuckled. "All right, folks, let's head back down the hill. We've had enough fun for today."

"No, man," Randy said. "I wanted to do some more manhunt, dude. That was cool!"

He grinned at Caitlin. She grinned back. Across the circle, I met Tobey's eyes, and they were smoldering.

"Everybody grab something," Doug called out.

"Help me with this one, Shannon," Marissa said.

She nodded her head toward a cooler, but her eyes were still glaring at Caitlin. I glanced around the group. It would have been comical if I hadn't been fighting a forest fire inside my chest. The Flagpole Girls were giving Caitlin looks that easily could have frozen Satan himself. The rest of the staff were looking as relieved and amused as if Caitlin were a mischievous kitten who had hidden herself in the laundry basket while everyone shouted, "Here, kitty, kitty!"

I snatched up the cooler handle so hard Marissa practically fell over.

"Sorry," I said.

"It's okay," she said. "I would be mad too if one of my sisters pulled something like that. You have more self-control than I do." She shot one more freeze-drying glance at Caitlin, but then her own mouth froze.

Before she could stop me, I looked over my shoulder and saw Caitlin on her tiptoes, hanging on to Adam's arm and murmuring into his ear. I couldn't tear my eyes away as he nodded—and folded his fingers around her arm and led her off to a bench.

"You ready?" Marissa said to me.

They sat down, face to face, and Adam leaned so close his lips almost touched her cheek.

"I can get Tobey to help me if it's too heavy," Marissa said.

Caitlin talked, and Adam listened with his eyes. Then he put his arm around her and pulled her into his chest. They fit together like two spoons in a drawer.

"What's the holdup?" Cheyenne said, coming up beside me. Her eyes followed my gaze. "Oh, gross. That totally makes me sick."

"Come on, Shannon," Marissa said gently.

I followed, but I didn't say a word.

CHAPTER FIFTEEN

I WANTED TO SAY PLENTY, MAKE NO MISTAKE ABOUT that. All the way back to the church, sitting on the very back seat, even though Adam had chosen to ride in the other van with Caitlin, the words I was holding back flamed in my chest.

You have them all fooled, Caitlin, you little tramp. They think you're this cute little bubbly thing with all this personality. Even Adam. But I know you, girl. And if they knew you like I did, they would quit believing you. They would stop trying with you because no matter how perfect they were, how good they tried to make it for you, how much they always protected you, you would still turn on them. You would still take everything—all the popularity, all the attention, all the love, all the Adams.

We had transferred from the church van to Tobey's car, and Tobey was pulling the car up to the front of my house, before I realized it wasn't really the staff I was raging at. It was me.

The thought seared through my throat like a charcoal briquette.

"Thanks for the ride, Tobe," Caitlin said, as she opened the door.

"Sure," Tobey said. She didn't smile as she watched Caitlin in the rearview mirror.

Caitlin looked at all our sober faces. "I guess since I've stressed everybody out so much already, I might as well ask one more favor."

We all waited.

"I would appreciate it if none of this got back to my parents," she said.

I flung open the car door, snatched up my bag, and stomped

up the front walk without a word to the Girls, without even closing the door or waving as Tobey pulled away. Caitlin was on my heels before I hit the front steps. She grabbed my arm with a cold, clammy hand, and I wrenched it away.

"Don't tell them, Shannon," she said through tightened teeth. "It's a done deal. They don't need to know."

I pressed my lips together hard. If I opened my mouth, I knew I wouldn't be able to control whatever came out.

Caitlin got up on the step higher than me and looked me in the eyes. Hers were swimming.

"I know I treat you bad," she said. "But just this one time, please. Even Adam said he thought—"

That did it. I hurled my bag away from me.

"I thought you went for a walk, Cait-lin!" I shouted at her. "If that's all that happened, then why can't they know? Because you're a stinking liar, that's why! You haven't told the truth since you were five years old. You tear everybody apart. You expect everybody to understand and let you do whatever you please, and then you dump on them—on purpose! And I'm sick of it! I'm sick of *you!* I hate you, and I'm not helping you—not now, not ever! If you want help, go to your doper friends and leave mine alone!"

I couldn't even see her at that point. I don't know how I got my hand to connect with her face. I only knew it did because I heard the slap and felt her cheek under my palm for a stinging second before I plastered my hand across my mouth and felt my knees give way. I was hitting the steps with an elbow and a thigh when I heard the front door fly open, heard the tangle of voices on the porch.

"What in the name of God?"

"Shannon! Caitlin!"

"Caitlin, did you push her?"

"No! She fell down—after she *slapped* me!"

"Stop your lying!"

"Look at my face!"

"What did you say to her?"

"Why is it always *my* fault?"

"Did you have to carry on like this in front of the whole neighborhood?"

"Shannon, are you all right?"

I felt my father's hand on my arm, and I opened my eyes. Our front porch spun, and I closed them again.

"Shannon, answer!"

Slowly I nodded.

"Look at me!"

I opened my eyes again. Dad's face was magenta with anger, but his eyes were twitching back and forth as he examined my face. He was as scared as he was mad.

How do you feel now, Big Mouth? Still want to go after everybody with your fingernails and teeth?

I shook my head.

"What?" Dad said.

"Nothing," I said. But I wanted to say plenty. Edith might be trying to plaster a layer of guilt a foot thick onto me, but my chest was still burning.

"She's a freak show," Caitlin said. She was breathing hard, surprisingly on the brittle edge of tears. "She just started to yell at me, and then she hauled off and slapped me one. Right here. Is it still red?"

"It's fine," Mom said without looking at her. "Could we please take this discussion inside?"

"What 'discussion'?" Caitlin said. "You're going to believe her over me anyway, so what's the point in even talking about it?"

"Oh, for heaven's sake." Mom planted her hands on her hips and pursed her lips. She shook her head as if she were refereeing one of our childhood spats. "All right, Shannon. Did you slap your sister?"

"I told you she did! See what I mean?"

"Yes," I said.

"For heaven's sake, why?" Mom said.

I couldn't answer her.

"Come on," Dad said. He scooped an arm under my knees to pick me up.

"She called me a liar!" Caitlin screamed. "Like she's so perfect! Like she doesn't puke every bite of food you make her eat! Like she isn't trying to get some guy's attention by acting all holy and Christian. If I'm a liar, she's the worst hypocrite on the planet!"

"She *is* a liar!" My voice matched hers scream for scream. "She disappeared for two hours today and had everybody looking for her…"

The story spewed out of me like hot lava while Caitlin stood rooted to the porch, eyes growing narrower and more hateful the more I erupted.

When I was finished, Mom opened her mouth, but Dad put up his hand so sharply he might as well have slapped it over her lips. Then he looked at Caitlin with his own eyes glittering.

"Is it true?" he said.

"What difference does it make what I tell you?" Caitlin said. "I'm not even answering that. The Favored One has spoken. End of discussion."

"Now, don't be silly," Mom said, voice shrill. "We always listen to your side."

"Not this time," Dad said. "Caitlin, go to your room."

By now, Caitlin's olive face was blotchy, and her voice was thick, but she wasn't crying. No way was she crying. She folded her arms across her chest. It was strange, but just then I realized she wasn't wearing her flannel shirt. Suddenly she looked vulnerable without it. I started to cave.

"Can't you think of anything original, Dad?" she said. "The go-to-your-room thing is getting kind of monotonous."

"This is only temporary, believe me," Dad said. He was inhaling and exhaling hard through his nose. "You've come to the end of the line. You start screwing with the people at the church—"

"John, language," Mom said between her pursed lips.

"Naughty, naughty," Caitlin said.

"Go. All of you. Get out of my sight," Dad said through clenched teeth. "Or I'm not going to be responsible for what happens!"

"I'm afraid," Caitlin said. Actually, I think she was. Her face was as tight as his, but her eyes couldn't hold a focus. When Dad went after her with his fists doubled, she retreated, swearing, into the house. Mom gave Dad a bewildered look and hurried in after her.

Satisfied now? Edith hissed at me.

I shook my head. Once I started, I couldn't stop. My hair was swinging across my face, stray strands sticking to the tears on my cheeks.

Dad's thick hands went to the sides of my face and held it still. They were cold and clammy on my cheeks, just the way Caitlin's had felt. "Hey, come on. Get hold of yourself. You're going to make yourself sick. Stop this now." His voice had calmed down.

I tried to slow down, too, but I was sure I was going to throw up if he didn't let me go. And being anorexic had nothing to do with it. "I'm sorry," I said. "I'm really sorry."

"Shh, shh-shh." Dad tucked my face against his chest and stroked my hair. "It isn't your fault. Something's going to have to be done about her, that's all."

"I just got so...I couldn't help it..."

"I know exactly how you feel. Why do you think I always send her to her room? It isn't punishment. I'm just afraid I'm going to knock out her teeth!"

He forced a laugh and pulled me out to look at me. "Why don't you go in and wash your face?"

"Dad, I—"

"Go on, now. You'll feel better."

I ducked into the downstairs powder room. The face that looked back at me from the mirror was white and waxy, just like everyone else Caitlin had pulled into her world that day.

It isn't all her, and you know it, Edith said.

I didn't argue with her. I was afraid to think at all.

When I emerged, hair brushed back in a ponytail so tight it pulled at the corners of my eyes, Dad met me in the downstairs hall.

"You want to ride to the store with me?" he said. "Your mom wants me to run over to the Safeway." He gave a wry smile toward the kitchen, where I could hear cabinet doors slamming and pans clanging against each other. "You know it helps her to cook when she's upset."

"What about Caitlin?" I said.

"Come on," he said. "Mom needs that ricotta."

If he had a reason for me to ride along, he didn't divulge it to me on the way or while we were searching the aisles for ricotta cheese and fresh Parmesan. When we got back in the car, though, he just sat looking at the keys dangling in the ignition. "I don't know what to do about your sister. You've had your little up-heaval lately, but all I have to do is bear down on you, and you snap right out of it. Not Caitlin." He shook his head wearily and smeared his hand across his face. "I've yelled, I've threatened, I've taken everything I could think of away from her, including her own home. We've done the counselor—that was a waste of time. We have people praying from here to New York State, for Pete's sake." He lowered his eyebrows at me in an attempt to be playful. "You have even tried smacking her silly, and that obviously had no effect on her."

"I shouldn't have done that," I said. I looked down at my hands.

"You can't be blamed for that. You don't know how many times I've had to practically nail my hands to the table to keep from whaling the tar out of her."

That wasn't comforting to me. Ever since I had seen the fear in my sister's eyes as she hurled her last insult at our father, I had felt like a piece of wood. The burning in my chest was gone, and I had no more energy to argue with Edith. I had expended it all exposing Caitlin to my parents, and what good had that done? I was stiff, powerless, and practically inert with guilt.

Dad pushed himself back from the steering wheel and squinted into the last of the sunlight disappearing over Peavine Mountain. "I thought maybe you could give me a suggestion."

I nearly choked. "Me?"

"I discovered something about you today. I always thought you were like your mother. You two seem to agree on everything. But when I watched you exploding this afternoon, when I saw that handprint on your sister's face…" He gave me a sideways almost-smile. "I think you're a lot more like me than I ever gave you credit for. You swallow it until you can't take it anymore and then—boom!—it's out there like a bomb nobody can dismantle."

"You're not like that," I said lamely.

Dad laughed a real laugh then. "Oh, honey, where have you been for the last sixteen years? Of course I'm like that. And most of the time I can keep it reined in, just like you do. But when something like this comes along, something I've never had to deal with before, it really gets next to me." He reached over and gave my shoulder a squeeze. "I thought since we seem to think alike, you might have some ideas that I hadn't thought of."

At first I shook my head—force of habit, I guess. Edith seemed to approve of that approach, because my head was silent.

Except for another voice, one I had never heard before. A soft, firm one that said, *You really ought to tell the truth. Otherwise, aren't you the hypocrite Caitlin said you were?*

I looked quickly at Dad to make sure he wasn't the one who had spoken. But he was still looking bewildered.

"Any ideas?" he said.

I waited for the new voice. There was nothing. Maybe it had been my imagination.

Freak Show, Edith whispered.

Maybe so. But that new voice had made more sense than probably anything I had thought—ever.

"I think she feels like she's been pushed into a corner," I said.

"What corner? What do you mean?"

"Well, she really is different from Colleen and me. She says she couldn't live up to your expectations the way we do—or at least Colleen does—so she just gave up trying."

Dad scowled. I shriveled up. So much for that voice.

"That Georgette woman has filled your head with a bunch of hooey," he said. "Caitlin has done more than give up trying; she never started in the first place. She's been running the other way ever since she could crawl."

I nodded miserably. Inside, for the first time maybe ever, my heart ached for Caitlin.

"If she doesn't like the way we do things, she's going to have to knuckle under until she's old enough to live her own life." Dad abruptly started the engine and jammed the car into reverse.

"I'm sorry," I said.

"Don't worry about it," he said. "I'll figure something out."

He apparently was starting right then because he lapsed into a black silence that kept me shrunken on my side of the car. He didn't speak until he turned the corner and headed down our street. Then we both blurted in spite of ourselves.

"What in the world...?"

"What happened…?"

I stared at the scene ahead of us: red lights flashing confusion, hoses strung across the street like thick ropes up onto the lawn.

Our lawn.

Dad realized it the same second I did. He wrenched at the door handle and cursed when it wouldn't give. He jammed his thumb at the lock button and finally wrestled himself out of the seat belt and out of the car. I watched, motionless, as his stocky body broke into a run.

When I realized he had half disappeared into a fog of black smoke, I came to life and hurled myself out of the car. A man in a heavy coat and a hat that reflected the fire engines' lights grabbed me by both shoulders.

"Whoa there," he said. "We have this area sealed off."

"Dad!" I screamed.

Just ahead of me, looking surreal in the billowing smoke, my father stood waving his arms Italian-style at another fireman.

"That's my house!" Dad was shouting. "My wife, my daughter!"

"No one is inside," the fireman shouted. He had to shout; we all had to shout. The fire engines' roar obliterated everything else. "Your wife is over there in the ambulance."

"Ambulance!"

"She just took in a little smoke. She's all right."

"My daughter…"

"We were hoping she was with you," the fireman said.

Dad finally stopped waving his arms and shouting. He stared at the fireman with one hand still suspended in air.

"No," Dad said. "No, she was upstairs in the bedroom. The only one on the third floor."

"She's not there," my fireman said. Still holding me by the shoulder he moved toward Dad. "We've searched thoroughly. That's the only room that actually burned. The fire started there."

Dad's face went gray. I'll never forget it; it drained of its golden-olive color even as I watched. When he spoke, it was as if he were forcing his mouth to move.

"She's not…"

"There is no evidence that she burned in the fire, no," the fireman said. "None whatsoever. Your neighbor called us in time.

The rest of the house has smoke damage, some water damage. That couldn't be helped."

"Shannon," Dad said, still staring down the fireman. "Go to your mother."

I nodded. My fireman took me by the arm and led me to the ambulance. Mom was sitting on a stretcher just outside its back doors, oxygen mask over her nose and mouth, the tears streaming because of smoke and fear. When she saw me, she reached out her arms and folded me in, and we both sobbed.

"We can't find Caitlin," she said.

"She didn't burn," I said. "I know she didn't."

"Your room is gone, your whole room is gone."

"That's okay. Are you all right?"

"I was in the kitchen. Caitlin was carrying on up there, cussing and swearing." She coughed.

A paramedic with her hair in a tousled bun came over. "Easy now, Mrs. D'Angelo. You're not breathing easy yet."

Mom ignored her. "Your father told me not to go up there no matter what. So I turned up the radio real loud to drown her out. Next thing I know, Barbara King from across the street is banging on the kitchen door yelling that our house is on fire and to get out."

She tried to cover her mouth and cry, but her hand hit the mask.

"Come on, lie down here," the paramedic said.

"I don't want to lie down! I want to know where my daughter is!"

"Mrs. D'Angelo?"

We both looked up at a burly man whose face was smeared with soot. Sweat made rivulets in it from his graying sideburns. He introduced himself as Captain Somebody. Everything was starting to muddle in my mind. I wanted to climb up onto the stretcher with my mother.

"Did you find her?" Mom said. She bolted up, throwing off the paramedic's restraining arm.

"No ma'am," he said. "The fire is completely out, and there is no sign of her. I think it's safe to say she was out of the house before that room went up."

Mom shook her head firmly. "No. I was in the kitchen. I would have heard her."

The captain gave a dry cough. "You didn't hear the window shatter when the room reached nine hundred degrees either. My guess is that she went out the front door after..."

"Then where is she?" Mom said. She brushed one of about a hundred disheveled tendrils of hair off her forehead, as if it were going to make one iota of difference in her bewildered appearance, and searched Captain Somebody's face with her eyes. "Where did she go?"

"I'm sure she'll be found." He patted her shoulder. "Has your husband arrived yet?"

"I don't know," Mom said. She looked through me and down the street. I stared at her for a second before I said, "Yes, he has; he's down there."

I pointed, and the captain nodded his thanks.

"She's still in shock," he whispered to the paramedic as he left. "Keep an eye on her."

I turned to my mother. "Why don't you lie down, Mom? Dad is here. It's going to be all right."

"We have to call Colleen," she said. But she lay back and stared dully at the sky. "We could use Barbara's phone. You could stay with Barbara tonight."

She babbled on like that until I was really scared. But all I could do was watch her and wipe her forehead. I didn't want to look up at the house, which no longer had a third story. Which no longer had my room.

The firemen had stopped firing blasts of water bigger around than my legs at our house. I don't know how long I stood there trying not to look at it, trying not to curl up into a ball and hide under the stretcher, trying not to think at all, when Dad came over and kissed Mom on the forehead and got her bawling like a baby.

"Go talk to that fireman, that one," Dad said to me.

On legs of wood I crossed to Captain Somebody. He was standing next to a pickup-truck-sized fire vehicle, and he put his foot up on its step as if he wanted to make me feel more at ease. It didn't work. "You shared the room with your sister?" he said.

I nodded.

"Did she ever burn anything? Play with matches? Anything like that?"

"She used to burn incense and candles," I said. "My mom caught her though. She isn't allowed to do it anymore."

"When was the last time, to your knowledge, that she lit a candle up there or a stick of incense?"

I searched back through my memory and told him.

"Do you know if she still had any candles, matches, anything like that?"

"My mom took it all away from her," I said. "She could have gotten more, I guess."

He looked at me closely "Would she have?"

I looked down at the toes of my white tennis shoes, now darkened with soot, and pretended to have to think about that. There was no need, of course. The question really was whether to tell.

Don't you think you've narked on Caitlin enough for one day? Edith said.

I don't know what to do! I told her.

The truth. It's time to tell everyone the truth, including yourself, that other voice said, the one that was so comforting, so safe, so sane.

"She probably would if she had a chance," I said in the direction of my feet.

"Did she have a chance?"

"She disappeared for a couple of hours earlier today."

I swallowed hard and hoped just as hard that he would thank me and get into his little fire truck and move on. He didn't.

"One more question. Is there any reason your sister would have set this fire on purpose?" he said.

Is he nuts? He'll send her straight to jail—if he ever finds her. The truth. Tell the truth.

I'm afraid! I don't want to do wrong! What do I do?

Shut up!

The truth.

"You're not required to answer," Captain Somebody said at my elbow.

"I can't answer," I said. "I don't know."

And that was as close to the truth as I could come.

CHAPTER SIXTEEN

DAD WOULDN'T LET ME PAST THE FRONT DOOR AFTER HE went in and inspected the damage with the captain. He smiled when he came out, and he told Mom and me it "really wasn't all that bad." But he said I ought to spend the night somewhere else.

When a Reno police car pulled up, I used the opportunity to use our neighbor's phone to call Marissa. She and her father were there to pick me up fifteen minutes later. Even at that, it was fifteen minutes too long. I heard too much of what the policemen had to say.

"This is her second disappearance," the taller officer said. "That's not good."

"She didn't even leave Reno the last time," Dad said, eyebrows threatening.

"She didn't run away. I would have heard her leave," Mom said over and over. Her distance from reality was getting scary.

When Marissa's dad's car pulled up, I was in it almost before it stopped. They were wonderful to me over at Marissa's. Her dad told me whatever I needed, I should just speak up, and he would take care of it. Her mother told Marissa to feed me before I blew away and then ran her hand lightly over my hair.

"*Pobrecita,*" she whispered.

"What does that mean?" I asked Marissa when her mother had left the kitchen.

"'Poor baby,'" she said. She cocked her head so that her dark hair splashed against her cheek. "But you aren't a poor baby, Shannon. You're handling this really well."

"No, I'm not." I looked away and fought the lump in my throat.

"Look at you. You're not all hysterical; you could even dial the phone."

I shrugged. "Why not?"

Marissa continued to cut tomatoes for the tortillas. I watched, a film blurring my eyes.

"Because you just lost everything you own. Because your sister is missing. Because you already had more to deal with than anybody ought to."

"I should just handle it," I said.

"Why?" she said.

"Because it's my fault, Marissa. It's so my fault!"

I put my arm on the table, and my face fell on it. The lump broke through, and I cried and cried. I was only vaguely aware that Marissa's hand rubbed up and down my back until I fell asleep. I was only vaguely aware of somebody lowering me into a bed.

It was a little embarrassing to wake up in the morning to find my eyes so swollen they were almost closed into slits. I couldn't even think about going into the kitchen where everybody would be gathered at the same table where I had sobbed uncontrollably the night before. But the minute my eyes opened, so did the bedroom door, and Marissa came in with a bowl of sliced strawberries. She sat on the edge of the bed.

"You don't have to eat it all," she said. "But you're looking a little white...well, a lot white."

"I can try," I said. I popped one slice into my mouth and squeezed it down with my tongue. "I'm sorry about last night."

"Why? Mama said she was glad you cried. She was afraid you were going to snap otherwise. Papa said you could stay here as long as you want."

"I should probably go home and help," I said.

Marissa put two more slices of strawberry onto my spoon and offered it to me. I edged it toward my mouth and somehow got it in.

"You know," she said, "the Girls and I were talking today."

"Already?"

"Well, yeah, we met at Denny's after we all got out of church."

I looked up at the window. A blanket had been draped over the curtain rod. "What time is it?" I said.

"About one." She cocked her head at me in that sweet way she had. "Anyway, we made some decisions, but we're only going to do this stuff if it's okay with you."

I could only nod.

"Of course we're going to pray for you. That, like, goes without saying. And we're going through our closets for some clothes for you until you can get your own. Brianna's going to sort through them and decide which ones will fit and all that. That's her thing."

"Clothes?" I said.

"Well, yeah." Marissa's eyes drooped at the corners. "Yours probably all burned up."

"Oh," I said. Maybe I wasn't any closer to reality than my parents.

"And Cheyenne's calling Doug to tell him, in case you don't feel like going to VBS tomorrow. Plus Tobey is going to be your wheels and take you anywhere you need to go."

"You guys would do all that?" I said.

Marissa smiled. "Why not?"

So I stayed at Marissa's that day and that night. I tried to go to VBS the next morning, but when I started across the parking lot, the voices, which had been so quiet for the last twenty-four hours, shouted in my head, one piling on top of the other like football players heaping themselves on me.

Well, you got what you wanted. Caitlin's not here. You can have Adam all for yourself. You like that, don't you?

I don't! I would kill to have her back here, to know she was safe!

It's okay to be angry with her, Shannon.

I can't be! I was the one who drove her away by being angry. I can't ever be angry again!

"Shannon, what?" Tobey was right beside me.

"I can't go in," I said.

"Gotcha," she said. "Where do you want to go?"

Wimp!

Tell the truth.

"I don't know," I said. "I just don't know."

"I think I do," Tobey said.

She tucked me back into the car, and she took me to Ms. Race's. When Ms. Race she saw me, her forehead crumpled. I sagged onto one of her floor cushions while Tobey spun out the story. When Tobey was done, Ms. Race took my hands.

"What do you need?" she said.

"I need Georgianna," I said.

"Then let's call her." She reached for the phone.

When Georgianna's voice came through the receiver, I settled back onto the cushions. It was almost like being in her office.

"All right," she said when I had finished the story. "Now let me be sure of what I'm hearing you say. You're thinking that because you couldn't hold back your anger at Caitlin anymore, that was what made her try to burn down the house and run away."

"Yes."

"I want you to look at all the straws that have been piled on Caitlin's back through the last several years. How many of those did you pile on?"

"I didn't really help her make new friends and all like my mother asked me to."

"Did Caitlin need you to do that?"

I shrugged. "I don't think so."

"I don't think so either," Georgianna said. "She ended up with the boy you wanted, didn't you say?"

I stiffened. "Yeah. She probably needed him more than I did."

"But I think you deserved to throw one tantrum. When you put that beside all the good things you have done for Caitlin, it doesn't seem like much to me. Your slap across the face might have been the proverbial straw that broke the camel's back, but you aren't responsible for the whole load, nor should you take the blame for how Caitlin reacted to it. Do you blame Caitlin for your anorexia?"

"No!"

"Why not?"

"Because I'm the one who listens to Edith when she yells at me."

"Uh-huh. So why should Caitlin be any different? Don't you think she has voices in her head too? We all have them."

"Nuh-uh!" I said.

Georgianna chuckled. "It delights me when you disagree with

me, Shannon. It has the ring of progress to me. Now, just because you are not responsible for Caitlin's actions doesn't mean you don't care about her. It doesn't mean you don't ask God to forgive you for your part in it. It does mean you don't carry around a bunch of guilt about this. Try to say no to the guilt."

"Okay," I said.

"How do you feel?" she said.

"I still don't know what to do."

"For right now, I want you to take care of yourself physically, and I want you to pray. And that's all I want you to do until tomorrow. Can you do that?"

"I can't eat. I've tried."

"How long has it been?"

I told her. Her silence was loaded.

"Would you mind if I enlisted one of your friends to help get some food in you? Marissa, was that her name?"

"I'm staying with her and her family."

"Wonderful. Would you mind if I talked to Marissa?"

"That's okay," I said.

"Have her call me," Georgianna said. We said our good-byes, and I lay back on the cushions and closed my eyes. Maybe, just maybe, it was going to be all right.

But you couldn't have proved that to me just then. Immediately after dinner, which Marissa and I ate by ourselves in her room after she talked to Georgianna, my father called and said Mom wanted me to come home. She missed me and needed me to be there with them. They had fixed up the guest room on the first floor for me. There wasn't that much water damage in that room, he said.

Marissa packed all the clothes the Girls had supplied for me into a suitcase, and she whispered, "I put your new dress in there too. Good thing you had it over here."

Dad did the cheerful thing all the way home, telling me that the insurance people had already been there and sent a crew who had cleaned up the debris. They had even been able to salvage a few things. It seemed CDs didn't die, only the cases did. Practically all of Caitlin's music collection had been saved, although there was no sign of her portable player.

"It must have melted to something," Dad said. "Some of that stuff looked like it came out of a Salvador Dali painting."

That was my stuff! I wanted to say to him. To my horror, my esophagus was burning again. For some reason, I was getting angry.

It's all right to be angry.

Hogwash! Be nice!

It's all right. People are praying for you.

I walked up the front drive with my hand over my mouth. Maybe I really was crazy after all. I hadn't told Georgianna about the new voice that was now speaking up as often as Edith was.

There was more reason than that to cover my mouth *and* my nose when we went through the front door. The place was saturated with a stench I can hardly describe. A combination of rotten bacon, burnt toast, and some concoction you would smell passing the chemistry lab at school. It was so nauseating, I gagged.

And it wasn't just the smell that made me sick. The house now had a dreariness about it, achieved by the smoke-tainted walls, the water-stained floors, and the piles of blackened trash in the front hall.

"See?" Dad said, pointing to it. "We've managed to save quite a bit."

"That's what you *saved*?" I said.

"Just be thankful no one was hurt."

I looked up to the first landing at Mom, and I put my hand back over my mouth so she wouldn't hear me gasp. And they called *me* anorexic.

She had to have lost five pounds since Saturday night, all in her face. She looked so gaunt her eyes were sunken, and even from the bottom of the steps I could see that they had a wild, disbelieving look in them.

She pushed the stubborn tendrils back from her forehead and hurried toward me. Her hand gripped the banister like a claw.

"Caitlin hasn't come home," she said.

"The police are doing all they can," Dad said. "I've been out putting up fliers."

"They'll find whoever took her," Mom said.

Dad sighed heavily. "No one took her, Bronwyn. She ran off; we know that."

He was speaking as if he were talking to a child, a child he had said the same thing to at least a hundred times. He watched her as she went to the front door, pulled the curtain aside, and peered out. She looked like a ghost, drifting to the windowpane to search for someone who had mysteriously disappeared. I shivered.

Dad put his mouth close to my ear. "Go on to bed. The guest room is made up. I'll see you in the morning."

I was glad to escape, but I couldn't sleep. I lay on one of the twin beds on sheets that smelled of rancid bacon, smoke, and Downy and stared at the ceiling. It looked so soggy I was sure it was going to fall on me before the night was over.

Although I didn't think the night was ever going to end. I tossed around like a plastic bottle on the waves and drifted in and out of weird, twisted dreams about my mother running from window to window and growing steadily smaller until she disappeared altogether.

I finally got up at five and met Dad in the kitchen. He smelled like Brut, but his eyes looked as if he had never been to bed.

"Is there anything you want me to do?" I said.

"There's nothing you can do. Just try to act as normal as possible; I think that will help your mother. She needs to have somebody to take care of or she'll really go crazy."

"I think I should go back to Bible school today," I said. "And I have an appointment with Georgianna afterward."

Dad's eyebrows lowered. "That leaves your mother alone practically all day."

"Oh," I said.

"Tell you what. I got her to take a pill last night so she'll probably sleep awhile this morning. Why don't you go to the church thing and then come home afterward. Call what's her name…"

"Georgianna."

"…and tell her you have to cancel for today." He started for the door with his cup and his briefcase, and then he turned to me. "I'm so glad we can count on you, Shannon. That really means a lot right now."

Georgianna had told me it was okay to be angry. So had that

new voice in my head. But nobody had told me what to do when I was.

I put on a white cotton Gap shirt and a pair of khakis that used to be Tobey's. Then I called Marissa and had her walk me through consuming an Instant Breakfast. I was feeling a little calmer when we got to the church, especially when Doug told me I didn't have to play the piano. They would just sing with Adam's guitar. I sat in the back and tried not to look at Adam.

In fact, I managed to avoid him all morning, until we were headed for the car. Marissa and Cheyenne were on either side of me, arms linked through mine, following Tobey across the parking lot, when he called out from behind, "Shannon, wait up!"

"Don't do it, Shannon," Cheyenne hissed in my ear. "He's so fickle."

"Cheyenne," Tobey said.

"I know, I know, 'Shut up.'" Cheyenne let go of my arm, but she did direct a glare at Adam before she went on to the car with Marissa and Tobey. Adam hurried up to me with his arms out.

"Hey," he said. "You okay?"

"Um…"

Tell the truth.

"No," I said. "Everything's pretty awful."

"I heard." Adam shoved his hand back through his hair. "What are we going to do?"

"What?" I said.

I didn't want to look at him, but I couldn't help it. His eyes looked just as kind and his freckles just as cute as they always had. Even though I wanted to hate him.

"Can't we do something to try to find her?" he said.

"The police are doing all they can," I said emptily.

"Evidently it isn't enough. Will you call me if I can do anything?" he said.

Tell the truth.

Be nice.

"I don't know what you could do," I said. And then I added, "But thanks."

When I climbed into the car, Tobey was giving Cheyenne the "shut up" look. Me, I burst into tears.

"What did he say to you?" Cheyenne said. "I don't care, Tobey, I'm going to give him a piece of my mind."

"No, don't," I said. "He likes Caitlin. You see how upset he is because she's gone. He never liked me anyway. It's okay."

"No, it isn't," Cheyenne said.

For once, the kid was right. I shook my head.

"No, it isn't," I said. Then I cried into Marissa's shoulder.

My mother was up when I got home. I was surprised to find her just sitting at the table. Dishes were in the sink from the night before, and there were no signs of lunch being prepared. She was just sitting there with a paper towel in her hand, crying without making a sound.

"Mom?" I said. "Did something else happen?"

"Isn't what's already happened bad enough?" she said.

"Of course," I said faintly. "Do you want me to fix you some lunch?"

She shook her head, and then she nodded. "Yes. Maybe some food would help. I don't know. I just can't eat. I keep wondering if Caitlin has anything to eat."

"Yeah," I said. I crossed the kitchen to the refrigerator.

"Where did you get that outfit?" she said.

"Tobey gave it to me," I said.

"What for?"

A pang went through me. "Because, Mom," I said, still peering sightlessly into the refrigerator, "all my clothes were lost in the fire, remember?"

"I pulled out some things," she said. "I've washed them several times, and I think they'll be all right."

"Mom, you didn't have to do that," I said. I managed to find some lunchmeat and the mayonnaise and emerged with them. She was still looking at me.

"You don't look like yourself in that getup," she said. "After lunch, you need to change."

I put the lunchmeat package down on the counter a little harder than I intended to. My chest was igniting again.

"You better let me make the sandwiches," Mom said. "It helps me to keep busy." She gently shooed me out of the way.

"I need to make a phone call," I said.

"Who are you calling?" she said. "Use the phone in here."

I pretended not to hear her and quickly ran up the stairs. The smell up there was even more nauseating than it was on the first floor, but I put it out of my mind as I picked up the phone and dialed Georgianna's number. Then I pulled the phone into the room that used to be Caitlin's, before she moved in with me, and shut the door.

"Georgianna?" I said when she answered. "Am I crazy?"

"No," she said without hesitation.

"Yeah, but you haven't heard about the new voice," I said.

"New voice? Tell me."

I did. She was quiet for an awful minute while I imagined her looking up the number for West Hills Mental Hospital.

"I like this voice," she said finally. "What's her name?"

"I don't know," I said.

"I think her name is Shannon."

It was my turn to sit in stunned silence.

"You think that's me?" I said.

"I do. She makes more sense than either Edith or your responses to Edith, which are usually made out of fear, never our best self."

"You think I can make sense?" I said.

"Absolutely I do. And it's amazing how fast you've discovered that. It must be the prayers."

"I still can't pray."

"Then it's all the prayers the rest of us are praying, my dear, because this feels like God to me."

Then I told her about my mother. Her silence was longer this time. "Remember yesterday I told you not to take complete responsibility for all of this?"

"Yes."

"Think about this question, pray about it: What can you reasonably do? And then let the rest go."

"I don't know."

"I know. That's for you and all of us prayer warriors to find out."

After promising to call her if I felt the least bit shaky, I went downstairs. Mom was lying on the couch in the den, one hand flung across her eyes, breathing heavily. Whatever Dad gave her was pretty powerful stuff, and I was grateful for it. I went into the kitchen, picked up that phone and called Marissa. She suggested a cup of tomato soup and some crackers, and she talked to me while I fixed it and ate it. Then she talked to me until the urge to throw it all up disappeared.

When I hung up, the house was strangely quiet. No clocks ticked, no radio murmured in the kitchen. Everything really was different—and it was never going to be the same again. That much I could tell.

And maybe that was all right.

I just want to know what to do to make it happen, I thought. *I'm supposed to discover it for myself, but I can't! I can't, Georgianna! I can't, God!*

But at least you're talking to Him.

I am? I thought. And then I stopped. It was the new voice, the Shannon-Voice, telling me I was praying.

I sat down on the kitchen floor, closed my eyes, and clenched my hands tight in my lap.

I'm scared. I'm angry. I'm guilty, God. What do I do? How do I take the responsibility I can take? Can I, or am I just too lame?

No answer shouted to me from above, although I did look up, halfway expecting it. All I saw was the phone cord dangling down.

What would you like to do? Georgianna would say if I were sitting across from her right now. *The first thing that pops into your head.*

I want. . .

I didn't finish the thought. I just stood up and looked up the number where Adam was staying.

THE FIRST THING ADAM SAID WHEN HE FOUND OUT IT was me was, "Did you find her?"

I tried not to let my heart sink. "No, but that's why I called. I think I want to try."

"Cool." If Adam was mad at me for being rude to him earlier, he wasn't showing it. "How can I help?"

"Um, did she say anything to you that might give us a hint about where she went?"

"Huh." I tried not to picture him shoving his red hair around with his hand in that cute way he had. "The only thing I can think of was she said, 'Adam, you were right about *wanting* to do the right thing instead of just having people *tell* you to do it.' Then she goes, 'And you were right about not wanting to mess up when you get close to God and let Him get close to you. My old friends don't even compare to these people here.'"

I found myself staring into the receiver. "Caitlin said that?"

"Yeah. So I'm thinking, maybe where she is has something to do with those old friends. Who did she used to hang out with?"

"Kids like her," I said. "I mean, kids who were into pot and stuff. But my dad already had the police check into them. Nobody's seen her."

Adam was quiet.

"You still there?" I said nervously.

"Did you ever have to decide whether to tell somebody something somebody told you not to tell because you think now you have to?"

"Huh?" I said.

He laughed. Adam always found a reason to laugh, no matter what. I couldn't help it. I was warming to him again.

"Okay, if I tell you something she told me…well, you just use it however you want to. In fact, maybe I should ask you if you want to know something that might get her into even more trouble."

"Just tell me," I said. I was beginning to surprise even myself.

"I don't know for sure," he said. "But I think she went to meet with some of them when she left Sand Harbor Saturday. Her shirt, that flannel one?"

"Yeah."

"It reeked of cigarette smoke, and I said that and she just about freaked."

"She did? Caitlin?"

"Yeah, it surprised me too. She never acted like she cared one way or the other what your parents thought. What you thought, that was another story. Anyway, I told her I would wash it for her."

"I don't understand," I said.

"Here's what I think happened. I think she went back to see her old friends one more time, just to see if I was right, that when you get close to God and let Him get close to you, you start not wanting to mess up so much. I think that's what she meant when she said those people couldn't compare to, like, the staff here."

Edith started to scream, but there was no need. I felt bad enough already. Caitlin had been about ready to turn around, and I had slapped her.

"But then I don't get why she would run away after that," Adam said.

"I do," I said. "I told on her."

"Oh," he said.

"It was mean; I know that."

"Hey, I didn't help her that much either, obviously, if that's all it took to erase it. Come on, Shannon, don't beat yourself up. Caitlin made her own choices. She has to take responsibility."

"Yeah," I said. "But—" Another head-clearing discovery came to me.

"What?" Adam said.

"It's hard to take responsibility when you feel like you don't have any control."

"Whoa," Adam said. "You're probably right."

I made it through the promises to tell each other if we got any more ideas and hung up just before I started to cry. It was the first time I realized what I'd been doing all along: seeing what it was like to be Caitlin.

It was a lot like how it felt to be me.

For the next twelve hours, everything seemed stuck in a sameness. That is, until we went to the church the next morning, and Adam was pacing the parking lot. When I got out of the car, he was right on me.

"Well, well," Cheyenne muttered as she passed.

We both ignored her. The urgency in his face made my stomach do flips.

"I have something," he said close to my ear. He stood with his big back to the church and pulled an object out of his shirt pocket. It was a cardboard coaster, the kind they have in restaurants.

"This was in the pocket of Caitlin's shirt," he said. "I was getting ready to wash it last night, and I found this."

Higher Ground Coffee Shop, it said. I put it up to my nose.

"Yeah," he said. "It smells just like the shirt."

"And a lot of Caitlin's other stuff," I said. "It used to gross me out."

Adam took the coaster from me and turned it over. "Look at this on the back."

Somebody had printed in felt-tip pen, "Seth."

"Do you know who that is?" he said.

"No. I didn't know any of her friends."

Adam looked at the other side of the coaster again. "Do you know where this place is?"

"No, but we could find out."

We headed for the church, where Tobey, Cheyenne, and Marissa were waiting but trying not to look like they were waiting at the door. All three of them were microscopically examining their fingernails. I had never known any of them to take that much interest in their manicures before.

"Oh hi, Shannon," Cheyenne said, as if she had just noticed our approach.

Adam grinned. I turned to Tobey. "You said you would take me anywhere I wanted to go, right?"

"Absolutely."

I stuck the coaster out in front of me. "Do you know where this is?"

Tobey frowned at it, and Marissa shook her head. But Cheyenne's eyes popped open. "You don't want to go there!"

"Why not?" I said.

"Because Tassie caught Ellie hanging out there once, and I went with Tassie to pick her up. It was gross."

"What do you mean 'gross'?" Tobey said.

"It's down on Fourth Street, and you can't even see across the room there's so much smoke. And it stunk."

She clipped her fingers over her nose. My heart pounded.

"Can you take me there after this?" I said to Tobey.

"Sure, I guess so, but I don't get it."

"I think they might know where Caitlin is."

Three pairs of eyes widened, and three heads bowed forward into ours. We were ready for action.

"Okay," Tobey said. "We'll jam out of·here as soon as we're done. I'll meet you guys at the car."

"Everybody be praying," Marissa said.

For the first time since I couldn't remember when, I didn't cringe at the thought.

"God, I know You love me," I murmured as I headed for the sanctuary. "Please help."

Like He's really going to, Edith said.

Oh, He'll help. He'll help, Shannon-Voice said.

"Amen," I said.

We were the first ones out of the building at noon, headed for Tobey's car. The feeling of hope was so sure.

"I have an idea," Marissa said. "Why don't we take Brianna with us? I bet she would know about this place. I mean, she lives close to Fourth."

When Brianna squeezed into the front seat with Tobey and Cheyenne and was introduced hastily to Adam, she said to me, "Good thing you came and got me, girl."

"That bad, huh?" Adam said.

She nodded to him and pressed her lips into a serious line. "It's going to be nasty, lots of smoke and swearing and raunchy music and all that. Don't look all shocked. Just go to the counter and ask somebody what you want to know, and then get out of there."

"Have you, like, actually been in there?" Adam said.

"Nuh-uh, honey, I don't do that scene anymore. But I been in plenty like them. Just don't hang out long enough for anybody to get real acquainted with your face, you know what I'm sayin'?"

"If it's that kind of place, then we ought to go tonight," Adam said. "That's when we'll learn the most."

"No way, boy," Brianna said. "Nuh-uh. You are askin' for trouble if you go down there after dark."

"But I have to find Caitlin," I said. "I have to at least try."

Adam slid the arm across the back of the seat and for an instant brushed my shoulder with his hand. Marissa looked at me sadly.

"Bummer," Cheyenne said.

"Okay, look," Tobey said. "Why don't we all get together and come up with some kind of a plan—"

"A Plan of Action!" Cheyenne cried. It didn't take much to raise her hopes.

We all waited for word from Brianna. She slanted her eyes back at me. "Six o'clock tonight at my place. My mama has Bible study tonight at the church."

"We can all pitch in for pizza," Tobey said. She glanced in the rearview mirror. "You need a ride, Adam?"

"I'll call the guys," Marissa said. "Cheyenne, you tell Diesel."

My mother was so absorbed in practically scrubbing holes in the drywall, she barely acknowledged me when I asked if I could go out. So at six o'clock we were all at Brianna's—Cheyenne, Diesel, Tobey, Fletcher, Marissa, Wyatt, Brianna, Adam, and me. Only Norie and Ms. Race couldn't make it because of a meeting about their trip. Even Ira was there. I had trouble looking at him. He sat tall in his wheelchair, but he didn't say much. I felt a pang of guilt.

Why should he even be here? You wouldn't help him. Why should he help you?

But Dad said—

Caitlin. This is about Caitlin.

Pizza arrived shortly after we were all settled in Brianna's tiny but spotless living room. I had eaten two tidbits of pineapple dripping with cheese that Marissa handed me before I realized I was eating without Edith screaming at me.

Who could hear me over all this racket? she said. *Don't worry. You'll regret it later.*

There's no time for that. Think about Caitlin.

I did.

I told them everything I knew about Caitlin's old friends. Adam reported what she had said to him. Brianna described the neighborhood surrounding the Higher Ground Coffee Shop. Diesel organized vehicles. Everyone contributed something while Marissa wrote it all down. The pizza was gone, and Reno was growing dark when a Plan of Action was formed.

Then we stood in a circle holding hands, and we prayed.

Cheyenne and Marissa stayed at Brianna's and promised to call the police if they didn't hear from us in an hour. Diesel and Tobey drove to Fourth Street in Diesel's truck, and they went into the Higher Ground first. Adam said Diesel looked big enough and scary enough to ward off questions. That made it safe for Tobey.

Adam and I rode with Brianna, Ira, and Wyatt in Ira's van. That was the part of the Plan that scared me the most. As we were leaving Brianna's apartment, I saw Brianna and Ira whispering in the corner. She was hanging on to his wheelchair, and he was trying to "drive" it forward. Pretty soon, they forgot to whisper.

"You're not going down there without me," Ira said.

"What good are you going to do me? You plannin' to run over some mugger with your wheelchair?"

"Who's going to know I'm paralyzed when they see me sitting in the van?" Ira said. "From the waist up, I look like a mean mother bear!"

"That isn't the only reason I don't want you to go and you know it," Brianna said.

"What's the other reason?" Cheyenne said.

Brianna glared at her.

"Is it because of me?" I said.

"No, it doesn't have anything to do with you," Brianna said, waving me off. "Ira's clean record is about the only thing he has goin' for him in the trial. If he gets involved in something down there on Fourth Street, he might as well stick out his hands and say, 'Put the cuffs on right here. I'm goin' to prison.'"

"What am I going to get 'involved in' sittin' in the van except watching out, just like you're going to be doin'?"

"That's all we *have* to be doin' for some cop to come up and start askin' questions," Brianna said. "Remember the night all you were doin' was driving down the street in your own neighborhood and the police stopped us and frisked us—just because they didn't think we belonged there?"

"You don't have to come if it's going to mess things up for you, Ira," I said.

Ira turned his brown, handsome eyes on me and smiled. "I would feel terrible if anything happened to anyone. Now, come on before Diesel and Tobey think we ditched them."

So we went, Brianna practically breathing fire and giving Ira smoldering looks at every stoplight. I was almost eager to get out of the van and head for the coffee shop full of pierced-and-tattooed people. That is, until I took a good look.

The building Brianna pulled up across the street from was a pawnshop, actually, with a clutter of dusty stereo equipment and musical instruments in the filmy display window. A set of stairs went up the outside of the building on the side, in an alley formed by the pawnshop and the bar called the Dog House next door. Brianna pointed to that second story.

"That's Higher Ground," she said. "There's a side door right at the top of the steps."

"We have you covered," Wyatt said as Adam and I climbed out. Somehow, it wasn't very comforting. Wyatt looked like a white-collar computer operator.

"You have to look the part," Adam said to me as we stood beside the van.

I realized he was carrying Caitlin's flannel shirt. "Put this on, and hang your hair down over your face some. No, just one strip."

He raked his hands around in my hair the way he always did his own. I could feel my face turning white. Under any other circumstances, I would have been having a ball.

"Sneer," he said.

"I don't know how."

"Think Caitlin. Do the Elvis-Presley-curled-lip thing."

I tried it.

"Yeah," he murmured to me as we crossed the street. "Perfect. Runs in the family." He, I noticed, looked like a drugged-out Huckleberry Finn.

I hugged Caitlin's flannel around me and felt the legs of Tobey's jeans flapping together. I followed Adam up the steps. The screen door to the Higher Ground was standing wide open, and people appeared to be bulging from it in clumps. The smell hit us like some kind of disgusting anesthetic. I willed myself not to cough.

We elbowed our way through the clumps of people, and I stood on tiptoes and eyeballed the room. Through the haze of smoke I spotted Tobey and Diesel at a table in the corner, but Caitlin was nowhere to be seen.

"Let's ask around," Adam said into the top of my head.

I nodded and trailed him as he ran interference for me through the tangle of people. He leaned on his palms on the edge of a table of four guys in bandannas and said, "Anybody seen Caitlin?"

All four shook their heads. We moved on to the next table and the next and the next. I followed Adam like a leech, but I noticed the crowd's fringes were watching us over their cigarettes.

"I'll take a few tables," I whispered to Adam.

He looked at me sharply, but I ducked away before he could stop me. Two girls were sitting at a table, leaning toward each other and talking with barely moving lips. I remembered a lot of Caitlin's questionable friends did that.

I said to them, "You guys seen Caitlin tonight?"

They looked at me, then at each other. It clearly meant, "Are you going to tell her?…I don't know, are you?"

One of them looked back at me while the other took a drag on her cigarette and stared at the wall as if I had disappeared.

"I don't know any Caitlin," she said. "Sorry."

Her black-lipstick lips curved into an unfriendly smile, and she picked up her cigarette and inhaled. I watched until she blew smoke out through her nostrils.

"What about Seth?" I said. "You seen him?"

Another look.

"Don't know any Seth either," the girl said. "What is this, roll call?"

"No," I said. "I just need to talk to one of them."

"Guess you can't if they're not here."

I backed up. "I'll keep asking."

"I said they're not here," the girl said. The smile vanished, and her eyes snapped.

"Move on, okay?" the other girl said. "Find a new career."

I definitely moved. I wanted to go straight to Tobey and Diesel's table and scream, "Help!" I did glance their way, and they quickly looked away. At least they had been watching.

Caitlin had no one watching over her; I was pretty sure of that.

I quickly selected another target table and went toward it. Behind me, at the girls' table, I heard an additional voice, a raspy one, join them. I couldn't hear what they were saying, but there was urgency in it. I forced myself not to look until I was across the room. When I did, they were talking to a pathetically thin girl who had, I could see even from there, a nose ring.

Get you one of those and then maybe you won't stand out like a sore thumb. What are you doing here? Get out!

I have to find Caitlin.

"You ready to go?"

I jerked up to see Adam at my elbow. His face looked flushed and discouraged. "We've asked everybody," he said.

"Not that one girl," I said.

"Which one?"

I didn't want to point, so I looked as pointedly as I could at the girls' table. She was gone. I craned my neck to find her, but Adam took hold of my sleeve.

"Come on," he said. "I think it's time to go."

I followed his gaze to the counter, which was a plywood affair equipped with a cash register. Three guys had stationed themselves there and were making no attempt to hide that they were watching our every move. They all had shaved heads, pierced eyebrows, and tattooed hands. They looked uncannily alike. In fact, everybody in the room looked alike. Caitlin was looking less like a stoner all the time next to this group of clones.

With Adam clutching my shirtsleeve, I grabbed on to the back of his and clung as he crossed to the door. We had to go through the knot again, those people who didn't seem to know what to do beyond stand there like question marks and squint through their own smoke.

"Excuse me, dude," Adam said.

Somebody grunted. A couple of people moved. I started through the narrow path they made, but suddenly I was shoved sideways. I careened into a guy wearing about twenty chains. One of them scraped savagely into my cheek.

"What the..." he shouted at me.

"Sorry!" I said.

I found my footing and groped for Adam. Instead, I found Nose Ring Girl. The nose ring actually moved as she flared her nostrils at me.

"Excuse me," I said.

She didn't move.

"She said, 'Excuse me!'"

Heads turned as big shoulders loomed behind Nose Ring Girl. A muttering of trouble stirred the room. Any minute now, everybody in the place was going to be looking at Diesel, towering over the girl.

"Get out of her way," Diesel said, sounding like a Harley revving up.

In spite of herself, Nose Ring Girl stepped aside. Tobey's hands whisked up to Diesel's shoulders and maneuvered him around while he twisted his neck and drilled his eyes into the girl.

"Come on," Tobey said to him. "We don't need this."

Diesel's eyes met mine and pulled me right out of the knot. Tobey got him out the door before I could grab on to him. Adam was right there, practically picking me up as he put his arm around me and got me outside too. Tobey and Diesel had already hightailed it for Diesel's truck.

"Is anybody following us?" I whispered breathlessly when we were at the bottom of the stairs.

"I don't think so. Don't look back. Just get to the van."

He pushed me out onto the sidewalk, and there we both stopped dead. No van was waiting for us across the street. Above us, the screen door banged.

"That's them," someone said in a thick voice.

I froze.

"No, where's that big dude? He's the one I want."

"Let's go," Adam whispered into my hair. He took my elbow and steered me down the sidewalk. My heart was beating so hard I could feel it up in my throat. I knew I was going to throw up, right there on the sidewalk. I probably would have, if a figure hadn't darted around the corner ahead of us and waved its arm frantically at us.

"Yes!" Adam hissed.

At that point, he practically picked me up and ran with me, leaving the jeers of the drunks on the sidewalk behind. It wasn't until we were around the corner, and I was being hurled into Ira's van, that I realized the person at the corner was Wyatt.

"What happened?" Adam said. Wyatt slid the door closed even as Brianna was pulling out onto Keystone Avenue.

"It's okay," Ira said. "Reno Police were just cruisin'. Brianna got cold feet and thought we ought to move."

"Cold feet nothin'," she said. "Ira was afraid they would spot you two comin' out and get suspicious. You're about as convincing as Dorothy and Toto."

"Ira had her pull out and draw their fire, so to speak," Wyatt said.

Ira grinned. "Pays to be black now and then. I knew they would follow us, and they did till we pulled into the drive-through at Kentucky Fried Chicken. I guess they figured that was right where we belonged, because they took off."

"What happened in there?" Wyatt said. "You both look like you just witnessed a murder or something."

Adam told him. I sank miserably against the seat. All that for nothing. We were no closer to finding Caitlin than we had ever been.

I shoved my hands into my pockets so no one would see them shaking. As I did, my hand hit on a piece of paper. Probably something Tobey had left in there, which was fine because I'd be giving these back to her momentarily. My mother would really have a fit if I walked into the house in these.

But I stopped and felt the paper again. I didn't remember its being there before I went into the coffee shop. I slid the paper out, and in the fleeting light of the street lamps, I opened it up.

Your girl is on Second Street, Seth's place, it read. *Go alone. Your boyfriend looks too wholesome. Don't show this to anybody.*

My heart raced as I shoved it back into the pocket. Adam did the arm-on-the-back-of-the-seat thing.

"You okay?" he said.

"Yeah," I said. "I think I need to go home."

CHAPTER EIGHTEEN

I DIDN'T CARE THAT MY MOTHER NEARLY FAINTED WHEN
I entered the house looking like a stoner. At least I remembered
to take off the flannel and stuff it down inside the jeans until I got
to the bathroom.

*Do you think your precious Georgianna would approve of your
sneaking around like this?* Edith asked me.

I don't know. But what else can I do?

Pray, Shannon-Voice said.

Oh right. Pray. A lot of good that's done so far.

But as I lay in the foreign-feeling guest room and stared at the
ceiling most of the night, I at least had the feeling *somebody's*
prayers had helped a lot. I had my first real glimmer of hope in
the note.

Obviously Nose Ring Girl had written it. She must have put it
into my pocket when she shoved herself against me. She had
given me instructions; I had to follow them.

Now how I was going to do it without telling anybody, I didn't
know. I seesawed back and forth between that and thoughts of
where Caitlin was sleeping.

God, I thought at one point, *I hope You're with her, wherever she
is. I'm doing what I can reasonably do, but she must think I'm not doing anything. God, bring her home.*

I finally fell asleep and was awakened at dawn by Dad standing over me with the phone in his hand. "It's Norie somebody," he
said. "What is she doing calling at this hour?"

"Sorry," I said. I waited until he left to say hello.

"I am definitely missing out on all the fun," Norie said to me.

"What fun?" I said.

"Look, Shannon, I feel really bad I wasn't there last night to help. Tobey called and told me what happened. What can I do?"

"It's really okay. I don't know what else we could find out."

Except what that piece of paper means.

"You need a ride anywhere?"

"No."

Except to Seth's.

I didn't know which voice was speaking to me. I didn't care. I turned an inner ear to it and then said, "Maybe you could give me a ride, only I don't know to where. Some place on Second Street."

"O-kay," Norie said slowly. "Can you give me more information?"

I gave her all I had. I ended with a firm, "But you can't tell anybody."

"No problem. My lips are sealed." Norie's voice had that brisk, take-charge sound. "Where and when do I pick you up?"

"Noon at my church."

"Got it. Meanwhile, I'll find out what I can. See you at noon."

I stayed as quiet as possible at Bible school that morning. Nobody questioned it, even Adam. They knew how worried I was about Caitlin. The truth was, I was scared half to death. Red Sam pointed out that my lips were blue.

When noon finally came, I told Tobey that Norie was picking me up, and then I ran to Norie's Jeep before Tobey could get the words, "Great! We can all go to lunch together" out of her mouth.

"Ready?" Norie said.

"Not quite," I said. "But go ahead and drive. I can get ready on the way."

As Norie wound the Jeep down from gentle, redwood-fence suburbia into neon-light downtown, I pulled the flannel and Tobey's jeans out of my music bag and donned them both over my other clothes. By the time we reached Second, I had the hair pulled down and the sneer properly in place. At the stoplight, Norie stared at me.

"Man," she said, "that therapy is amazing stuff. You're, like, transformed."

"Right," I said.

"No kidding, you look brave."

I sure didn't feel it. The section Norie was driving us into made Fourth Street look like upper-middle class. The pawnshops and cocktail lounges had bars on the windows, and haggard-looking men slept on the sidewalks in front of them.

"I did some research after I talked to you this morning," Norie said. "A guy I did an article on for the paper last spring owed me a favor. Anyway, he said he connected the name Seth with a couple of the crack hotels down here."

"Crack Hotels?" I said. "Is that like a chain?"

"Not the kind of chain you're thinking," Norie said with a grunt. "No, we're talkin' crack—you know, cocaine, drugs."

"In a hotel?"

"They used to be hotels. Now they're just places where druggies hang so they won't be out on the streets snorting or shooting up or whatever."

"But Caitlin doesn't do hard drugs," I said.

Norie just looked at me and pulled into a parking place in front of an abandoned house with its roof caved in and a needless sign that read "Condemned" hanging on the front door.

"Is this it?" I said. My voice was barely audible. My heart was pounding so hard it hurt.

"No." Norie nodded across the street to a two-story brick building that seemed to stare down at us out of glassless eye-windows. "That's it."

I swallowed. Norie cocked her head at me. "You sure you're up for this?"

Do what you can reasonably do.

I took a deep breath and looked back at her. "I am. Can you look tough?"

A slow smile spread across her face. "Oh, baby, can I look tough. Wyatt is scared to death of me. Come on."

We crossed the street with all the cockiness we could muster. I felt almost confident—until we pulled open the front door.

We were plunged into semidarkness and a horrific smell. We had gone beyond mere cigarettes.

Norie put her hand over her mouth. "Everything from feces to marijuana is stinking up this place."

I looked around to make sure no one had heard her. Luckily, not too many people inside were into listening to conversations. Individuals were slumped in every conceivable corner and on the steps, too, and a hall stretched endlessly in front of me. Most of the doors were open, and distorted sounds seemed to emanate from each one.

One of them twisted its way right to me.

It sounded like tin cans in the dryer. Nine-Inch Nails.

Like a magnet, it pulled me down the hall. I was conscious of putting each foot in front of the other and keeping my eyes straight ahead as I moved past rooms that spewed torrents of anguished swearing and ones whose occupants merely moaned. I only had ears for Nine-Inch Nails. I didn't know where Norie was until I heard her call faintly, "I'll keep an eye on the front door."

Finally, after what seemed like hours, I reached the right door. It was one of the few that was closed, and the music seemed to be screaming to squeeze through the cracks around it. I looked at the knob for a long moment before I could get my hand to touch it.

These people are drugged out. No telling what they might do.

I have to find Caitlin.

You can't do this! You don't have the guts.

Slowly I reached for the knob. It turned under my hand. And then it was wrenched away.

I watched my hand jerk away from it, felt a viselike grip go around me from behind. Heard a male voice like a rattling chain in my ear. "What do you think you're doing?"

I screamed. I couldn't move my arms. Whoever it was had them pinned against me, but I could kick, and I did. My foot connected with something, and the man swore. I screamed some more.

It was a wonder I heard, above the noise of the two of us, the raspy female voice that shouted, "Seth, turn her loose. She's havin' a bad trip, man."

I kept kicking, though I lowered the screaming to a whimper. The big arms let me go, and I dropped to the floor with a thud.

"Let me handle her," the raspy voice said. Then somebody turned me over and looked hard into my face. It was Nose Ring Girl.

The signal in her close-set eyes was clear: *Work with me, or so help me I'll kill you.*

I squeezed my eyes shut and kept up the crying. It wasn't that hard.

The man swore some more, and then I heard his footsteps fade off down the hall.

When they disappeared, I heard the door creak open above me. Nose Ring Girl pulled me up and shoved me into the room.

"You have two minutes to get her out of here," she rasped to me.

I looked back at her. The door closed, leaving her face beyond the door. I turned back around and gasped. A mattress was in the middle of the floor. My sister Caitlin was on it.

I flung myself over to her and shook her like a rag doll.

"Caitlin!" I whispered hoarsely. "Caitlin, wake up! It's me! It's Freak Show!"

She didn't even moan. Her eyes were closed except for two small slits at their bottoms. I pulled one lid up, and her eyeball rolled back.

"Oh no!" I said to her. I didn't have to pretend to cry now. I sat up on my knees and ripped the "tough" hair out of my face.

"What do I do?" I whispered to the smelly, vacant room. "Dear God, what do I do?"

I looked around. The only other object in the room was Caitlin's portable CD player, endlessly droning out her song over and over. She obviously had it on repeat, so there was no telling how long she had been this way. In a shudder of panic I flung myself at her again and put my face close to her nose. She was breathing but not that well. I had to get her out of there—in less than two minutes.

The room had a window, and we were on the first floor. I ran to it and pried it open. It faced the alley, and it wasn't much of a drop to the ground.

I crawled back to the mattress and got Caitlin up against me from behind so I could drag her from under the armpits. Her head lolled heavily, and she moaned.

"Keep talking to me, Caitlin," I whispered.

Somehow, gasping and grunting, I reached the window.

Getting her up to the sill and out, though—no way. My arms were like rubber bands, and I was seeing black spots before my eyes.

Do what you can reasonably do, right now.

I was way beyond "reasonably." As gently as I could, I laid Caitlin's head on the floor and flung my leg over the window sill. Closing my eyes, I slid out. I was running almost before I landed on the ground. Norie was probably out here someplace. She wouldn't have left me, but she probably hadn't stayed in the hall when she saw Seth moving toward her.

I rounded the corner and stopped dead still. Norie was flat against the front of the "hotel," with a huge man looming over her. He had hairy arms the size of tree trunks, and he was yelling in a voice like a rattling chain. It had to be Seth.

I jerked myself away from the corner and tore back down the alley. Somehow I got myself back into the window, but by now the black spots were almost blanking out my eyesight. I leaned over Caitlin, picked up her head, and gingerly smacked her cheek.

"Come on, Caitlin. I know you hate me, but wake up. Come on, wake up."

"Come on. Let's get her out of here."

I convulsed like a shot rabbit.

"Hurry up, somebody's coming!"

Wyatt hoisted himself in through the window, minus his glasses and clad in pants big enough for both him and Fletcher to get into. Fletcher, however, had his own. He climbed in behind Wyatt. They went for Caitlin's limp form like a couple of soccer players after the ball.

"Get out, and we'll hand her down to you," Wyatt whispered.

I slithered out the window yet again and held up my rubber-band arms. Caitlin was in them, and we were both on the ground, as Wyatt and Fletcher rolled out the window and grabbed us both, somehow, in a fumble of arms and legs and flying gravel.

"Somebody came in the room!" Fletcher whispered. "Let's move!"

By then, Wyatt had Caitlin in his arms and was pounding down the alley, away from the street, with her arms and legs flopping lifelessly. Fletcher snagged my flannel in his fist and dragged me along after them.

I chanced a glance over my shoulder, but no drugged-up, tattooed people with shotguns were chasing us. And no Norie.

"Where are we going?" I said to Fletcher.

He didn't answer. He didn't have to. We were at the other end of the alley, and a Jeep was screaming to a stop right at the opening. A door unlatched and flung itself out, and Wyatt dumped Caitlin in and climbed in after her. Wyatt pulled the front seat back to reveal Adam, who reached out and pulled me in onto his lap.

"Go!" he yelled.

Norie, in the driver's seat, jammed down on the accelerator, and we leapt down Third Street with the door still swinging open. Adam closed it and searched my face.

"You okay?" he said.

"Yes, but Caitlin—I think she's dying!"

"God, don't let her die. Please, just hold her in Your arms till we get to the hospital," Wyatt was saying from the backseat.

I stuck my hand back there and felt her curls in my hand. "Please, God," I said. "Please, please, please."

CHAPTER NINETEEN

FOR THE NEXT SEVERAL HOURS, IT SEEMED THERE WAS nothing I could "reasonably do." Everybody else was doing it for me.

Norie called my parents on her cell phone on the way to the hospital. They reached the emergency room, white-faced and blue-lipped, ten minutes after we did.

All three of us had to hover on the perimeter of the curtained area while white-coated people carried on a frenzy of activity around Caitlin. They pumped, prodded, and electrified her, and barked questions at us, until a guy with his white coat flying out behind him hurried in and said, "The girl in the waiting room said she was found in a crack hotel."

My parents both looked at me as if I had checked her in there myself. "I found her like that!" I said. "I'm sorry!"

The next thing I knew, I was back out in the waiting room with a circle of Girls around me. I didn't hear a thing anybody said. I just went from one pair of arms to another, sobbing—until I reached Georgianna's.

"Let it go," she said softly. "Just let it go. It can't hurt you. You're strong."

She kept talking until I stopped crying. Then I went limp in her arms. About then, the double doors swung open, and Dad came out, holding Mom up, both looking like dishrags. I held my breath.

A doctor floated out after them and bypassed them to get to me. "Shannon?" he said. When he took the chair beside me that Tobey vacated for him, his nametag was at eye level. *Kevin J. Bogen, M.D.*

"Your sister says to tell you thank you," he said. He still had the same kind, gray eyes and the same soft, sympathetic mouth.

"She's alive?" I said.

He didn't say, "No, idiot, she spoke to me from the dead." He did say, "She's out of danger. She'll be in ICU until she's stabilized, and then we'll take it from there."

The rest was a blur. I must have fallen asleep on the chairs because I woke up with new sunlight streaming across my face and my father sitting next to me as if he had been there a long time watching me sleep.

"Have you been up all night?" I said.

He nodded, but he smiled. "And it was worth every minute. Caitlin's doing much better. They'll keep her here until they're sure she's stable, and then we'll move her to inpatient rehab for four months. After that, about a year of daily outpatient sessions plus Al-A-Teen meetings."

"For what?" I said.

"For drugs, honey," he said.

I stared at him. He said it like he had already digested it and was moving ahead.

"For just one time of hard drugs?" I said.

"It isn't a punishment, Shannon," he said. "She's going to get the help she needs. She's been into the hard stuff for a long time. She told us that last night. We just didn't know how deep, until she hit rock bottom and for once didn't start to dig!" Suddenly Dad's eyes took on a shine that, to my amazement, seemed to come from tears. "She said she really wants to change. I tell you, that was music to my ears, and your mother and I are going to give her everything she needs. I don't care how much it costs or how long it takes. She wants to get better, and I know she will."

I couldn't say anything. I was trying to sort out the grunts and moans my Voices were waking up with.

"I know we can count on you to be supportive too," Dad said.

"Well, yeah," I said. "But I—"

"Don't worry about the how's. They have a full staff over at inpatient who are going to walk us through everything. They make it a family matter over there."

"Family therapy," I said.

"They're just going to teach us how to help Caitlin through this, is all. I wouldn't call that therapy."

I put my hand up to my chest. It was beginning to burn.

Somehow I managed to keep it from exploding until Dad dropped me off at the house, checked on the construction crew working on the third-floor room, and drove back to the hospital. Then I marched into the living room, sat down at the piano, and started to pound. I banged and I hammered until my fingers ached.

But my chest was still burning, and a Voice was screaming in my head—and I didn't care whose it was.

Caitlin's ready for help now so Caitlin gets therapy and family therapy and the new room to replace the one she burned down. Caitlin needs my support. Didn't Caitlin already get my support? Didn't I risk my life going into that crack house—and my friends', too? And still it's, "Shannon, we know we can count on you. All we have to do is bear down on you a little, and you snap right to. You don't need that Georgette woman filling your head with nonsense. You just do what we tell you, and everything is fine. But Caitlin, now, she needs special treatment. We found that out when she set fire to the house and ran off and tried to kill herself."

I slammed my hands down on the keys. The B above middle C twanged, and the key sagged lifelessly below the rest. I sucked on my finger.

I was still seething inside as I stomped to the kitchen and punched Georgianna's numbers on the phone. I barely gave her a chance to say hello before I started blurting.

"Well then," she said when I was done. "That was some pretty healthy anger."

"That burning thing in my chest all this time—that's anger?"

"That's anger being held back," Georgianna said.

"But I don't know what to do with it!" I said. "Every time I let it go, all I do is make a mess."

"Maybe we should try to figure out what you're most angry about. Is it really that Caitlin is getting all the attention and support now, while you're expected to carry on solo?"

The answer came to me even as I spoke. "I think it's more the same thing that made Caitlin angry."

"What was that?"

"Not having control. I did all this stuff, and it's still not right." I was on a roll now. "Like with Ira. He was there for me the other night, even though you could tell he was worried about going to jail. But I'm not allowed to even sit in the courtroom for him. Not that it would make any difference, but I just want to do something, and I'm not allowed to."

"Then I would say do what you can reasonably do about that," Georgianna said. "Without disobeying your father."

I was on the front porch later, still groping around for what that could be, when Adam showed up.

"I skipped out after music," he said. "I had to come see you."

"Wow," I said. It was lame, but I was too tired to care. I scooted over on the swing, and he sat next to me.

"I'm sorry you had to get dragged into all that yesterday," I said.

"Are you kidding? I loved it."

I had a flash of realization. "I don't even know how you guys found me!"

"I get to tell the story?" His eyes glistened.

I nodded and felt a tiny glimmer of happiness.

I won't tell you the tale the way he did—it took him an hour or more. Basically, what happened was this.

As soon as Norie saw me walk down the hall of that crack hotel, she called Wyatt on her cell phone. He already had Fletcher with him. They grabbed Adam and came right over. Norie met them outside and said she would stall anybody who came out front if the guys would go down the alley and peek in windows. Who should she have to stall, of course, but Seth? My first question was, How did she get away from that gorilla? She wouldn't have, it turns out, if it hadn't been for "that girl with the nose ring" who came out front and said for him to come in because somebody had said the cops were on the way. No cops ever showed up, and I chalked that up to Nose Ring Girl's ability to lie under pressure.

Anyway, just as Seth went inside, Adam flagged Norie down and said they had found us. The two of them got in the Jeep and hauled buns to the other end of the alley where nobody coming out the front of the hotel would see them. It sounded so simple, but one slip-up in timing, and it could have been, as Adam put it, "curtains" for any one of us, including Caitlin. That, we decided, was God.

"You were so brave," Adam said to me.

"That must have been God, too, because I was so scared."

"Yeah, well, you saved the Cait-Lou's life. Can I go see her? I have something I want to give her."

When he left, I sat there for a while, wondering if what he wanted to give her was the song he had written.

Don't be selfish, Shannon, Edith said.

Stop it! I said.

I put my hands on my head. I had to concentrate on what I could reasonably do to gain some control over my own life. I didn't want to fold up under Edith again.

It didn't come to me until Brianna called me late in the afternoon, wanting to know how I was doing and scolding me for going back to that part of town.

When I asked her about Ira, her voice changed from right-on-top-in-charge to down-at-the-bottom-and-fighting-for-life. "It's not going too well in court. They've been through so much fighting and arguing, and now it's coming down to Ira's word against some dead boy's—and they've about made him out to be Saint Peter himself."

"I'm sorry."

"His lawyer says it's too late in the game to put character witnesses on the stand. He's done all he can. He says all we can do now is be there to support him."

The hot feeling surged up in my chest again. But this time it didn't threaten to explode. I thought of something I could reasonably do.

"What time does court start tomorrow?" I said.

"Nine," she said. "Why?"

"Just wondering," I said.

When we hung up, I called my father in the ICU area. He came to the phone, sounding out of breath.

"Listen, honey, we'll be home shortly," he said. "I was just helping them move Caitlin to a regular room. She's out of ICU!"

"Great," I said. "Can I ask you something, Dad?"

"Can't it wait until we get home?"

"No," I said. "I just need to ask you real quick. Um, I want to go to Ira Quao's trial tomorrow. It's his last day."

After an impatient sigh, he said; "We have talked about this before, Shannon."

"We never talked about it. You just said I couldn't go, but we never talked about it."

"You're sounding like Caitlin."

"Would things have been different if you had listened to her?" I said.

There was a stunned silence.

"I'm sorry," I said. "I wasn't trying to be smart. I just want to go. He was there for me when I was trying to find Caitlin. He put himself in danger. It could have messed things up for him bad, but he helped her. I just want to repay him."

Again, silence. I didn't know what else to say.

Please, God, let him say yes, please.

"All right now, you listen," Dad said. "You can go to the courtroom, and you can sit there with your mouth shut for whatever good it will do. And then you will come straight home. Don't talk to any reporters—do not say your name to anyone…"

I didn't listen to the rest; it was too ugly. I had already done what I could reasonably do.

My parents didn't say anything about the trial when they got home. Mom, in fact, didn't seem to know about it. She was too busy inspecting what the workmen had done and telling me what to wear when I went to see Caitlin, and, worst of all, how sweet Caitlin's "little boyfriend" was.

"That cute Adam from the church staff. I know he's leaving to go back to wherever soon, and he's actually a little old for her, but it's enough to boost her confidence. You should have seen how she lit up when he came into the room."

Pray, my Shannon-Voice said. *Or you're going to spontaneously combust.*

The first thing I saw when I walked into Caitlin's hospital room was this huge bunch of balloons that said, "God loves you!" tied to the end of the bed.

"Tobey and those guys brought these," said a voice from behind them.

Reluctantly I peeked around them. Even when I saw her, I wasn't convinced it was Caitlin. She was a shrunken version of the sister whose very being had always shouted, "I'm doing it my way, fools!" With the IV going into her arm, she wasn't doing anything her way.

Her eyes dropped to her lap. Yeah, this was definitely an impostor.

"How do you feel?" I said.

"Like Jell-O," she said. "Thanks for coming."

"It's okay," I said.

She dared a glance up at me. "You really didn't want to, did you?"

It was my turn to look down.

"I know I've really messed things up for you," she said. "But I want you to know I appreciate what you did, coming to get me out of there. It blows me away. I didn't think—"

"It's okay," I said. But I was staring at her. Of all people, she was the only one to thank me.

"And," she went on, "I didn't start that fire on purpose. Honest. Everything else is my fault. I pawned your ring. I used the money to buy drugs from Seth. You can go ahead and hate me—you should. But I didn't burn up the room on purpose. I lit some incense and candles and left them on just to make you and Mom mad. I really didn't intend—"

"It's okay, it really is," I said. "I think I'm going to tell Mom to just give you the new room. I'm kind of getting used to the guest room. I could fix it up the way I wanted to."

"The way *you* want to? Good luck," Caitlin said. "You know Mom."

"Yeah."

"But see, Shannon." Her voice was tear-filled. "I think family therapy, you know, over at rehab, I think that could really help her. They sent somebody over here tonight, after Mom and Dad left, a woman from the staff. She was way cool, and she told me that even though I've made some really stupid choices and I have a long way to go before I'm, like, 'fixed,' she said it's a family problem."

"I don't think Dad knows that's what it's about," I said.

She rolled her eyes and changed the subject. "Adam was here earlier."

"Mom told me," I said woodenly.

"I bet she also told you he was my boyfriend." Caitlin shook her head. "I tried to tell her he's just a friend. He brought me a new flannel. I told him thanks, but I didn't really want it. That's too much like my old life. I think I'm going to, like, start all over."

"That's—that's good," I said.

Caitlin looked at me closely. "At first I only wanted him because you did. And then I did have a crush on him for a while," she said. "He was the only reason I kept going to the summer program. But I figured out he's more like a big brother to me. It's you he likes, you know, for girlfriend material."

I could feel my face going cloud-white. Caitlin laughed— maybe the first real laugh I had heard out of her, maybe ever.

"What?" I said.

"You look like a bowl of porridge," she said. "Come on, admit it. You guys are perfect for each other. Too bad he's leaving Saturday."

"He is?"

"Well, yeah. Friday's the last day of VBS. I'm missing everything. The staff party Friday night, everything."

I was still gnawing on "he's leaving Saturday."

"It's a bummer," she said. "But you could just about have any guy you wanted. Except for those who don't like them heroin-model-thin. Have you told your friends about being anorexic?"

"Yeah."

Caitlin's eyes drifted to the balloons. "I wish I had friends like that."

"Don't you?" I said.

"No. You saw what kinds of losers I've been hanging out with."

"What about Nose Ring Girl?"

She splattered out a laugh. "Who?"

"That girl with the pierced nostril. She told me where to find you. She got Seth off of me when I found out what room you were in. She even got him off Norie out in front of the hotel."

"Jocelyn did all that?" Caitlin nodded thoughtfully. "Whoa. I bet she's in all kinds of trouble. Dad said they arrested Seth this afternoon, and a whole bunch of people who were in the hotel."

A nurse came in then with a little cup of pills. I said good night to Caitlin and went down to the end of the hall where the phones were. I fumbled through the phone book, found the number, and dialed.

"Higher Ground," someone barked into the phone. I could imagine his shaved head and pierced eyebrow.

"Jocelyn there?" I said.

"Yeah, just a minute."

My heart raced just being on the phone with that place. My "tough lessons" from Adam must have paid off, though, because a raspy female voice said, "H'lo?"

"Hi," I said. "This is Caitlin's sister. I just wanted you to know that she's all right, and she's at St. Mary's Hospital in room 304. She would really like it if you came to see her."

She didn't answer. All I heard was a loud click.

At least I'd tried.

I went to court for Ira the next day. We all prayed in a circle outside beforehand, and during his closing statement, Ira's lawyer surprised us all.

"I want to call your attention to something, ladies and gentlemen," he said to the jury. "You have heard the testimony of a number of Dillon Wassen's 'friends,' attesting to the nature of his character. But have you seen them since? In fact, are any of them in the courtroom today, waiting to hear about the fate of his supposed killer?"

He gave them a moment to sweep their eyes around the courtroom. There wasn't a skinhead in the place.

"On the other hand," the lawyer went on, "not a day has gone by in this trial that at least two of Ira Quoa's friends haven't been here, sitting through as much dull, boring testimony as you have, and probably yawning a lot less. And look out there today. I see nine decent, alert, law-abiding teenagers who have given up a summer vacation day to be here to support their friend. None of them looks as if he or she has even entertained the notion of violence. I'm sure not a one of them would know a crack dealer if he or she fell over him."

I almost laughed. It was amazing how deceiving appearances could be.

While we were waiting for the verdict, I used Norie's cell phone to call Caitlin. That's when she told me Jocelyn had come to see her that morning.

"I don't know how she knew where to find me," Caitlin said. "I was so blown away I forgot to ask her. She didn't stay that long, but do you know how hard it was for her to come here?"

I hoped my smile didn't come through in my voice. "Yeah, I think I do."

Right after that, the jury came back and said, "We find the defendant Ira Saban Quoa not guilty."

We all squealed, and rushed over to hug Ira, wheelchair and all.

The next good thing that happened was a little quieter, but it meant just as much. Tobey was driving me home, and she suddenly looked at me and said, "You remember when we all talked about our summer goals at the graduation party in June?"

"Yeah."

"Did you have this goal in mind then? That you were going to get on top of your anorexia?"

"No," I said. "I thought I deserved not eating then. Sometimes I kind of still do. I have a long way to go. What about you? Did you reach your goal yet?"

"To bring somebody to Christ?" She shrugged. "It's hard to tell with the little kids we're working with. I guess I would have to say no."

"I guess I would have to say yes," I said.

She looked at me, a quiz on her face.

"You brought somebody to Christ," I said. "Me."

"You were already a Christian!"

"But I was, like, drifting. I didn't realize until now that you brought me back. You kept talking about it. You prayed for me when I couldn't pray for myself."

"Yikes," she said softly. "That's awesome."

"Yeah," I said.

Then, of course, there was the staff party for VBS. I was trying on every outfit the Flagpole Girls had given me, when Mom came in holding something behind her back.

"I didn't have time to make you something new for your party," she said, "so this time I fudged a little, and I bought you something."

With a wide smile and a flourish, she brought out a long piece of pink-and-white striped seersucker fluff. All I could see were the snippets of white eyelet lace. She wrinkled her nose at me. She was pleased as punch.

And I was miserable. I couldn't imagine myself putting on that candy-striped dress. It wasn't that I thought it was ugly, or that I just didn't want to do it because my mother had made up my mind for me. I just suddenly knew it wasn't me.

"Try it on," she said. "I'll be so glad to see you in something that looks like you for a change." She went through the fabric and located the tags. "It was nice of your friends to lend you their things but—"

"Mom," I said, "don't take off the tags."

"It's all right, if it doesn't fit, I can alter it real quick."

"No, Mom," I said. "I really appreciate your buying it for me and I don't want to hurt your feelings…"

She stared at me. "What?" she said. "Shannon, just say it. I hate it when you pussyfoot around like that."

"It's not what I would have picked out," I said.

"Oh, don't be silly. It has your name all over it."

"Maybe it used to," I said, "But—"

"That's because you've been wearing everybody else's clothes."

"Mom, please," I said. "I would just like to pick out my own stuff. Would that be okay?"

"Fine," Mom said. She pursed her lips so hard they went white, and she spread the dress out on the bed and started to fold it. "But don't think I'm going to the Gap to buy you things, because we can't afford it. Especially not with the bills we're going to have with Caitlin."

"I'm not expecting you to," I said. "You could still make me stuff, but I'd like to pick out the fabric."

"And let me become your personal seamstress?" she said. "Sewing to order?"

I stopped. I just didn't know where to go from there. I was starting to feel panicked.

"I'm sorry," I said.

Her eyes were moist as she picked up her little folded package and made for the door. "You wear whatever you want to tonight."

I was stung as I sank down on the bed.

Now you've done it, Edith said, as if she had been bursting to say something for hours.

I really did feel as if I had done something wrong. But the Shannon-Voice whispered, *Open your suitcase.*

Edith had nothing to say, so I opened the suitcase Marissa had packed for me. There was the beautiful, silky dress with the green lace jacket.

The party was completely cool. Doug had the pavilion in the churchyard all decorated, and there was so much food even Randy couldn't finish it off. I didn't spend a whole lot of time looking at it.

Everyone did a double take when I walked in, and then they told me I was beautiful. Then Doug gave out awards to all the staff—funny ones. I got the Liberace Award for playing the piano.

Adam sat by me most of the evening, but just when it started to get dark, and we were all settling in for quiet, do-you-remember-when kind of talk, he disappeared. Right after that Doug sent me on an errand into the meeting room.

The minute I pushed open the door, I knew something was up. The room was dark, but then, not quite. A soft light came from somewhere. I reached up to snap the light switch, but somebody said, "Don't touch that!"

I jumped, and then I giggled. It was Adam, calling to me from across the room.

I crept over like I was afraid something was going to come out and bite me. Adam just waited by the light. Candlelight. On top of the piano.

When I reached him, he pulled me to the bench beside him. I didn't ask any questions as he rubbed his palms on his pant legs.

"I have something for you," he said.

He settled his fingers on the keys and began to coax a tune with them. It was simple, it was playful, and it was vaguely reminiscent of something I had heard before.

He started to sing.

"She smiles when she's supposed to;
She's the kind of girl you give a rose to.
So I tried to win her with a stunt on the potty.
By the look on her face, she thought that was shoddy.
Then I tried again with an ice-cream sundae,
But she wouldn't speak to me until Monday.
My friends tried to tell me that I would regret it,
'Cause when it came to her, I might as well forget it.
But I knew every time I listened to her play
That she was a girl I needed, so I'd pray,
'Dear Lord, won't you let her see what's in my heart?'
He said, 'Take her up on the rocks for a start.'
I knew He was right while I was watching her sleep.
Still, shadows over our love, they had to creep.
And now it seems that time has run away,
But I want her to know, my heart is here to stay."

After a few final, tinkling chords, he did a big glissando down the keyboard and laughed. But I could see even his freckles looked shy.

"I loved it," I said.

"Yeah, well, if I could stay longer, I'd probably love *you*. I mean it, Shannon. You're—you're just special."

All the usual answers, the "nuh-uh" and the "not me!" and even the "I am?" ran through my head, but I ignored them all. I didn't know what *to* say, mind you, but at least I didn't say any of them.

"Was it lame?" he said.

"No," I said. "You could never do anything lame."

He grinned, put his arm around me, and hugged me in close. I sighed into the smell of borrowed toiletries and smiled.

I know what I'll tell Georgianna, I thought, *the next time she asks me what song I would be if I could choose one.*

The last good thing happened the next morning at the crack of dawn. We all went to the airport to see Norie and Ms. Race off to Costa Rica.

Norie looked pink-cheeked and excited, which doesn't happen often, and Ms. Race was all teary-eyed as she hugged us.

"This is the first of a lot of good-byes, isn't it?" she said. "Brianna, Ira—it's going to be so different without them."

"I don't want to think about it," I said.

"But do," Ms. Race said. "Think about the good parts. We have a whole new school year to look forward to."

I nodded out of a long, happy glimmer.

When Norie and Ms. Race were gone, the rest of us stood there, kind of hanging on to each other. I don't know what anybody else was thinking. I was trying to come up with some of those good things. The Shannon-Voice gave me some.

Adam really likes you. He's going to e-mail you.

Surely Dad won't make you stop seeing Georgianna now that Caitlin is in therapy too. It won't hurt to ask.

And if I get to stay with Georgianna, maybe, just maybe, the time will come when I'll be excited about going to the table—first Jesus' table, then maybe everybody's.

Plus Norie, Cheyenne, Fletcher, Wyatt, Tobey, and Marissa will still be at school in September.

Not only that, but we'll have another See You at the Pole Day. Even more people could show up this time. And, hey, don't forget this: There will always, always be God.

Look for Other Books in the Raise the Flag Series
by Nancy Rue

Book One: *Don't Count on Homecoming Queen*
Tobey suspects Coach is up to something sinister at King High, and only the Flagpole Girls can help her figure out what to do!
ISBN 1-57856-032-2

Book Two: *"B" Is for Bad at Getting into Harvard*
Norie's faced with the chance of getting the grades she's worked so hard to attain, at a tremendous cost. Will she cheat or find another way?
ISBN 1-57856-033-0

Book Three: *I Only Binge on Holy Hungers*
Cheyenne only wants to fit in. Shoplifting seems to be the means to an end. It will take her Christian friends to help her find the way out.
ISBN 1-57856-034-9

Book Four: *Do I Have to Paint You a Picture?*
Brianna and the Flagpole Girls learn that keeping the peace is rough business when the rumblings of racial tension escalate into real-life violence.
ISBN 1-57856-035-7

Book Five: *Friends Don't Let Friends Date Jason*
When Marissa finds out that the first boy she's ever fallen for is a user, she learns that a healthy self-esteem is worth more than an inflated ego.
ISBN 1-57856-087-X

Book Six: *When Is Perfect, Perfect Enough?*
Shannon's wonderful Christian family is falling apart because her sister Caitlin has gone wild. Will her parents ever see the "good kid" in Shannon hiding in the shadows?
ISBN 1-57856-088-8

Join millions of other students in praying for your school! See You at the Pole, a global day of student prayer, is the third Wednesday of September each year. For more information, contact:

See You at the Pole
P.O. Box 60134
Fort Worth, TX 76115
24-hour SYATP Hotline: 619/592-9200
Internet: www.syatp.com
e-mail: pray@syatp.com